KU-400-892

Praise for *Flamingo*

'*Flamingo* is the most wonderful, life-affirming, readable book about two families who quite by chance end up living next to each other'   MARY ANN SIEGHART

'Beautifully written, witty, clever, and a proper page-turner'   FELICITY HAYES-McCOY

'I LOVED this. I read it in a day. It is vibrant and glorious, full of life and colour and pain and love'   JULIE COHEN

'I love Rachel Elliott's books. I love the way her stories are populated by characters who don't quite seem to neatly fit into the mainstream . . . You come away from reading a story such as this not feeling quite so bad about yourself . . . Utterly exquisite, heart-wrenching and heart-warming'   *NB Magazine*

'What a lovely book *Flamingo* is. It's a wonderful exploration of family and friendships and how covering up the truth can lead to unnecessary pain. Beautifully written, it kept me gripped as the truth began to unravel'   JULES SWAIN

'*Flamingo* is as gorgeous inside as it is on the outside'   SARAH TURNER

'Heartbreaking and funny at the same time. The observations of internal worlds – how we all think and feel, our fears and insecurities – are so accurate and nuanced, and also incredibly kind. Tender and beautiful, this novel is full of profound intimacy. Just wonderful'   NIGEL WELLINGS, psychotherapist and author of
Nothing to Lose, Why Can't I Meditate?
and *Present With Suffering*

'A brilliant and well-written book that I can't recommend enough!'   OWEN HOLLIFIELD

'A very special book. *Flamingo* is one of those novels that's hard to describe, because there's so much in it. It's only when you have read and thought about it that you can really start to appreciate what an incredible author Rachel Elliott is, and how layered and nuanced her novel is. I loved it'
CLARE, *Two Fond of Books*

'*Flamingo* is a beautiful story of love. You get close to Daniel, Rae, Leslie and the others . . . You want to keep them in your heart, listen to them, sit down at that table and be a family together. The writing style is magnificent: stimulating, intriguing, musical, like a song. A brilliant book – this is a five-star for me'
NAZA THE BOOKWORM

'It's really different, fresh, endearing. It's about managing to be in a family and being seen for who you are – all the struggles of that. An easy read yet there's so much emotion. Bravo!'
PHILIPPA HALL, *The Quick Book Reviews Podcast*

'This was such a breath of fresh air for me. Daniel's experience of homelessness is raw and emotional and the journey he goes on is so compelling. I love that the characters are flawed, as we often are in life, which made them seem so tangible and real. There is heartbreak and laughter within these pages, and everything in between. Rachel captures the human experience so perfectly and the raw emotions leap off the page. It's brilliant and I thoroughly recommend!'
JOANNA WRIGHT, *Books and Lovely Things*

'I adored this intelligent and nuanced novel, and Rachel's prose is beautiful . . . I loved it for many reasons, but her ability to have you laughing out loud on one page, and genuinely moved on the next is a rare and wonderful talent'

Years of Reading Selfishly

'I couldn't put it down. Every now and then a book stands out as not just amazing but absolutely exceptional and *Flamingo* is that book. It tells the story of determination, desire, heartbreak, loss and redemption and does so in a way which will have you giggling one moment then sobbing the next. I absolutely adored *Flamingo* and was devastated when the story finished and I had to go back into real life'   *Intensive Gassing About Books*

'Poetic, lyrical, it pulled me in. You really start to feel a part of it – this story, this family . . . I would highly recommend'

The Bert's Books Podcast

'I don't know if I can find the right words to express how much I loved this book . . . told in fragments like half-forgotten memories and with such beauty it could be a poem. The writer conveys perfectly how certain people can hold space for and heal wounds in each other. I was enchanted by this story and it will keep a special place in my heart'   *The Lotus Readers*

'This is a moving story, beautifully written – a story that shows in times of despair that there is always hope, love and kindness around'   *Zoe Bees Books*

'An enchanting and charming read . . . Even after I had finished it I was still thinking about the characters. It's a story that people may find comfort in, a tender story that in time will heal us'

Echoes in an Empty Room

'I loved the rich and well-developed characters . . . A book I've been unwilling to put down. I'll definitely be recommending this gem'   *Little Miss Book Lover 87*

By Rachel Elliott

Whispers Through a Megaphone

Do Not Feed the Bear

Flamingo

RACHEL
ELLIOTT

FLAMINGO

HEADLINE PUBLISHING GROUP
An Hachette UK Company
Carmelite House
50 Victoria Embankment
London EC4Y 0DZ

TINDER
PRESS

First published in Great Britain in 2022 by Tinder Press
An imprint of HEADLINE PUBLISHING GROUP

First published in paperback in 2022 by Tinder Press
An imprint of HEADLINE PUBLISHING GROUP

1

Cataloguing in Publication Data is available from the British Library

Paperback ISBN 978 1 4722 5947 9

Designed and typeset by EM&EN
Printed and bound in Great Britain by Clays Ltd, Elcograf S.p.A.

Headline's policy is to use papers that are natural, renewable and recyclable
products and made from wood grown in well-managed forests and other
controlled sources. The logging and manufacturing processes are expected
to conform to the environmental regulations of the country of origin.

MIX
Paper from
responsible sources
FSC® C104740
www.fsc.org

For Jac

CONTENTS

liminal, not criminal

He is cross-legged on the floor of the public library, deep in cookery, holding a book of old recipes, gripping it tight, his tears tapping out the code of how lost he is on its sun-bleached cover.

He is soft rain.

He is a filthy shirt.

He is two nights on a bench, one night in a doorway, two nights under a tree after years and years of mattress and cotton sheet.

The book in his hands is simply called *Fruit*. It's hard and heavy, a book to be used and passed down, built to last. On the front cover, there's a still life painting: a table draped with cloth, a ceramic jug, a plate of apples and pears.

For a second, he has the sensation that he is a boy sitting in a church, holding a bible.

He has never been to church.

And his own kitchen table, his jug and plates, where are they now?

The library is quiet this morning. Silent slo-mo papery room.

There is no one close but Daniel Berry is not alone. The bodies of these books have thick spines and buttery fingerprints. A man can do worse for company than cooks and celebrity chefs, and he imagines them lined up with offerings: a pot of strong coffee, bowls of broth and noodles, bread and flapjacks straight from the oven.

He closes his eyes, and it scares him, so he opens them again.

He feels like he is outside in his pyjamas.

Sometimes the only thing to do is keep perfectly still.

He remembers being knocked off his bike last year, how he lay on the road for a long time, too scared to move, to discover what damage had been done. After a while it was sort of pleasant, looking up at the sky, watching the clouds from inside a private bubble of shock.

His stillness now, it's something like that.

Funny what the mind does. How it leaps from chefs to flapjacks to pyjamas to falling off a bike and watching clouds, all without him moving a muscle.

Also, he is not dead. This is what he thinks next. He is not dead, but he is a body in the library.

Very Agatha Christie, Daniel.

It's true, he thinks. He is a warm living damp body in a public library. He has dragged the wet swamp of himself in here and no one has stopped him.

As a boy, he was often in the library. His mother would come with him sometimes, but mostly she would leave him while she went off to run errands – this was the story she used to tell, a tale of bills to pay, letters to post, things to buy from the market. By the time she collected him on her way home, he would be the proud temporary owner of a pile of books, he had a way to fill the hours and the hours, a way to avoid the packs of other boys who didn't take kindly to newcomers. He was frightened of these burly boys, fascinated by them too. The way they would sit for ages on a wall, languorous and slow and short-sleeved in the sun. They made the passing of time look easy. They made being a boy look easy.

Just when they began to notice him with friendliness instead of suspicion, even throwing him the occasional *All right, Dan* as he walked past, it would be time to move on again.

Will there be a library? he would say to his mum.

And Eve Berry would say yes, don't worry, I've checked and there's definitely a library.

What would she say if she could see him now? If she could *smell* him now?

Mainly, he smells of fear.

He reaches out to the shelves, places his hand across two spines, strokes them as if they are wood he has just finished sanding, a job well done, smooth and good and real.

This helps, just a little, he can feel it helping.

He listens to the sounds around him, tries to tune in to something other than himself.

Health and safety warning for all visitors to the library this morning: please be careful not to trip over the poor excuse of a man on the floor of the cookery section, or step in his puddle of sorrow. We hope to have this mess cleaned up as quickly as possible.

How the human mind will turn on itself. As a species we think we're so evolved, so superior, and yet hidden inside the cave of the human mind, we're all beating ourselves with sticks.

Tears come, again.

He is an empty stomach.

He is the urge to steal.

He is a boy's facial tic, a twitch of the nose that should be long gone.

Excuse me, a voice says.

Daniel looks up.

There is a woman standing beside him. She crouches down, puts her hand on his shoulder.

I just want to say, she says. Whatever it is that's hurting you right now, it won't last forever.

His mouth opens, he doesn't speak.

Trust me, she says.

And the weight of her hand on his shoulder.

He will feel it through these filthy clothes.

He will feel it through pyjamas.

He will feel it through a clean T-shirt, a soft jumper.

He will feel it through all the seasons as they manifest around him, in the skies and underfoot, in blossom and birth, in hibernation and awakening, in the simple air, in snow and sunlight, in resilience and rot, in a flourish and a fading, in the many guises of an old tree, in every living thing.

Over time, the story changes.

Sometimes, in his mind, she is not a woman at all.

She is a pool of still water.

She is a rush of colour and flight.

Like a kingfisher, here then gone, that no one saw but him.

I found him in the library, check-shirted, cross-legged.

I had gone in for a novel, something hard and fast and stark, preferably overwhelming.

I found him in the library, a crumple of salt and blue eyes.

Silver-brown stubble on olive skin, that was him.

Mousy hair, rough hands.

He was staring at a book as though it were a map, or a photo of someone he loved.

But this man was not the first thing I noticed.

It was his small companion, beside him on the dirty carpet.

A ceramic sheep.

He kept looking at this ornament, as if it was speaking in a small sheepish voice, as if they were having an important conversation.

Unlike this time last year, no one has started a fire in the back garden using shoe protector spray, a lighter and someone else's coat. There has been no physical violence. No one has deliberately thrown the past in someone else's face, as far as Rae can tell. A successful party by this family's standards.

And now a bell is ringing. An old brass bell, once owned by a town crier. The bell their mother likes to brandish when she wants to demand attention.

We've all been summoned to the lounge, a voice says.

Tell me it's not what I think it is, another voice says.

I'm afraid so. Hope you remembered your earplugs.

As a gift for her husband on his eightieth birthday, Sherry is about to serenade him with her special a cappella version of 'I Want to Know What Love Is' by Foreigner.

Please no, not *again*, Leslie wants to say. Must you sing this every year on my birthday? It's not special, it's painful. I had more fun when I went for the snip, if you can remember that long ago – yes, that's right, that *is* what I'm saying. Going into hospital to have the tubes that carried my sperm cut and heat-sealed, *that* was more enjoyable than standing in front of our entire family, their partners and ex-lovers and all the other randoms you like to invite, and trying to work out what to do with my face. They're looking at me, you're looking at me, *everyone's* looking at

8

me – it's excruciating. You know I'm a quiet man, Sherry, I've always been more reserved than you. The perfect gift for my eightieth birthday? That would be you *not* singing 'I Want to Know What Love Is' by Foreigner.

Please, not again, Rae wants to say. Honestly Mum, I don't know how to say this, but your rendition, your *highly unique* cover version, well basically it haunts me, it floods my mind at the very worst moments, like when I'm trying to sleep, like when I'm working, and sometimes honest to God I even hear it during sex, not that there's been much of that lately. You have to stop singing it, Mum. You have to make it stop.

But who would be so selfish as to silence a caged bird, whose song is her only freedom? A woman who *feels* like a caged bird, that's what she often says to her husband.

Let me out let me out let me out, she shouts.

Darling, you know where the front door is, Leslie says.

I just need to vocalise my sense of entrapment. That's enough for me. It's a release in itself, she says.

No one's trapping you, my dear, he says. You're free to leave whenever you like.

Life's not that black and white, Sherry says. Emotions are not that simple.

For me they are, he says.

Well maybe *that's* what traps me, she says.

What? he says.

Your simplicity, she says.

Leslie smiles and looks back at his sudoku. He is a patient man with a nervous twitch in his left elbow, which juts out when he is feeling stressed. Once, after queueing in a post office for forty-five minutes, he elbowed a teenager in the head and was accused of assault.

*

The Marsh family and their guests are perched on the sofa in the cosy – i.e. small, cramped, suffocatingly cluttered – living room of 4 Abigail Gardens. They are squeezed into armchairs. They are sitting on the floor, waiting.

It's fine, Rae tells herself. This get-together is almost over. Not long now until she can grab her trainers, jump on a bus and forget these people exist until the next unsolicited reminder.

Who invited the postwoman? her sister says.

The answer is engulfed by a power ballad.

Sherry makes a theatrical, what some might call *experimental* start, part song, part spoken word. If you have ever heard an a cappella version of 'I Want to Know What Love Is', you will understand how curiously arresting it is: a release of heightened emotion, an act of oversharing, teeming with eerie pauses.

Now she loosens up, finds her groove, gets into it.

She sings about heartache, if singing is the right word, which it isn't.

Rae turns to look at the stranger beside her, who seems to be crying. This makes her laugh, not because she is cruel or insensitive, but because she is, in this moment, traumatised.

She pulls a neatly folded square of tissue from her cardigan pocket and offers it to him.

His name is Rufus. She has no idea if this is his real name, presumes it isn't, but who knows.

Rufus mouths *thank you* while nodding slowly and unfolding the tissue as if it were a secret note. He is a picture of earnestness, but not the kind Rae likes in a person, the serious-minded studious kind. His earnestness is mawkish and disorientating. It makes her feel travel-sick.

And now the best/worst bit, depending on how easy you find it to witness desperation:

With outstretched arms and a glossy grin, her mother begins to flap her hands up and down. She resembles a pop star, inviting a huge crowd to get up and sing along. But she is not a pop star. She is sixty-five-year-old Sherry Marsh in her faithful trouser suit and silk blouse, standing on a purple rug in front of a gas fire, its fake briquettes spilling onto the floor, most of them half chewed during puppyhood by a neighbour's golden retriever. Inside her jacket, the sleeve of her blouse is still torn from when she snagged it on a holly bush after too many ginger wines in the Dog and Duck.

As usual, no one moves. This is how it always goes.

Until it doesn't. Thanks to Rufus, who jumps to his feet and starts singing.

Sherry is illuminated. She is emboldened. She is happiness personified. Once a year since 1988 she has invited her family and friends to get up and join her in song. In *this* song. And no one ever has.

There are many ways to describe this, depending on your outlook on life, depending on whether your glass is half full or half empty.

1. Foolishly persistent.
2. Wonderfully persistent.
3. A moving display of love and optimism.
4. A cry for help.

And now Rufus is right beside her, looking into her eyes.

She picks up her brass bell, shakes it about, carries on singing.

Sometimes, a moment of joy is so surprising, so overwhelming, that if a bell is close to hand why the hell wouldn't we ring it.

The word *cacophony* does not suffice. The word *discordant* does not suffice. There is no word for how Sherry's notes don't even come close to those sung by Foreigner, for how this surge of joy has inserted a brutishness into her voice that is frankly quite scary – and this, mixed with the sound of the old bell, mixed with Rufus's overzealous baritone ...

Rae remembers the huge headphones she used to wear as a child, often for hours on end to keep everyone at bay, plugged into the empty pocket of her corduroy trousers. She had loved those headphones, and those cords for that matter – they were gold, with a square patch sewn onto the left knee by Eve Berry, her mother's friend, who had attempted to capture the likeness of Wonder Woman in embroidery. And yes, fair enough, this superhero embla-zoned on jumbo cord could in fact have been any woman with long brown hair, but to Eve and Rae she was Wonder Woman and this was all that mattered.

Embroidery is an underrated art form, Rae thinks. Because she is highly skilled at psychological off-roading, at heading off down any available track; how else to distract herself from moments like this? So much better than having to experience the odious assortment of emotions aroused by her mother: disgust, fear, pity and contempt, all rolled up in the shabbiest kind of love, and that's just for starters.

Rae glances at the curious duo, who seem to have devi-ated from the original song, their heads thrown back in untuneful anarchy.

She looks away, decides to focus on the painting hang-ing on the wall, one of the few objects in this house that she actually likes. It's a painting of a blue kitchen, a bright window, a long table. On this table there is fresh bread, butter, cheese and fruit. There's a jug of water and a bottle of something Spanish, sweet, profoundly alcoholic, this is how Rae has always seen it. It's a still life, but to her it's anything but still. As a girl she would lie for hours on the sofa, staring at this painting, imagining all kinds of different people entering its kitchen, lighting candles and gathering around its table. These people would eat and drink until the early hours. They would talk about all the best parts of being human, like cinema, sea and forests. They would lean in close, fall in love.

Now she notices Pauline looking in her direction. Is that *hatred* on her face? Oh come on. How was she to know that Rufus would supply backing vocals? That he would egg their mother on, *inflate* her?

Her sister is mouthing something now.

What? she mouths back.

WHAT THE FUCK? Pauline shouts.

Rae vows to make an official complaint to Stranger of Mine, otherwise known as SOM, through which she hired Rufus. She hadn't asked for an extroverted singer who would make himself as visible as possible. She had specifically requested a *soft furnishing*. I'm looking for a male this time, someone to attend a family function with me across an afternoon and evening, she wrote. I need him to serve as a kind of cushion. You know how soft furnishings absorb sound in a room? Well I would like him to absorb the audible impact of my family, to limit their reverb, so to speak. This is the brief, I hope it makes sense. I look forward to hearing from you. Kind regards, Rae Marsh. PS The improvements you have made to your app are excellent, well done.

It brought her pleasure and a rare sense of importance to type the word *brief*, to feel that she was giving someone instructions. It also gave her a secret to keep from her family, something else to put between them, which made her more distant, safely out of reach.

Rae is addicted to the Stranger of Mine app. She can't resist hiring a Stranger to sit with her in the cinema, walk with her through an arboretum. What appeals to her most is the lack of pressure. She doesn't have to make an effort, be a good conversationalist, wonder if they might want anything more – and if not, *why* not. But even better than this, there is no boomerang effect, which is Rae's term for what it feels like to get to know a new person. You reveal something about yourself, while believing that this revelation belongs to that moment in time, to that particular conversation, and then *BAM* – the next time you meet there it is again, coming back at you, hitting you in the face when your new friend refers to it all of a sudden. Getting to know a person – the continuity, the unpredictability – is alarming, to say the least. And with SOM there's no continuity. No boomerang. The person Rae arranges to meet is simply another body beside her as she goes about her business, to be sent on their way when she says so, never to be seen again.

I think you can go now, Rae says to Rufus in the hallway.

He looks at his watch. Really? But I was just popping to the loo. I don't have to go yet.

Don't worry, I'll still pay for the whole time. Actually, I've already paid online, so –

Honestly, I'm happy to stay.

Just go, she says.

But why? Have I disappointed you?

She considers saying yes, you're as mad as my entire family, I don't know why I bothered. In fact, I want my money back.

You've been fine, she says. But please leave.

Are you aware that you haven't smiled once since we arrived? he says.

Excuse me?

I don't care if you give me a bad review. Some people need a mirror holding up to them. You have a really interesting family and you're a miserable sod. I wish *my* family would sing.

What the hell do you know about my family? You think coming to one party tells you anything?

Lovers' tiff? Pauline says, squeezing past on her way to the kitchen for another Bacardi and Coke.

He is *not* my lover, Rae says.

Too right I'm not your lover, Rufus says. No wonder you have to hire a friend.

What happens next is something that will haunt Rae for years, despite her attempts to block it out. Again and again she has witnessed the members of her extended family losing their tempers, slamming doors, arm-wrestling to win an argument, everyone apart from her father always hurling their weight around, making a racket. Throughout all of this, she has considered herself to be quite unlike them. A black sheep in a separate field, dignified and intelligent, chewing on better grass. A light drinker, in control of her emotions. Certainly not boorish or violent. Certainly not someone who would raise her hand to a stranger in her parents' hallway, slap him across the face –

They both stumble backwards in shock.

Oh my God, Rufus says, his hand pressed against his left cheek.

Fuck, Rae says. I'm so sorry. I've never hit anyone before, I don't know what happened. It was the weirdest reflex. I am *so* sorry.

Now Rufus is crying, muttering something about hating his fucking job, wishing he'd stayed at Sainsbury's, why must everything turn to shit.

Rae is an open mouth, a buttoned-up cardigan, a cracked mirror.

Rufus was full of song and now he is distraught.

How life changes in an instant.

You're not supposed to judge me, she says.

What?

You're supposed to be neutral and impervious.

Impervious?

Yes. It means –

I know what it means.

You insulted me.

Does that justify violence?

It was hardly violence.

If I were a woman and you were a man, would you call it violence then?

Rae grimaces. Because he's right. Do you need a hug? she says.

A hug?

She nods.

No I do *not* need a hug, he says, moving forward just the same, sobbing into her shoulder.

Sherry emerges from the lounge and spots her daughter embracing a man. What a sight! Like morning sunshine through her ill-fitting curtains. Like discovering a rare antique being sold unwittingly for 50p at a car boot sale. She rushes towards them, throws her arms around Rufus.

And then there are three.

Group hug, Sherry says.

Jesus Christ, Rufus says, spinning around.

Oh, are you crying, dear? Sherry says. Why are you crying? What has my daughter done to you?

I'm afraid she just hit me.

Rae?

That's right.

Our Rae?

She slapped me in the face.

Well what are you crying about that for? What kind of man are you? For goodness' sake, I'd like to slap you myself. You arouse passion in a woman who's usually as bland as a Rich Tea biscuit and just stand there crying?

He does *not* arouse my passion, Rae says.

Oh shut up, Sherry says.

Don't tell me to shut up.

Your generation, you're always crying. Do you see *me* crying? Don't you think I'd like to be bawling my eyes out?

Silence.

Rae and Rufus look at each other.

I actually really like Rich Tea biscuits, Rufus says.

Thank you, Rae says. Then she pauses, glances sideways at the wall, at the lilac flock wallpaper coming undone. Why did she just thank him? You're doing it *again*, Rae. Being submissive. You are not a fucking Rich Tea biscuit!

She calls a taxi, and on the way into town, Rufus makes them stop at McDonald's so she can buy him a Happy Meal to apologise. She has never said sorry with junk food before. The taxi drops him five streets away from his house because he wants to safeguard his privacy, says he doesn't want her turning up in the middle of the night to slap him in the face again. For all he knows she might have a problem, a compulsion, she might be one of life's slappers. She laughs at this and slips two £10 notes into the pocket

17

of his jacket, which feels wasteful and exciting, as though her evening has been far more illicit than a family party. Consider this a tip, she says, while a wide-eyed taxi driver watches through his rear-view mirror. You won't take this any further will you? she says. I really am terribly sorry for what happened. Well, you'll just have to wait and see won't you, Rufus says, enjoying the sensation of power, of knowing something she doesn't, of having something on her. Then he and his Happy Meal are gone and she is sitting in the back seat of a taxi by herself. Nice one, love, the taxi driver says. I beg your pardon? she says. Good for you, he says, women's lib and all that.

At home, Rae showers and changes into an old T-shirt, makes a cup of camomile tea, reads four poems aloud to calm herself down.

After tonight, she will try to forget about the slap, and about her family in general. They are simply people she knows, people she spent too much time with until she was eighteen. They have little to do with her daily life. They do not represent or define her. And it's highly unlikely that she will *ever* hit another human being again – it was a blip, that's all, an involuntary misdemeanour, entirely out of character and no doubt caused by a deficiency of some kind. She will visit the doctor and ask for a blood test, buy a good multivitamin, go back to having porridge for breakfast (she is sure she was calmer when she ate porridge). And she will buy herself the biggest pair of headphones she can find, at least as big as the ones she had when she was a girl, and wear them as much as possible.

As she tries to sleep, she thinks of those old headphones. She used to plug them into the back of the enormous stereo in the lounge and sit beside it, but mainly she plugged them

18

into her trouser pocket. Those cords were fantastic, she thinks. Eve made such a good job of that Wonder Woman. Eve also used to make biscuits and bring them round in special cellophane wrapping, tied with ribbon. Once, she even made Rae's mother a skirt. She was sensible and generous, quite unlike her future replacements, all the other friends and neighbours who spent time with Sherry Marsh over the years. The endless cackling, the Babycham nights, the underwear parties.

Rae pulls the duvet up over her head.

She imagines herself living on a small island, where she makes her own clothes and candles, grows her own vegetables and has a cat named Esther. The island is hard to reach, any visitors arriving by boat can be spotted from a distance. No one can arrive unannounced or uninvited.

This island is called Petula, and Rae has been going there for as long as she can remember. It's part of her psyche, her landscape.

Who else knows about the place? No one really. Only Eve Berry in fact, the one person she told, because she was wholly trustworthy, able to keep a secret, this was something you just knew about Eve.

They were on the beach, out on one of their day trips. Ever since her mother became friends with Eve, day trips to the coast were a regular occurrence. They would get bundled into the back of Eve's old Mini – Rae, her little sister, Pauline, and Daniel, Eve's son. It was hot, it was a squeeze, it was the summer of 1985. Eve had bought them sweets for the journey, a paper bag full of flying saucers, lemon bonbons and giant white mice.

Now they were all in the sea, apart from Rae and Eve, who were on a blanket by themselves. Eve was good company. She was attentive, and sort of even, meaning her moods and her voice were all on one level all of the time, this was how Rae saw it. Her mother's voice and moods were unpredictable, scattered, a frenzy of litter. She made Rae feel tense and untidy.

That afternoon on the beach, Eve was wearing a yellow bikini and a grey cardigan. The cardie looked so soft, Rae wanted to reach out and touch it.

Can I tell you something incredibly private? she said.

Of course, Eve said.

Rae moved closer, just a little. She glanced at her mother, who was bobbing about in the sea, then back at Eve. I have an island that I go to, she said.

An island, Eve said.

Uh huh.

That's nice. Is it near here?

Oh no, it's miles away.

I see. And is it *your* island?

What do you mean?

Do you own it?

I do.

It's all yours, completely yours.

That's right.

Sounds amazing. What's it called, this place?

It isn't called anything. I've never thought of giving it a name.

That's okay. A thing can be nameless can't it, Eve said.

Rae thought this over. She listened to the music coming from the tiny radio beside them. A woman was singing about downtown, how it's a good place to go, a place that will make everything feel better.

Who sings this? she said.

Eve didn't answer, which was unusual. She was gazing at the sea, watching Rae's mother swim up and down while

20

Pauline and Daniel paddled nearby, quite separately, two six-year-olds who looked like they had never even met.

Eve? Rae said.

Sorry darling, what did you say?

Who sings this song?

Petula Clark I think.

Petula Clark. That's a nice name. Unusual.

It is isn't it. Sounds like a type of flower.

Rae smiled. My island will be called Petula, she said. But don't tell anyone will you, not ever, do you promise.

Eve laughed, in a friendly kind of way, a way that felt like an invitation to laugh along with her. Which Rae did. And it felt very grown up. She didn't really know why they were laughing, except that it was something to do with the joy of music and secrets and giving things a name.

I love it, Eve said. And don't worry, mum's the word.

Then she looked away, asked Rae if she fancied a swim. And it was over. A perfect moment here then gone, a glimpse of adulthood, of what it might be like to be a woman like Eve. Rae was nine years old, and she was every age she would ever be, just for a second, that's how it felt. Something like a whole life flashing through her. On a blanket on the sand, she felt completely naked.

Tonight, thirty-three years later, in her own bed in her own flat, Rae's mind has become busy with this and that. All of which is mist over sea, obscuring Petula.

Petula being her talisman, companion, defence.

Her ladder down to sleep, her childish thing.

(If childish is a clean ocean, a lighthouse, a picnic on a rock.)

Finally, the memories clear and her breathing deepens.

She is there. Inside her wooden house on the island.

Esther, her black cat, who follows her around like a faithful dog, is asleep on her lap.

Rae watches the birds from her chair by the window, and just as she too is about to fall asleep, something catches her eye. There is a framed photograph on the sideboard, Rae is sure it wasn't here before. This house on Petula changes and shifts about, of course it does, all places do; there have been paintings, sketches, even a tapestry on the wall. But there has never been a photo. Because Rae comes here to forget other people, not to be reminded.

Such an effort sometimes, even in a daydream, to get out of a chair and walk across a room.

Before she reaches the photo, Rae knows who it is. She recognises the bikini and the cardie, the attentive tilt of the woman's head.

And seeing Eve again, it feels like peace itself.

All night, she dreams of freedom.

He is two nights on a bench, one night in a doorway, after years and years of mattress and cotton sheet.

There is a portable radio on a wall in a street in a suburb in which Daniel walks alone.

As he arrives at the solitary radio, he wonders who it belongs to and why it has been left here, switched on. Doesn't anyone mind the noise? Funny how no one has stolen it on their way past. He thinks about taking it himself, but it will only be something else to carry. Maybe he could barter, swap it for a meal, if he were that kind of person. He pictures a man walking into a fish and chip shop with a portable radio and walking out with battered cod. He is not that man.

He lets his rucksack drop to the floor, then stands and listens.

A woman is talking about the weather. We can expect to see temperatures of up to 27 degrees in parts of England by the end of this week, she says. That's warmer than the French Riviera, the Costa del Sol. In fact, this could well be the hottest May since records began.

The woman talks about traffic on the roads, how thousands could head for the coast.

She says something about shorts and flip-flops, how it's time to dig them out.

23

Daniel pictures people everywhere, poised with spades, about to unearth their summer wardrobes from dry soil.

And don't forget to wear sunscreen, she says.

He doesn't have any sunscreen, nor does he plan to buy any. It's no longer what he considers an essential item. He thinks about how people give tea and coffee, sandwiches and soup to those who have nowhere to live, but does anyone ever give them sunscreen?

Them, Daniel? says the woman on the radio. Haven't you been sleeping in a doorway and on a bench for the past three nights?

Thanks for pointing that out, Daniel says. His nose twitches.

Well honestly, how long are you going to wander around like this? Other people are driving to the coast, Daniel. They're restocking their fridges, buying sunscreen. I'm concerned that you don't have a plan, that you're not even capable of hatching a plan.

Hatching? You make it sound like an egg.

Well I suppose it sort of is, when you think about it, she says. It's the beginning of a new life. For a plan to emerge you need to brood for a while, let it develop – you need to *incubate*.

What a curious DJ you are, he says.

I prefer the term *radio presenter*, she says.

He hears an engine, turns to look. It's a grey van with the words ALAN DAVIS PLUMBING on the side. The van parks beside him and a man gets out.

All right mate, he says.

Hello, Daniel says.

Alan Davis grabs the radio by its handle, rolls his eyes, says he'd forget his head if it wasn't screwed on, and this baby wasn't cheap, it's virtually indestructible, battery lasts

24

for ages, break my heart if I lost it, well not break my heart exactly, but I'd be bloody upset let's put it that way.

It has a very good sound, Daniel says. Warm and bassy.

Alan looks pleased. You're my little workmate aren't you? he says to the radio. Can't believe I left it behind while loading up, I'm always doing that.

Daniel's stomach hurts, it feels a bit like a stitch but it isn't. And the blister on his foot is aching again. He wonders if Alan Davis has any painkillers in his van. Is that a weird question to ask a stranger? Can this plumber tell that he has been walking for four days with no destination?

Yesterday, Daniel hitched a lift. He had never hitched before, didn't really expect a car to slow for his arm and his thumb, but it did. He travelled with a stranger to the motorway services, the ones he used to stop at when he too owned a van with his name on the side.

DANIEL BERRY, PAINTER & DECORATOR

These services are not the usual bland pitstop. There's a farm shop with artisan bread and local delicacies, designer gifts, even clothes – but most importantly, a shower.

He stood for a long time in the warm water.

He bought a cup of tea and a sausage roll, and found half a ham sandwich in the bin, still in its packet, which he discreetly removed while pretending to empty out his tote bag.

As he shook crumbs from the bag, turned it inside out and back again, he stared at the ink drawing of books printed on the side, and the writing beneath it: *David Hockney, A Bag Full of Books.*

The sight of this bag disturbed him. It looked familiar and strange, like something he used to own when he was someone else. It was his and not his, a tote bag that he had or hadn't bought from the Strand Bookstore in New York, during a minibreak that he had or hadn't taken. Before last week he would push it into the pocket of his jacket, take it into town to hold his shopping. He had bought it because he loved David Hockney, especially the paintings of swimming pools, which reminded him of something he couldn't put into words, a parallel life maybe, that's how he had described it to Erica. A few months later, after visiting an affordable art fair, she had come home with a painting by a local artist – a man diving into an outdoor pool, a woman lazing on a sunlounger. For you, she said. I know it's not a Hockney, but I thought we could put it on the bedroom wall so we can see it when we're in bed.

Erica Yu, Daniel's ex-girlfriend. Australian, beautiful, prickly. A curious blend of giggly and often humourless. Erica is no longer in the picture, and she is the *whole* picture, every bullish brushstroke, painting him into a corner.

As he drank his tea, Daniel felt glad that he had come to the services. For once he had made a good decision. The transience was a comfort. He felt at ease, no different to anyone else passing through. As he sat on the grassy bank, gazing at the fields, he was simply a man taking a break from a journey, a man taking his time. There was no need to panic.

Unable to even comprehend the vulgarity of your current situation? Its emotional foulness, its filth? In a time of crisis, just come to our motorway services! All yours from 6am to 10pm. Take a walk, sit by a lake, drink tea, eat a bloody good pie. Everything will be all right.

He placed a little ceramic sheep gently on the grass beside him. There you go, he said.

Thank you, the sheep said.

Later, he hitched his way back to the small city that

26

now had nothing to offer but memories. He was like a cat, returning to its old home after its owners had moved, curling around the legs of ghosts. But Daniel isn't as brave as a cat. He feels weak and scraggy-minded, can't bring himself to go near the cottage, to see other people inside it, painting the walls, sprucing it up. Instead he paces through nearby suburbs, takes lifts in strangers' cars, sleeps outdoors in the perfect ominous night with the weather and the moon, the foxes and the litter, the uncanny echoes and the cider fights.

Do not look the truth in the eye, Daniel. Do not do not do NOT.

Are you okay? a voice says.

Sorry?

Alan Davis has one foot inside his van and one foot out. Just checking you're all right, he says.

I'm okay, Daniel says.

You waiting for someone?

Sort of. Not exactly.

Fair enough, Alan says, sensing complication that he doesn't need.

Daniel watches the van pull away. He stands beside the wall, looks down at the space where the radio had been. Its absence hurts. Something else, gone. It had been so warm and bassy. And what strikes him now is the extreme importance of a radio, how it can be a reason to stop, a place to land, someone to hold on to; like reaching out in the dark and a voice saying *I'm here, I'm just here*. A portable radio is bloody miraculous, he thinks. As well as somewhere to live, every homeless person should be given a small radio, some batteries and a pair of headphones. Alongside food, water and shelter, we need a friendly voice.

Daniel listens. All he can hear now is the faint sound of traffic, a window being closed, a seagull overhead. Not a single human voice, despite the fact that he must be surrounded by people. Inside their houses they are cooking dinner, washing up, putting children to bed, watching TV, reading. They are cleaning, worrying, talking on the phone, stroking furry animals. They're feeling ugly, feeling attractive. They are fucking, quick and slow, generous and careless. Mainly, they are staring at screens. They are trying to compose sentences. They are comparing themselves to other people. They are asking if anyone has seen their glasses.

Daniel is also quite sure that right now, at this very second, someone close by must be putting a clean cover on a duvet, plumping pillows, throwing a soft blanket across a bed.

He sits on the wall and imagines this, a sight so commonplace, unremarkable, but not to him. Whenever he changed his sheets and made his bed, he always saw it as a moment of love and good fortune. His oldest duvet cover, soft and worn, was the thing he would have saved in a fire.

Seriously? Erica said, when she asked him this question. That's what you'd grab if the house was on fire – some old bedding?

Yes, he said.

That's weird, she said.

Is it? he said. Just because it isn't what you'd take?

I'd take my laptop and my old photographs, she said. Photos can't be replaced. You can easily buy a new duvet set.

I don't have any photos, he said. Anyway, it was the first thing I bought after all those months of sleeping in my car. I still remember exactly how I felt when I made my bed and got into it. It was quite a moment.

He turned to look at her, wanting her to ask a question, make a space for more detail, a space for him to unfold before her. *What was that like? How did it feel?* But Erica didn't ask questions like that. This was something he had noticed when they first got together, how her questions were mainly about their everyday life – how his day had been, what he fancied for tea, where they might go at the week-end. Or, in a fairly sweet tone, she might ask why he had said or done something in a particular way; she was the queen of disingenuous questions. And sometimes he craved a deeper kind of interest. He wanted her to ask what he had been like as a boy, why he moved away from Wales after his A levels, why he slept in his car for almost six months. Instead, she embraced his history as if it were a series of facts, head-lines, bullet points – no investigation required. If he had turned his life into a book and given it to Erica, she would have held it firmly in her small hands, run her fingers down the contents page and index, gazed lovingly at the cover, then placed it on the coffee table in a prominent position. She would carry it in her bag sometimes, as if she wanted to keep it close, or might finally read every page, but she wouldn't open it again, and she would never speak of having carried it with her, and he would never say that he knew.

Now he pictures their bed. He wonders if anyone has bought it yet, wonders who is sleeping in it now.

He pictures the iron bed frame and the mattress – the first big items he and Erica bought together when she moved in. The mattress was made from linen, cotton, hemp and wool, among other things. It was natural, breathable, medium tension. I think you love this bed more than me, she said. I think I might love it as *much* as you, he said, back in 2012, Year of the Dragon, year of stupid excitement, year of day trips to Ikea.

How did Ikea always steal a whole day, even when they only went for one thing? They would eat meatballs, chips and gravy, followed by cake, while looking out at the car park. It shouldn't have been fun, but it was. The amount we've eaten today is grotesque, Erica said after they had queued with an overflowing trolley, then paused for a cheap hot dog, paused again to buy ten packets of Swedish biscuits, before returning to Daniel's van with thirty-two items they didn't really need – and without the item they had gone for.

Here's a question, Daniel:

When is a bed not a bed?

When it's a pocket-sprung desert island.

After Erica left, a month before he did too, the cottage and everything inside it changed. His corner of the world turned against him. He was a castaway in his own bed, stranded in his own room.

He thinks about the roses, wonders how they're getting on without the sound of his voice. It's only been a few days, but maybe they've noticed his absence? He has always believed in the intelligence of trees and flowers, always treated them like companions. He would tell them what he'd been doing, what was happening in the world; sometimes, he would even read them poems. And why not, what a way to start the day, hard to think of anything better than barefoot in the garden with a poem and a plant and a mug of strong tea.

They can't hear you, Erica would say, by the kitchen door in her pyjamas.

Now he kicks his heels against the wall. It's only a matter of time before someone comes over to ask what he's doing, why he's sitting on private property, loitering on a quiet street.

He waits.

And nothing happens.

I could be a potential intruder, he thinks. For God's sake, I could be *anyone*.

He begins to sweat.

There is a kind of whooshing sound, coming from nowhere and everywhere.

It's the sound of his own body, the whoosh of fear.

He doesn't know where to go.

The wall seems to be getting higher, or maybe his legs are getting shorter, further from the ground like a boy's legs.

He remembers the boys from his childhood. When they sat on a wall they *owned* that wall. And now he no longer owns anything. Apart from these clothes, this rucksack.

And why is that exactly? a woman says.

He looks around.

It's me, she says.

Who is me?

Don't you recognise your friendly radio presenter? Anyway, I want to know, she says.

What, he says. What do you want to know?

Why did you give all your things to charity? Your beloved bed, the swimming pool painting, all your brushes and tools. How could you bear to stand there while they took it all away? Even the bedding you would've saved in a fire.

I don't know, he says.

It was quite extreme, she says. I mean, I applaud your gesture, the hospice will make good money from selling all your things, but there's no going back, what's yours is someone else's, what's gone is gone.

Daniel pictures the men from the charity shop loading his possessions into their van.

Take everything, he said. I've boxed it up, used bubble wrap, it's all labelled.

Did someone die? one of the men said. If you don't mind me asking.

Daniel shook his head.

And the van drove away with all the things he and Erica had bought together.

What a wild donation.

He stood on the kerb and waved.

He imagined a harvested heart, beating on ice in a box in the back of the van.

Later that week he locked the cottage door for the last time, posted his keys through the letterbox.

He walked to the charity shop.

Where else would he go?

It was part of an old factory; red brick, urban regeneration. This building was the home of community projects – a bar, a theatre, a hub for local artists. And across three floors was Aubrey's, run by the local hospice. A poster in the window said *Buy pre-loved – help us give someone a good death*.

Aubrey's was organised into bedrooms, kitchens, living rooms. It was like wandering through a museum, or some kind of installation, an exhibition about love and home and history, all the shifting shelters we make.

And there was Daniel's life for all to see, their sofa, chairs and coffee table, their lamps and vases, their entire kitchen from cups to colander.

Christ, Erica. Look at all our stuff in here, it's so bloody eerie. I feel like I'm on the set of a TV show that we once used to star in. It's all still here, it's not too late.

He sat on their sofa and waited.

A cold wind blows from the radio presenter's mouth, just for a second.

Daniel rubs his hands together but they are not his hands. The skin is so rough and dry, its sound is new, high-pitched. Sandpapery, he thinks, looking down at his own hands.

Then he looks up.

All the stuff with my mum, he says. I still can't believe it.

I know, the radio presenter says, I know.

And the landlord, the fucking landlord.

It's all right, she says. It's all right. I'm here, just lean into my voice.

It was the longest I'd lived anywhere, he says. I'd built an archway in the garden, bought a little woodshed, painted it pink. You should've seen the wild flowers, we had so many bees. It was our home. It was a game, a hot bath, a medicinal whisky. It was a bright forest, a brilliant den, but you have to go and you'll never choose when.

Breathe, Daniel, the radio presenter says. Slow down, take a *long deep breath.*

Then she just left, he says at the end of his breath.

I'm so sorry, she says.

He shrugs. His bloodshot eyes, his odd socks.

Where will you sleep tonight? she says.

33

In the park, he says. I was in there earlier, I found a private spot under a tree behind the tennis courts.

Private, she says. In what sense of the word exactly?

You know what I mean.

Fair enough, she says. You choose to snooze in the dark of the park.

Choose, he says. In what sense of the word exactly?

Interesting question, she says. And by the way, what's with the sheep?

He rummages for his pet, his pal, his memento. He opens his fingers and there it is, smiling in the palm of his hand.

The thing you gave away, and then didn't, she says. Look at you. I see you, I see what you are.

And what am I? he says.

You're a dropped boy, left behind like an old wooden toy. That's you isn't it, Daniel Berry, she says.

He smiles.

Dropped overboard whistle snore, black of night a son no more, he says with a surprising swell of volume, a surge of aliveness, as his hand moves to the side of his head, where all of a sudden it hurts.

They are playing 'Can't Buy Me Love' on the radio again. Didn't they already play this an hour ago? Rae is sure she has heard it twice since she got up. Either that or 'Can't Buy Me Love' featured in one of her dreams last night, and has lingered in her consciousness like sinister background music.

Over the past week, Rae's dreams have been disturbingly vivid, so long and intense that she wakes up exhausted. Camille, her psychoanalyst, was excited to hear this news and called it *a significant development*. It means something important is finally happening in the bowels of your psyche, she said, her fingers pressed together like a woman in prayer. *Finally?* Rae said. *Bowels?* she said. Camille smiled, told Rae it would be best if she ignored the content of her dreams and paid deep attention to the tone. Content is a red herring, a box of old hats, she said. Rae squinted at her therapist, who was bright and mischievous and French. Do you mean, she said, that focusing on the content of a dream is *old hat*? Precisely, Camille said. Pay attention to the atmosphere, the emotion, the texture – what's left on top of you when the dream is over.

These linguistic glitches, spoken in that soft accent, are a big part of why Rae enjoys going to therapy. She replays them in her mind throughout the day, the endearing sound of Camille's sentences, the way she tries so hard to translate her French psychoanalytic insights into terms Rae will find useful. I always try to remember you are my layperson, Camille said. Concepts like transference mean nothing to you. Which makes you a lucky woman, Rae Marsh!

Rae tends to leave her sessions feeling perplexed and at sea, which is how she likes it. Perplexed is always an improvement on what she is feeling when she arrives, and she likes being at sea, it's an antidote to how landlocked she usually feels.

You throw me into the sea and I find that helpful, she once said to Camille.

And you are the most intriguing patient, Camille said. You like to have saltwater hair, *oui*?

The chaos of their conversations. The fetch of their waves.

Rae couldn't remember the last time she had salty hair. She hadn't swum in the sea since she was a child. And this struck her as extremely sad. Because the years when she swam in the sea were the very best years. And there were only three of them.

Clever Camille, always tapping into her sadness like that.

This morning, Rae's dream has left her with a profound sense of irritation. She is not a fan of the Beatles, and she certainly doesn't want to hear their songs in her dreams. That's bordering on nightmare territory quite frankly, and is bound to be Freudian in some way, because Rae's mother is *obsessed* with the Beatles. Sherry Marsh discovered a long time ago that if you are prepared to pay for the pleasure, plus the postage, you can find all kinds of Beatles merchandise on the internet. Which is why the house that Rae grew up in is now full of Beatles toilet roll, Beatles toothpaste, Beatles jugs, Beatles wallpaper, Beatles candles, Beatles lampshades, a Beatles washing-up bowl, Beatles dusters and boxes of Beatles matches. Sherry prefers her merchandise to be functional. I'm interested in the juxtaposition of fandom and domesticity, she once said to Rae and her father, a sentence that silenced them both. Did Sherry Marsh just use the word *juxtaposition*? You never cease to surprise me, my dear, Leslie said, grabbing hold of his wife and kissing her.

Is love really that simple? Rae thought, as she grimaced and turned away from her parents. Can a kiss be bought with a surprising word? Are people this easy to impress?

In her first-floor flat, Rae makes a pot of coffee and tries to forget about the Beatles.

It's a Sunday, and yet she has a meeting. Most irregular. She has been invited to meet Sally Canto, founding director of Stranger of Mine, following a complaint from one of its employees, Mr Rufus Willoughby. While they would usually ban any member of the public who hits a member of staff, or abuses them in any way, Rae has been a loyal customer since the beginning, and everything in life is complicated, nuanced, so instead of making a rash decision, Sally Canto would like to discuss this matter in person.

Why had Sally suggested a Sunday? Rae felt insulted by this. Yes, she used SOM as regularly as other people used Uber or Deliveroo, but it was rude to extrapolate from this, to box her in as the kind of person who didn't have plans to spend the weekend with friends or family, a lover or a hypoallergenic dog. Which she didn't, of course, but that was not the point.

She stands by her kitchen window, looks down at the communal garden. This garden is one of the things that persuaded her to buy this flat last year, to make the commitment, put down roots. It's long and narrow, with winding paths and archways, little areas to hide in.

Bruce Springsteen is playing on the radio now, 'Born to Run'.

She opens her mouth to sing, closes it again. Because Rae Marsh does *not* sing. Even the thought of it makes her feel unwell, makes her feel too much like her mother's daughter. It takes a lot of effort to maintain the degree of separateness that Rae requires to function well in life, and singing would threaten that, make her feel like a rotten apple, shaken by song from her mother's dubious tree.

But what is a soul without music, Rae? This question sits tight in her muscles, is posed by a stiff neck, a sore back, a tension headache.

So Bruce sings by himself, and she looks down at the garden, jigs about to the saxophone part of the song, thinks how good it is.

Sally Canto is waiting in the park, beside the bandstand, just where she said she would be. She is eating an ice cream.

You must be Ms Canto, Rae says.

Please, call me Sally. Can I get you a Mr Whippy? I was going to wait until you arrived but I just really fancied one.

No thank you, Rae says. Is that some sort of supersize Mr Whippy?

Sally smiles. I know the ice cream man, she says.

Without any awareness of doing so, Rae compiles a first impression:

Sally Canto is a woman who eats ice cream at 10.30 in the morning. She has no qualms about being messy, just look: see that drop of ice cream on her shirt? Does she look bothered, is she searching her bag for a tissue to wipe it off? No she is not. This hint of unruliness is endearing, but the urge to remove that stain, to grab a wet wipe and rub it all over Sally's chest, is overwhelming. She may not even have paid for that drippy Mr Whippy, things just drop in her lap, quite literally, probably.

Shall we walk? Sally says.

Sure, Rae says.

They set off along the path just as day trippers spill from a bus. These visitors begin to take photos straight away, snapping flowers, trees and squirrels, a frenzied spaniel, two teenagers kissing.

Talk about manic, Sally says. Did you notice how they didn't even look around before they held up their cameras, didn't even get their bearings?

Like pent-up animals, Rae says, reading the slogan on the side of the bus.

GET OUT & ABOUT WITH TMN

What's TMN? she says.

Take Me Now, Sally says.

I beg your pardon, Rae says.

TMN stands for Take Me Now, Sally says. They run social events, days out.

Now, just ahead of them, two women run towards each other, squealing. Their squeals are not equal, in volume or gusto. It's as though one of these women has just found herself joining in, mimicking her friend's welcome for the sake of politeness, and now seems shocked by her own behaviour. They hug for a long time, a tight squeeze, it looks painful, airless. When the hug ends, the more eager of the two pats her friend's face all over as if to check she is really there. Hello hello hello, she says. Hello my dear, the other one says, flinching now, leaning backwards, pulling away from those toddlerish hands.

Sally and Rae have slowed right down, they're making no secret of their nosiness. It strikes Rae that this is a moment of intimacy, the way she and Sally have instinctively changed their pace to observe these women. Rae spends a lot of time walking with strangers, and knows only too well that this shared pace and interest rarely happens. She is often left behind while she watches a bee on a flower, stops to see which book is making someone laugh.

This is rather apt, isn't it, Sally says.

Sorry? Rae says.

The unwanted touching of another person's face, Sally says.

Oh, Rae says.

She feels betrayed, hurt. Further detail about Sally Canto: she knows how to burst a bubble.

I'd like to apologise for that, Rae says. It was completely out of character. I can only assume that a lifetime of irritation with my family had built up in my system and was released in a kind of gesticulative burp.

Gesticulative burp? Sally says.

That's right, Rae says, aware that what she just said was bizarre, but this is one of those times when she must stick to her own rule: commit to your piffle. If you want to come across with any degree of authority, you have to stick to your story once it's out there, speak it with confidence, conviction and passion. Commit to your piffle, your baloney, your drivel, your bosh, your bollocks, your cobblers, your crapola. Never draw attention to the fact that you don't believe in what you're saying.

Well that's a new one, Sally says. I've never heard someone liken a slap to a kind of burp.

Haven't you? Rae says.

That's actually quite inventive, Sally says. So do you often experience irritation as trapped wind?

Rae thinks it over. She can't believe they're already talking about trapped wind, but she takes it as further proof of the intimacy quickly burgeoning between them. Her bubble is back. Long live the bubble.

I do actually, she says.

Rufus must have really pissed you off, Sally says. What did he do?

He called me a miserable sod.

And was that a fair comment?

Possibly, yes. But he also said it was no wonder I had to hire a friend.

Ah. He didn't reveal *that* in our one-to-one.

Your what? Do you mean meeting?

That's right. He said he did his best, even joined in the karaoke.

There was no karaoke.

No singing?

Well, there *was* singing, sort of, but not karaoke. My mother sings by herself, a cappella. The same song every year.

Sally grimaces. He also said he liked your family very much, and when he told you this, you hit him.

That was not what happened. And anyway, he's supposed to be impartial.

That's true, and he's been given a warning for that, not for the first time either. He struggles with restraining his opinions. But this doesn't excuse the fact that you hit him, and pretty hard by the sound of it. The thing is, I don't want to fall prey to socially conformist double standards.

Sorry? Rae says.

41

If you were a man and you'd slapped a female employee, we wouldn't even be having this conversation. You'd no longer be able to use our services, simple as that, Sally says.

That's what Rufus said.

So what do you suggest?

Just as Rae is about to answer Sally's question, to make a case for remaining a loyal user of SOM, to reassert herself as a calm and logical person, something happens. She imagines slapping Sally across the face. The scene in her mind is as vivid as her recent dreams. She pushes her hands deep inside the pockets of her three-quarter jeans.

Look, Sally says. I did need to check you out, to take Rufus seriously, but I'm not here to cut you off.

Oh, Rae says.

Everything's fine, Sally says. I'm sorry if I worried you. Do you fancy a coffee?

Rae has no idea what's going on.

At a table for two there is no further mention of Rufus. They drink coffee, eat almond croissants. Sally tells Rae about Stranger of Mine, how the idea came to her one night as she dined alone in her local Italian restaurant.

The wine was so good, Sally says. Just the house wine, but really lovely. That's the good thing about dining alone, you can order the house wine.

What do you mean? Rae says.

Well, no one orders the house wine if they're with other people do they, Sally says. It looks tight, like you don't care what you drink and know nothing about wine.

I'm always happy to order house wine, Rae says.

Interesting, Sally says. I always go for the third on the list, maybe the fourth.

Rae wonders where this is going. She is still hungry after her croissant, would order a toasted teacake if she were alone, but she isn't.

And it was during my second bottle that it came to me, Sally says. How sometimes you just want another body beside you, not for sex or anything like that. Just the presence of someone who doesn't know you, doesn't expect you to be who you normally are, to pick up the threads of a long conversation and keep sewing sewing sewing. For heaven help us if we want to change the pattern, the material, the stitch.

Rae's heart has gone off-piste. Instead of the usual one two, one two, its rhythm is all over the place. To her relief, it settles. Must have been the coffee. Nothing to do with the fact that sitting with Sally in this moment is like sitting in front of a mirror.

I've always been drawn to embroidery, she says.

Sally laughs. See, that's *exactly* what I mean. What you just said was random. You didn't try to empathise or agree with me. You have no interest in pleasing me, in investing in something we've built over time. I like that very much.

Rae tries to sip from an empty cup. She wonders if anyone pleases Sally Canto, thinks it's probably unlikely.

That evening at the restaurant, I just wanted to share a meal with someone, to eat together by candlelight, Sally says. I didn't want to be alone, or with anyone I knew. The company of strangers is so precious, Rae. We can be whoever we want to be – surely this must be good for the brain? I'm convinced that time spent with strangers creates new neural pathways, that SOM is helping to slow the decline of the human brain, caused by the fact that so many of us now exist in a giant hyperconnected echo chamber. I've been thinking about ways for SOM to sponsor neurological research into this. Familiarity not only breeds contempt, it destroys brain cells.

I find that fascinating, Rae says.

I thought you would, Sally says.

I do. There's a lot to be said for anonymity, privacy, disconnection.

And *this* is why we're here, Sally says. She picks up her cup and clinks it against Rae's. To you, she says.

Me?

Yes.

Why me?

I've been following your progress.

My what? Rae says. She wasn't aware that she had made any progress, in any area of her life.

All the contact you've made with SOM since we launched. And you've made *a lot* of contact. All those long essays full of feedback and new ideas, they were incredibly useful.

Do you mean my emails? They were hardly essays.

They had introductions, conclusions and references.

I like to be thorough.

Well, I think we should consider all of that as a kind of high-level induction.

A what?

You know more about my business than anyone. You're its target user, but you've also helped shape and drive the project. We made vast changes to the app after your assessment. To me, it's as if you're already part of SOM.

Already? Rae says.

I'd like you to *officially* join us, Sally says.

I beg your pardon?

I'd like you to join the company. I know you already have a job – you're a copywriter aren't you? Freelance, I believe.

Rae nods.

Well I'm here to make you an offer.

I thought you were here to tell me off. What about Rufus?

This is nothing to do with Rufus. Anyway, our IT person says he's applied for a job at Argos.

How does he know that?

She knows what everyone's doing.

Rae shivers. The thought of being spied on like that. The thought of Sally following her progress. The thought of *anyone* following her.

Is this a joke? she says. Are you recording this on your phone?

Sally shakes her head. You're not very trusting, are you, she says.

Anything could appear on YouTube, Rae says. You have to be careful these days.

This isn't a joke, it's a serious offer.

Right. Okay. Well, this is all very sudden and unexpected.

Of course.

I need to go off and have a good think, Rae says.

Sally's voice is quieter now. Rae has turned her down, lowered her volume, is refusing to listen to what she is saying about money, flexible hours, a desk in their friendly office, the co-authoring of articles and papers about modern neurological decline.

Rae remembers something her mother once said: If anyone you don't know comes up to you, just shout STRANGER DANGER!

Her entire body is saying no. Because Rae is a woman who knows only what she is not, who is defined by what she isn't. Her life has unfolded in the negative. *She* has unfolded in the negative. And now Sally Canto wants a yes.

I do hope you'll say yes, she says.

Home again, Rae goes straight into the garden.

She walks across the grass to the patio, unfolds a deck-chair, sits down.

She closes her eyes.

And now she is back on her island. The place where she can say yes without fear of being smothered or overwhelmed.

Yes, she says to Petula.

Yes to your trees, your birds, your clear water and leaping fish.

Yes to your slow boats, your middle of nowhere, your refusal to keep up with the times.

He is two nights on a bench, one night in a doorway, one night under a tree.

Under a tree. It almost sounds romantic when you put it like that, the idea of sleeping in the great outdoors, against the body of a faithful old tree on a balmy night, looking up at the stars, nowhere else to be, no responsibilities to speak of.

And yes, you could lift a person from a good life, drop them here and they would probably be fine, as long as you remembered to tell them it was temporary. An experiment, that's all – turn a life upside down, wrong side up, head over heels just for one night, all in the name of adventure.

People pay a lot of money to be pulled out of their comfort zones, to be reminded that they are not defined by the life they have built. Daniel once worked for a man who paid £2,000 to be dropped in the middle of the woods for five nights with nothing but water, dried food, an inflatable mat and a tracking device. He was one of a group of ten who had booked this experience, and were deposited one by one in different places, scattered throughout a vast woodland, miles away from any house, village or town. On the sixth day, if they hadn't reappeared at one of the collection points around the edge of the forest, they would be retrieved from the wild. Then they would sleep for a night in a yurt, sit around a campfire and share their stories in a group facilitated by Harvey Pembroke, who marketed himself as a fear-breaker, and preferred to be called HP like the sauce.

Do you still feel blocked? HP asked them. Do you still feel numb, distraught, anxious? What aspect of yourself did you tap into? Have you experienced a sense of expansion? Connected with your wildest primal self? But what I really want to know, he said, while handing out bottles of the darkest ale, is whether you experienced your own fearlessness.

Daniel remembers this story now as he tries to stand up after his first night under a tree. You'd think it would be less uncomfortable than a bench or a doorway, but it isn't. He aches all over. He remembers how he used to ache when he slept in his car, but he was younger then, only eighteen. Now he's a forty-year-old man, recently wounded; his back hurts in a way it has never hurt before, in brand new places. HP would approve: after four nights of sleeping outside, Daniel is certainly discovering new aspects of himself, both physical and emotional. Like how it feels when an animal comes out of the bushes and hurtles across him, its feet digging into his chest as if he is nothing more than a raised bed of soft soil. Like how it feels to be told to move to another tree because this one is taken and is always taken. How it feels to be mid-shit when a group of teenagers arrive and find it hilarious and take his photo. And how it feels to allow himself to think, just for a minute, that there may be no end to all this. No one is coming to collect him, to hand him clean clothes, sit him down beside a campfire and talk to him about *personal growth*. He will shit and they will find it funny. He will sleep and animals will sift through him. He will keep on learning about the after-dark ownership of benches, doorways and trees.

Fuck this, he thinks. He grabs the clothes he slept beneath, the papers he slept on top of, pushes it all into his rucksack and walks to the cafe he and Erica used to go to, late morning for brunch. Erica would always have a mocha and the vegetarian breakfast, he would have a flat white, a full English.

He stands before a table laid for two, thinks can I, honestly, is this wise. Then he pulls up a chair, sits down.

Déjà vu, Daniel Berry.

As always, this cafe smells of bacon, sausages and eggs, all being cooked behind a long counter. We're going to stink when we leave here, Erica used to say. Daniel hopes this is true, hopes the smell of fry-up will overpower his own smell, which can't be good right now.

He orders a black coffee and his usual breakfast.

While his food is being cooked, he leaves his jacket on the chair and takes his rucksack to the men's toilets, where he washes his face, brushes his teeth and rubs a wet wipe over his body. He looks better now. Still hairy, creased, a musty kind of stench. But better.

The food comes quickly. He butters his toast, shakes HP sauce onto his plate.

Turn a life upside down, wrong side up, head over heels.

He wonders if this is his own sentence or something he once read.

There is a difference between upside down and capsized.

Wouldn't it be great, he thinks, if every thought you had was a line from a novel, not related to yourself or your own life, pure fiction running through you, words about other people, easy.

That would be called reading, Daniel.

Good point, he thinks.

He wishes he had a book to read now, to hide behind and crawl into, world within a world. He will buy one later.

He remembers the second-hand bookshop he and Erica used to visit.

Please take my memories and replace them with lines from a book, he thinks. But which book? This is the all-important question.

Until it isn't.

As he eats, he listens to his own mind, which, it strikes him now, is a bit like the radio he found on the wall yesterday, but a weird twisted supersonic hi-tech lo-tech kind of thing, preloaded with maps and pathways and channels, full of the internalised past, grasping at the future, buzzing with electricity, waves and vibrations, emitting random broadcasts, static, memory muzak, white noise on an infinite loop, churning out thoughts beginning with an I as if the I is all that matters when actually it isn't, as if the I is solid and consistent, when actually it isn't.

He remembers something his mother once said, a long time ago, about liquids turning to solids and solids turning to liquids. She was telling him about science, all the things he would learn at school. And things are not always what they seem, she said, your body isn't what you think it is. What is it? he said, looking down at himself. It's mainly water, she said. And this struck him as truly miraculous, miraculously true. He thought she was saying that only *his* body was mainly water, that he was somehow more watery than everyone else. So he would lie in bed at night, worrying about turning into a puddle in summer, freezing into a statue in winter. This anxiety lasted several weeks, until the subject came up again, but it wasn't so bad. It made him feel special, deeply connected to river and sea, it somehow felt right.

Anyway, he thinks now. Returning to the human mind. The most important thing in life isn't to find a person on the same wavelength as yourself, it's to find a person who isn't disturbed by your own unique frequencies. Ha! I may have nowhere to live right now, which bizarrely and disgustingly means I get looked at as if I'm some kind of lowlife, someone who has brought it on himself, this wandering like a stray dog, but I still have the odd useful thought.

And another thing, he thinks.

Looping back now, to the issue of how he wishes his memories could be replaced with lines from a book, and which book that would be –

Connected to that, but more *pressing* than that, is this:

When a person is lifted from their life and then dropped, what's the most important thing? Is it (a) where and how they land, or (b) what state they were in before they were dropped?

Which is to say: were they (a) strong and healthy and ready to survive a crisis, or were they (b) weak, fractured, already broken?

a, b, a, b,

which is it now, we shall see

He butters his toast and thinks about Erica.

He wishes he had never met her. Wishes he had been better when they were together. Wishes he could meet her all over again.

I'm afraid the patient has multiple fractures.

He thinks about his childhood, all the moving from place to place; his mother's fear, her curious sorrow, all of it eventually displaced by the books she threw herself into.

He is muttering, and has no idea that he is doing this.

Buttering and muttering.

Lower the noise, where is your poise?

If he could see himself now, shame would enter this cafe. It would burn him up, drench him, blow him about, make him want to hide underground. For shame contains each of the elements: fire, water, air and earth.

He is hot, dehydrated.

Jesus, Erica says, from behind a newspaper. Can you imagine being the only person to survive a plane crash?

I read about that, Daniel says. It's bizarre isn't it.

Everyone else was dead, she says, but this guy, he just walked away with scratches and a broken arm. Can you imagine how he must have felt?

Daniel smiles.

What? Erica says.

Nothing, he says. It's just nice that's all, coming out for breakfast like this.

Erica does that thing, that thing he loves, a sort of long slow-motion blink, her eyes closing in a look of pleasure that always reminds him of a cat somehow, soft and sleepy and content. Her nose is scrunched-up, and she is smiling, and all of this is for him. It comes and goes in seconds, and it moves him every time, this thing she does.

We should go and see a play, she says. We haven't seen a play for ages. Or a band for that matter. We're getting boring, Dan.

We're not boring.

Okay, we're in danger of getting boring.

Choose a play and I'll come with you.

What if I want *you* to choose?

Then give me the paper and I'll see what's on.

No, I'll choose. But let's go out for dinner beforehand, she says.

Fine, he says.

Now he looks down at his empty plate.

He looks at the empty chair, where Erica was and is and isn't.

He runs his hands over his head, pushes his hair this way and that, sending dirt and dust into the air.

It lands on his plate.

His filth, here for all to see, like sick-joke pepper.

His filth, like weather coming down.

Filthy weather we're having, Daniel.

Ugh, he says.

He looks at his hands, his fingertips grey from his own hair.

What the hell is he doing in here? What if Erica comes in with someone else and sees him like this?

Someone else.

This thought shocks his stomach.

She's lovely, Daniel. She's so bloody sparkly. Of course there'll be someone else.

After only a few weeks?

You're so naive. She probably had someone in mind when she left, if she wasn't already seeing them.

No, that's ridiculous. It wasn't like that, not at all.

So why hasn't she been in touch? You don't even have a forwarding address – don't you think it's a bit strange?

Yes, he thinks. It *is* strange. He doesn't even know where she is staying, where she lives. How can this be something he doesn't know?

Where are you, Erica?

This room is a ship and the wind is up. Hold on tight, Danny Boy, more weather's coming down.

Grief, like that scurrying night-time animal, its sharp frenetic feet and the swerve of his mind, its backwards and forwards, its tilt and sway, hot airless pendulum ship, feckless yo-yo travel-sick.

Ugh, he says, lowering his head.

He puts his hand on his stomach, throws up all over the table.

> *a, b, a, b*
> *which is it now, we shall see*
> *hot airless pendulum ship*
> *feckless yo-yo travel-sick*

Two days from now, Daniel will speak those words aloud to a woman he hasn't seen for thirty years. He will tell her how this used to happen when he was a boy, and does she remember, the rush of rhyme and nausea and pain in his head, and afterwards a kind of peacefulness, as if he had stepped into a warm breeze on an empty beach.

Being sick in that cafe, in there of all places, was one of the lowest points of my life, he'll say.

And this woman will say well, it could've been worse.

Could it?

Definitely.

Have *you* ever vomited in public?

And she will say Daniel, do I look like a woman whose life has been so small that she's never thrown up in public? Now drink your tea, have one of these Jammie Dodgers and tell me more about this fuckwit called Erica.

Rae has agreed to a tour.

Her tour guide is Sally Canto: bubble burster, privacy killer, opportunity giver, how dare she.

How dare she *see* Rae, notice her, invite her in? She was perfectly happy being Stranger of Mine's customer, client, user, hiring other people for genuinely platonic one-off encounters.

Rae is waiting in reception. The receptionist is nice, her name is Pam, after Pam Ayres she says, because her mother loves Pam in a really big way, and who wouldn't, she's so adorable and funny isn't she. Do *you* like Pam Ayres? she says.

Of course, Rae says from one of four enormous grey armchairs. Who wouldn't, who doesn't.

Exactly, Pam says. Can I get you a lemon water while you wait? A tea or coffee, an espresso, mocha, mochaccino, babyccino?

Aren't babyccinos for babies? Rae says.

Why should babies have all the fun? Pam says. No-frills frothy milk is for everyone surely. We have semi, skinny, soya, oat, rice, hemp, flax, almond, cashew or coconut.

No thanks, I'm okay for now, Rae says.

Pam is humming. She is one of those people who hums to fill a silence, who is clearly uncomfortable with silence.

Which to Rae is inconceivable and tragic. She gazes at the tall windows and sliding glass doors, watches pedestrians marching at high speed with beakers at their mouths, brightly coloured sippy cups, the sort she had as a child. Infantilisation, she thinks. Yet another example of.

So what do you do? Pam says.

I'm a freelance copywriter, Rae says.

Oh wow. So what are you working on right now, anything interesting?

I'm writing some stuff for a make-and-do company.

A what?

They teach people how to make and mend things. There's a lot of knitting involved, workshops and classes.

I *love* to knit, Pam says. I have my knitting right here, look. She reaches down, lifts a mustard-coloured rucksack from under her desk, knitting needles and wool poking from the top. I'm knitting a pair of boxers for my boyfriend to watch telly in, she says. Boxers for box sets, I call them.

That's catchy, Rae says. *Boxers for box sets*, I like that.

Pam looks happy. She rearranges the stationery on her desk, places her little wireless keyboard right in the middle, just so. It's a kind of celebration, this putting things in order.

We all go to yoga on a Thursday evening, Pam says.

Oh right, Rae says, deliberately neutral: *never show enthusiasm for group activities, never provoke an invite*.

It's a bonding thing, Pam says.

Rae shivers. I heard that people are doing yoga with goats now, she says quickly, to change the subject, to talk about anything other than bonding.

Goats? Pam says.

They climb on top of people while they're doing their poses. I'd probably go to yoga if there were goats, Rae says.

Wow, Pam says. You should reach out to Sally with that, it's so blue-sky. We could branch into it couldn't we. Who says the Strangers for hire have to be humans? They could easily be goats.

Thankfully, a side door opens. In Rae's mind a herd of goats rushes through it, out towards freedom.

Ready for your tour? Sally says.

Oh yes, Rae says, trying to move, but the armchair is cavernous, she is stuck.

I am forty-two years old and fairly fit. I do not get stuck in armchairs.

Sally smiles. We had those shipped from Norway. They're called the Engulfers. Don't worry, no one can get out of them, it's not just you.

Jesus Christ, Rae says, struggling.

What can I say, Sally says. Love hurts.

Love? Rae says.

I *love* those chairs, Sally says, helping Rae to her feet. If I'm feeling a bit tubby, I sit in one then stand up really fast, over and over again. We also use them to lower cortisol levels in the workplace. Every member of staff has to sit quietly in an Engulfer for fifteen minutes twice a day.

Rae tries not to yawn. She can sense a wave of exhaustion, so close she can smell it. She knows it's Petula. Her island, doing its thing. The surrounding water, calling her home.

Don't do this, Petula says. You love to work alone, ideally from home, do you really want to join this merry band of babyccino drinkers with their Engulfers and knitted underwear? It's like a nightmare! You're going to get stuck in a chair, stuck for life watching box sets in woolly knickers. Come home, choose me, *choose your island*.

Rae follows Sally up some stairs into what looks like a loft-style apartment. Exposed brick walls, sofas, colourful rugs; long wooden tables, red chairs, big copper lights hanging from the ceiling.

So people work anywhere they like in here, depending on what mood they're in, Sally says.

Rae trails behind as Sally speaks the name of each person they pass. This is Jamie, this is Su, this is Carla –

Hi, Rae says, as people look up from their laptops.

Off to the side, there's a kitchen with two espresso machines and a Smeg fridge. There are other rooms too. This is a quiet space, Sally says, strolling past a doorway. And this is another. We respect and nourish introverts at SOM. And here we have our meeting room, and this one's for intense face-to-face, hence the two chairs.

Do the Strangers ever come here? Rae says.

They come in for clinical supervision with a psychotherapist – group sessions *and* individual, Sally says.

Really?

Of course. We all have clinical supervision. You have to when you serve the community like we do. It's not easy, meeting new people all the time. It can trigger emotional issues, touch the heart.

I see, Rae says.

Then Sally looks excited. Oh, there's something else too. Come this way.

Rae follows her again, back into the main office and through another door.

Voilà, Sally says. Our reading room.

Goodness, Rae says.

I thought you'd like it. Go inside, have a proper look.

Rae wanders in. This room is smaller than the others but far more impressive, with floor to ceiling bookshelves.

The books are ordered by category: fiction, psychology, neuroscience, night sky and poetry.

Intriguing, Rae says, taking a battered copy of *Strangers on a Train* from one of the shelves.

Are you a fan of Patsy? Sally says.

Rae has never heard anyone call Patricia Highsmith Patsy before. It sounds odd, as if Sally herself is friends with the dead writer, or feels like she is.

I think Patsy's excellent, Rae says.

Sally's smile shows all her teeth.

In the kitchen, Sally makes two green smoothies. The wooing is in full swing. Sally wants to play to Rae's strengths, put her centre court, this is what she is saying.

I'm thinking *head of process,* she says, placing an envelope on the table, followed by a smoothie.

Written on the envelope: *Offer for Rae Marsh, please say yes!*

I need you, Sally says.

Oh I'm sure you don't, Rae says.

I do, I need your eyes. I want you to look at everything, all of our processes: our advertising, our website, logo, the tone of the brand, the Strangers themselves. I want you to tighten us up, help me take a next step. We're doing well but we're in limbo.

How are you in limbo?

We're straddled between two worlds, Rae: a successful business on one side, a meaningful business on the other. And I want *meaning.* I want research, articles, public discussion. I want us to challenge the ethos of social media, how it thrives on familiarity and tribes, on the whole idea of *I'm like you, I like the same things, I believe in what you believe.* If we're going to fight dementia, our brains need to be snapped out of this sickly inertia. Looking in a mirror does nothing for grey matter.

Dementia? Rae says.

Absolutely, and why not, Sally says. In terms of evolution, the human brain has entered a phase of rest, the lethargy of overfamiliarity, and it's *dangerous*.

I wouldn't say we're in a phase of rest. More a phase of *unrest*, Rae says. We're hyper-vigilant, bombarded. I think the human brain is in a phase of trauma, Rae says.

Oh that's good, Sally says, her eyes bright. You're wasted as a copywriter.

I like it actually, Rae says.

Sally ignores this, says we're all plugged in, that's how it seems right now.

Reality does feel simulated, Rae says.

It does, Sally says. Because it *is*. I mean, what's true and what isn't?

Now there's a can of worms, Rae says. She sips her smoothie. To her surprise, it's fantastic.

WOMAN WOOED INTO MAJOR LIFE CHANGE BY LIQUIDISED KALE

I like talking to you, Sally says. I'd really like to get to know you, Rae.

Me? Rae thinks, still drinking.

Shit, she thinks. She doesn't know what to make of Sally. This woman clearly knows how to build a successful company, she's unusual and interesting, but her quest to help the human brain seems a little ambitious. And anyway, what about Rae's *own* brain. What do you need, brain? she thinks. Does *this* head want to be head of process?

A change will enliven you, Sally says.

Can Sally see inside her head? Why does she think she needs enlivening?

I have my own psychoanalyst, Rae says. She's French.

Do you? Well good for you. Do you speak French?

No, we do it in English. But the thing is, I don't want my own process muddled by seeing a different therapist.

That's fine, I understand. I'd be happy to pay for some of your sessions, if you'd like to use them to discuss your work.

That's very generous.

I'm glad you think so.

The kitchen falls silent.

OFFER OF FREE THERAPY TOO GOOD FOR FRUGAL WOMAN TO REFUSE

They look at each other, then look away. No one hums, tries to fill the space. The silence is simply itself, vast and open. And Rae relaxes, just a little. It's like visiting an old friend, sitting in this kitchen. A friend who says sweetheart, let me enliven you, I'll make you something raw and green and cold. It also feels a little like a blind date, and meeting a stalker, and meeting a genius, and meeting a psychopath.

Such confusing multiplicity.

Rae imagines what it would be like to come here every day. It might be helpful to be somewhere instead of nowhere, to feel that she belongs. Seeing as she has a slight *issue* when it comes to place. Seeing as every single time she is anywhere at all, she feels like she is nowhere.

Take last night, for example. Rae was in a bookshop, listening to an author read, and ten minutes in she was no longer there. She had the sensation that her body was made of wax and she was trapped inside it, up on a ladder, peering through its eyes. She often feels like a puppeteer, trapped inside a giant puppet, detached from the flow of life.

She hears Sally's words: *I'd really like to get to know you, Rae.*

But if she does, Sally will find out what she is: not head of process, only a thing stuck in a hot and sticky head.

On her island, Rae is never a thing. She is fully human, with a woman's body, like that song, 'A Natural Woman'. Yes, that's exactly it. On Petula she is a natural woman – somewhere, not nowhere.

So what's it gonna be? Sally says.

If in doubt, vomit it out.

Daniel feels better for throwing up, physically if not emotionally.

Later that morning, in the supermarket, he wanders around the fruit aisle, decides to buy a peach and a plum.

There is a little girl, holding her mother's hand. She stares at his trainers, her gaze moving up over his clothes before settling on his face.

She studies him for a long time, this little girl.

Hello sad man, she eventually says.

Freya, shush, her mother says.

Hello there, Daniel says.

He is sad. Even a girl can see. Or maybe it's only the girl who can see.

You're right, he says. Thank you. I *am* sad.

It feels good to say this, to be seen this way.

The girl's mother is not as positive. If there was an award for the maximum number of negative emotions expressed in a smile, she would definitely win. It's quite an assortment, a facial feat. He can see disgust, pity, fear, disapproval, contempt and anger, all in her mouth and eyes. How complicated it must be to love her.

She pulls her daughter away.

But I want to talk to the sad man, he can hear the girl saying.

He walks to the frozen food aisle, opens a freezer door and pushes his hands inside, waits for it to hurt.

Better.

Now he is in a charity shop.

It's not the charity that took his furniture, his trinkets, his white goods, even his washing-up bowl.

This one raises money for the human heart.

A sign on the wall says BEAT HEARTBREAK FOREVER.

Daniel has been thinking about the issue of clothes and how to wash them. Over the past hour, this has been his sole concern.

I'd like to buy these. Do you mind if I keep them on? he says at the till, as he waggles two paper tickets at the shop assistant. The tickets are still attached to the trousers and shirt he is now wearing. And I'd like to donate these, he says, handing over his own bundled-up clothes. They'll need a good wash I'm afraid. Sorry about that.

Don't you worry, the shop assistant says. She takes his clothes and places them on a shelf behind her. Those look good on you, I think they're designer.

Are they? he says.

I reckon, she says.

Well, this is the first time *I've* ever worn designer gear, he says, flattening the shirt with the palm of his hands.

The shop is quiet. It smells of wet newspaper and bananas, not altogether unpleasant.

She studies his appearance, mainly his face. Such watery eyes, as if he's waterlogged somehow, or maybe watered down, she thinks.

He blinks quickly, one two three. His nose twitches.

She watches these tiny tremors. She has seen them before, on her own face. She remembers a friend once pointing them out, and how embarrassed she felt. It's all right, her friend said. You've experienced an earthquake, a seismic event, and these are the aftershocks. It makes sense really, doesn't it. It's logical. Or, *geo*logical. So don't be embarrassed.

The kindness of this friend, who is conjured between them now; a phantom, a hope.

Would you like a hot chocolate? she says. We have a new machine, it's instant. I'm just going to get myself one. You can take it away, we have paper cups.

Are you sure? he says.

She nods.

Okay then. Thank you.

She tells him she won't be a sec, and while she is gone he listens to the radio, wonders where the radio is. He spots it up high on a shelf, a waterproof duck, like the one his mum used to have in her shower years ago. 'Pretty in Pink' is coming from this duck. Now that was a good film, he thinks. Then he thinks about the shop assistant, how trusting she is, leaving him alone by the till like this.

Now she is back with two cups of hot chocolate. It's not the best in the world, she says, but it's also not the worst.

Thanks so much, he says. What do I owe you, for this and the clothes?

Absolutely nothing, she says. It's on me.

Oh no, I really couldn't. You're a charity.

Well exactly, she says. Anyway, it would make me happy if you'd let me do you a small favour.

She smiles and he notices her teeth, how they are white apart from one, which is gold.

You're admiring my golden central incisor, she says. It's a 20-carat permanent crown. I got it after my husband died.

She tells him a story about a dead husband and a gold tooth, bought with the money he left in an ISA. It's a symbol of my love for him, it was so bright and precious, but dark in many ways too, she says. People don't expect a middle-aged woman with highlighted hair and M&S clothes to have a gold tooth, you know? But seeing the shock on their faces when I smile, somehow it makes me feel better.

You're a very interesting woman, he says.

Why thank you, she says.

She holds out her hand for the taking, for the shaking. Her shake is firm, vigorous, it makes him smile.

I'm Marie, she says.

Daniel, he says.

Well you go careful, Daniel.

You too, he says.

That night, alone in the park in another man's outfit, he thinks about what we wear of each other. Marie's gold tooth: a symbol of love and life interrupted, of no longer being who she was. And him, well that one's easy: his mother's eyes, her long fingers, her silly after only one drink.

Mum, he says aloud.

And saying the word *Mum*, what difference does it make.

He is a howl.

He is sandpaper.

He looks up at the full moon, a defiant lantern in a blown-apart room.

He falls to his knees.

No, that's not true, let's watch this again:

He puts one knee on the ground, then another. This movement is slow, deliberate, something he has decided to do.

Sometimes there is nothing but the sense of having made a choice.

What on earth are you doing, Daniel?

He leans forward and begins to dig a hole.

As the soil flies over his shoulder he is making something happen, he is vital and strong, he is an animal on a moonlit night, he hadn't known he could make a hole this deep with only his own hands.

Wash me clean in mud and moon. These are the words in his mind as he stands with his hands on his hips, nails full of soil, admiring his creation.

It's really something, this hole. Who knew that a moment of satisfaction could be found in uprooting a neat lawn, dismantling a picnic spot?

For God's sake, Daniel, it's a hole in the ground on a bright night. It's hardly something to feel proud of. You've been lied to, left, you have nowhere to live. Jump in why don't you, I'll happily cover you up.

Leave him alone, the little sheep says.

It's a feisty fellow, this ornament.

This park in the city has known Daniel for a long time. As a single man, he would cycle through on his way into town, stop at one of its benches on the way home to eat the lunch he always bought from the same stall at the market. Then, he appeared with Erica. They walked hand in hand through all the leafy avenues, met friends for lunch at one of the picnic tables, came here for fireworks and music, sunshine and frost, the quiet falling of snow.

Once, on their way back from seeing a French film at the cinema, they fucked in the rain in this park. Erica asked him to take off his shirt. He was half naked in the cold mist. This park had seen it all before. When they got home they peeled off their wet clothes and took a long hot shower, and as he looked at her standing there, pink-faced and laughing, hair full of shampoo, his chest hurt from happiness. Later, under the duvet, he told her this. She called him cheesy and laughed. And her laugh wasn't the same as the one in the shower, it wasn't even close. There was a shrillness to it, like a warning, subtle but definitely there.

In front of his hole in the ground, Daniel takes a deep breath, lifts his chin and howls.

This sound raises him up, straightens his shoulders.

He is wolf, he is song.

There's a creature in the distance, he can see its silhouette. A fox, watching him. He waves. Then he howls again, long and loud.

It's a song of separation. A call, a cry. A port in a storm in the mouth of a man. Accidentally a little bit joyful.

He steps down into the hole, sits with his knees against his chest, and waits under the all-seeing stars.

We see you, Daniel Berry.

Later he wanders from tree to tree, searching for the one from last night.

When he finds it, he makes a bed from newspaper and folded clothes, uses his rucksack as a pillow, his jacket as a blanket.

He is two nights on a bench, one night in a doorway, two nights under a tree after years and years of mattress and cotton sheet.

He tucks the little sheep just inside his rucksack, close to his face, and somehow then he sleeps.

Once again, he dreams of Erica. His sleep is fitful, comes in fits and starts, fits of love and brokenness, all her hissy fits thrown back at him.

Make them stop, these dreams are too hard.

Keep them coming – it's her, it's her.

Where are you living now? he says.

I don't really want you to know, Erica says, casual and hard and cold.

For a second in this dream he is a bird drenched with oil, staggering across a beach.

Then he is himself again, and she pulls him close and kisses him.

Oh, he thinks. She does want me. She *does*.

And a whole future opens in his body.

Until he wakes to a licking.

What the –

Tiny fast tongue on his cheek and his neck, *what are you who are you?*

He opens his eyes to a small dog. Behind the dog, two men.

One of the men unzips his trousers and pisses all over Daniel.

It goes right through his supposedly waterproof jacket.

(He hadn't thought to ask if it was urine-repellent when he bought it.)

The dog backs away now, the man zips up his trousers and laughs and then –

He wakes to a licking, wakes to a kicking.

Kick a man while he's down, why don't you.

Dirty fucking loser, the man says.

Which technically is true.

Then it stops, and a hand reaches out for his rucksack, his pillow, his everything.

There is a no inside Daniel. It begins in his belly and thighs, moves fast into his chest and arms.

No, Daniel shouts. You are not taking my sheep.

What sheep? the other man says.

Daniel grabs the arm that's reaching for his rucksack. It's quick and hazy and dark, how he pulls and twists.

He hears the words *Jesus Christ* as the man pulls away.

As one springs back, another springs forward.

Daniel glances at the dog, its tail down, scared.

Hole in the ground, look what I found, he yells.

Which confuses the fists, dancing in front of him, boxing ring style. But not as much as when Daniel barks.

He is a piss-stained jacket, a barking beast.

He throws his head back and howls.

(For dear life.)

(For any kind of life.)

Because there was a time when he had everything. And now, everything that matters, *gone*.

He is liminal, not criminal. And yet he may have just broken a man's arm.

He hears one of the men say *not worth it mate* to the other, then *what a bloody nutter*.

Afterwards, clutching his rucksack to his chest, Daniel returns to the damp earth of his hole in the ground and wonders what to do. He hurts all over.

It's light out here now. Pretty soon, commuters will be passing through.

He looks down at himself, at the way he is sitting. It reminds him of sitting in a boat made from sand on a beach when he was a boy. He remembers being highly impressed by the boat, carefully built by his mother, who carried buckets of water from the sea all afternoon as her sculpture came to life.

For you, she said when it was done.

And he sat in the boat and looked up at her.

This is amazing, he said. I mean, all the detail, it really does look like a *real boat*.

She looked proud, happy. It's a boat that knows its way to the most stunning island, she said. And he saw her wink at Rae Marsh, who was lying on a blanket nearby, in jeans and a jumper even though it was hot.

In a hole that will get him nowhere, Daniel has a thought.

He pictures the library.

Silent slo-mo papery room.

Safety.

And now he is cross-legged on the floor of the public library, deep in cookery.

He is holding a book of old recipes, gripping it tight, his tears tapping out the code of how lost he is on its sun-bleached cover.

He glances down at the little sheep, sitting beside him.

I'm so sorry that man urinated on you, the sheep says.

(Because it's wise enough to know that this was worse than the kicking.)

Thanks, Daniel says.

I wish I could've made them stop. I felt so powerless, the sheep says.

Daniel's eyes sting.

He is an empty stomach.

He is the urge to steal.

71

He is a boy's facial tic, a twitch of the nose that should be long gone.

He closes his eyes, and when he opens them again there is a woman walking slowly towards him.

She crouches down, puts her hand on his shoulder.

Whatever it is that's hurting you right now, it won't last forever, she says.

He looks into her eyes.

Trust me, she says.

And he does.

This woman with a warm hand and a soft voice, he does, he trusts her.

Because she reminds him of someone he once knew. A woman who used to sing all the time, make rude jokes, bring out the best in his mother.

A woman who made them fearless for a while.

He gets up, wipes his face with his hands, picks up his piss-stained jacket, his rucksack and the sheep.

He walks to the train station, buys a one-way ticket and tries not to panic over the cost.

The journey will be long but he doesn't care.

Up on the breezy platform, the idea of leaving is all around him.

He takes a deep breath, steels himself.

Go back.

Keep going.

Daniel watches through the window as the train picks up speed.

It's too easy and too difficult.

The stepping aboard, the speeding away.

He watches the fields and the trees, all the back gardens with their fences and sheds and trampolines.

There is a girl, alone in her garden, bouncing on one of these trampolines. The sight of her is both joyful and sad.

He looks down at his ticket:

OFF-PEAK SINGLE

VALID FOR ONE JOURNEY TO THE FEARLESS YEARS

(VALID VIA ANY PERMITTED ROUTE)

the fearless years

Eve Berry is hanging out the washing in slow motion. Her bare feet are damp from the grass. She shakes the creases from a pillowcase while staring into the space in front of her. The garden smells of summer rain, makes her think of patchouli, olive groves, old wooden toys. The pillowcase smells of apples and she brings it close to her nose, breathes it in while peering over the top at her six-year-old boy.

Daniel is inside his Wendy house. He is sitting cross-legged, watching her through one of the plastic windows.

She pegs the pillowcase to the line and waves.

He waves back.

The house, known in gendered retail terms as a *play tent for girls*, was left behind by the previous tenants, along with a child's tea set, a fishing rod and a pack of cards. Daniel was mainly interested in the tent, brand new, still in its box.

Can I come in? Eve says.

If you like, Daniel says.

She climbs inside and he zips the door shut.

He has placed the tea set on a square of cardboard, and they stare at this in silence, the teapot, cups and saucers, all in miniature.

The Wendy house soon becomes hot and airless. Eve unzips it in a rush and crawls back out.

What's wrong? Daniel says.

I'm claustrophobic, she says.

Pardon?

I'm not sure it's healthy for you to spend so much time in there. Come out now, get some fresh air.

I like it in here, he says. It's my home.

It's not exactly your *home*.

Can I keep it?

Of course you can.

But won't they come back for it, the other family? Won't they take it?

They're not coming back. They've moved away now, they'll be settled somewhere else.

So it's mine.

It is.

And can I take it with me when we move?

We only just got here.

How long we will stay?

I can't answer that question.

Why can't you?

Well, nothing's ever certain in life, not really.

She sees his nose twitch. You sneezy again? she says.

Can you zip me back in? he says.

Okay, but don't close it completely, all right? I'm worried you're going to suffocate. Do you want a comic to read?

No thanks. I'm going to look at the tea set.

Really?

He nods.

She drags the zip upwards, leaves a gap at the top.

He pushes his small hand through the gap, waggles it around.

She takes his hand and kisses it.

Her lips are on his knuckles, and it strikes her yet again that she grew this person in front of her, this brain, this skeleton. His hand was once a speck of bone, a speck of boy. During her pregnancy she imagined him deep-sea diving, her baby floating near the bottom of the ocean, suspended in saltwater, which made her the wider world: his climate, his shore, his sandbank, his reef. This was the image in her mind as she lay in bed each night, thinking is he okay, is he healthy, and does he feel the cold when I do, does he feel hungry when I do.

Eve was sixteen when Daniel was born. Her love was loud, bright, determined: a revolution.

I'm sorry, she whispers now.

Then the hand disappears, and she hears him shuffling about on the plastic groundsheet, making himself comfortable again.

Eve wonders how to get rid of the tea set without Daniel noticing.

Thing is, it's disturbing.

Some objects are portals to the past, best discarded. This one reminds her of her mother's *special* tea set, the crockery she saved for best, for other people, for those she wanted to impress. It was white, with tiny blue birds all over it, flying from one garden to another, Eve had thought, or maybe from one country to another. She had loved those birds, but she was never allowed to touch them. They lived in the darkness of a kitchen cupboard, never to be seen until a visitor called round.

Once, when she was small, and her mother was napping upstairs, Eve took the whole set from the cupboard and carefully placed each cup, saucer and plate on the living room floor in a circle, finishing with the finest piece of all:

the teapot. Then she sat in the middle, and the room was full of birds flying around her, all of them brilliant blue. She had been learning about birds at school, and she loved the weird names for when many of the same type gather together. Her teacher had written some of these on the blackboard:

MY FAVOURITE COLLECTIVE NOUNS FOR BIRDS

an asylum of cuckoos
a trembling of finches
a prayer of godwits
an exultation of skylarks
a scold of jays
a murder of crows
a descension of woodpeckers
a booby of nuthatches
a wisdom of owls
a charm of goldfinches
an unkindness of ravens

What the *hell* do you think you're doing? her mother said, her lips dry from sleep, her voice rough and deep with horror at what Eve had done. Can't I even take a nap without you causing chaos? she said.

Which was a strange thing to say, because she was always napping, always trying to revive herself from the stresses of being a parent, and there was never any chaos, not even in the wildest dreams of her afternoon naps.

I just really like the birds, Eve said.

Apparently, this did not justify her behaviour, her impudence, her *selfishness*.

When the tea set was back in its rightful place, there was a smack. This punishment disturbed Eve far more than any previous smacks she had received. If it had happened straight away, as soon as her mother entered the room, it would have been less painful, or at least easier to understand – a loss of control caused by a fit of bad temper. But after yelling at her daughter, Gail Berry had set about the task of carrying her precious china back into the kitchen, and Eve had helped. They had worked together, moving from room to room in reparative silence. Briefly, they were a team with a shared purpose, it was tense and sickly, but it was simple, harmonious, rare. When her mother gently closed the last of the kitchen cupboards, Eve thought it was over, they had put things right. She didn't expect her mother to turn in the way she did, to march across the room, lift her dress and slap her across the thigh. The smack itself wasn't especially hard, but its sting was in its timing, Gail Berry was clever that way.

Eve taps on the front door of her son's private world.

Anyone home? she says.

Who is it? he says.

It's me.

Who is me? Please be more specific.

She smiles at his use of the word *specific*, all the effort he puts in to saying it correctly.

This is Eve Berry. And who's that?

This is Daniel Berry.

Well, Daniel Berry, I wondered if you might like a cheese and pickle sandwich.

Okay.

Do you mean yes please?

Yes please.

And where would you like this sandwich? Would you care to join me on a blanket on the lawn in about ten minutes?

I would.

Excellent.

Mum?

Yes.

Are you still there?

Obviously, otherwise you wouldn't be able to hear me.

Can I have a rabbit?

A rabbit?

Yes.

Why do you want a rabbit all of a sudden?

It's not all of a sudden.

Well you've never mentioned one before.

We have a garden now, so we can have a rabbit can't we.

But we may not always have a garden. And then what'll we do with our rabbit?

She waits for him to reply.

Someone might grab it, our rabbit, he says.

She grits her teeth. Not again. This thing he does when he is stressed, this rhyming thing. After the rhyme he usually feels queasy or has a headache, and when this passes he seems happier than usual, as if the rhyme has somehow renewed him.

BOY'S MOOD LIFTED BY INVOLUNTARY RHYME, CLAIMS MOTHER

Sounds like a tall story, she thinks.

BOY SITS PRETTY AFTER DITTY

Now she's doing it too. Compulsive, once you start.

A FIT OF RHYME, A STITCH IN TIME

Run rabbit run let's play in the sun, he says.

Everything's all right, Daniel, she says quietly.

Funny how his episodes of rhyme always make her think of a drenched dog, shaking itself dry.

She sits on the grass, waits for his voice. Maybe this isn't a stress thing after all, she thinks. Maybe this is a seed of talent, and her son will progress from spasms of rhyme to artful soul-stirring poetry. He's already bookish, shy and emotional, halfway there surely.

Something in her bones says *unlikely*.

Something in her bones, deeper than any language, says *you know it's your boy's nerves, curling like burnt paper covered in rhyme. The stench of a burnt curl makes him feel sick, and then he is ashen, and then he is better.*

Eve listens to a bumblebee, traffic, a dog barking in the distance.

She glances over at her washing, blowing in the wind.

It's good to have a washing line, she thinks. Good to have their clothes drying out here in the sunshine instead of hanging around a flat. All things should be outside as much as possible.

She unzips the front door of the Wendy house.

Daniel, she says.

What what what, he says.

Why don't we go for a picnic. We can visit the big park, see the lake, what do you think?

Will that make you happy? he says, which sounds odd coming from a boy's mouth, unbearably heavy.

Come on, she says.

He sits there for a few seconds, reluctant and suspicious, but also wanting to visit the big park, see the lake, eat a picnic.

His mother pulls a stupid face, which he tries to resist, but he can't. She is always pulling stupid faces and he always finds them funny. A few years from now they will annoy him, make him roll his eyes and sigh, and the loss of his laughter, the easy ability to win him over, will be just one of Eve Berry's sadnesses.

Is that a smile, Daniel? she says.

No it's not, he says, clambering out of the Wendy house. He zips the door closed and stands beside her.

Do you feel all right? she says.

Yes thanks, he says.

She is kneeling on the grass, her hands flat on her lap. She looks at his floppy hair, his big eyes, his yellow T-shirt with a lion on the front. This lion is brown and orange, and she remembers how he had named it Bryan as they stood together in Woolworths, choosing his summer clothes. I love his smile, Eve said, it's a picture of goofy goodwill. Daniel didn't know what this meant, but he liked it. Maybe that should be his name, he said, we could call him Goofy Goodwill. He thought about this for a moment. No, Bryan the lion, he said.

Why are you crying? he says to her now.

I'm not crying, she says, jumping to her feet. Shows what you know doesn't it.

In the park, after feeding the ducks, they sit on a blanket and eat hot bacon sandwiches from the cafe.

Mum, he says.

What.

Who is Abigail?

Abigail?

From the sign.

The street sign?

He nods.

She's not a real person.

Is she like the Queen?

Sorry?

Does she own our street, like the Queen?

I think we need to discuss the role of the monarchy, sweetheart, she says.

So why is it called Abigail Gardens?

It's just a random name, probably chosen by the council or the developers.

Oh. And why do we live at number three?

She turns to look at him, tries to read between the lines, see beyond his questions about numbers and names.

Number three was available to rent, she says. Don't you like it?

I like it, he says.

Do you, or do you just like the Wendy house?

He smiles. We have two gardens, he says. Not one like I said before. A back garden and a front garden, they're both ours aren't they and no one else can use them.

That's right, she says. But I don't think we need to get all territorial about it.

What?

She is about to explain, to make a joke involving the phrase *get off my land*, but realises he won't understand. It's too easy to forget how young he is, she is always doing this, speaking to him as if he were a man.

Nothing, she says, and kisses his cheek.

As she pulls away, she notices how he lifts his head and sits up straight. Has her affection just made him feel taller, or has he tightened up against it? Eve wonders these things as if one discounts the other, when both of them are true.

They sit quietly, eat their sandwiches.

They watch a group of teenagers playing rounders, a girl flying a kite, a woman jogging in circles around the park. The woman passes their blanket once, then twice, a wheezy flash of yellow nylon and pink shoe.

Eve nudges her son. What's that one? she says, pointing at the sky.

He says hmm, let me think.

She says he knows this one, he definitely knows it.

Is it a seagull? he says.

That's right.

But we're not by the sea.

The name's a bit deceptive, they often come inland. I blame all the litter and landfills, she says.

Daniel moves closer to his mother, ever so slightly. Will it take my sandwich? he says, remembering a seagull on the beach, how it stole an ice cream from a girl's hand.

I don't think so. It's going now, see?

They look up for a while, and Daniel eats his sandwich super fast, just in case.

Do you remember all the starlings we saw last winter, flying together? she says.

Murmuration, he says, because he knows his mother, knows the next thing she'll say.

Well done, she says.

More than a hundred, all doing stunts, he says.

Could have been more than a thousand, she says.

Why *do* they fly together like that?

For safety, I think. And they talk to each other about where's best to sleep and find food.

They must have lots of friends and family, he says.

I suppose so, she says.

Why haven't we got any?

Daniel, don't keep asking me that. I've told you the answer before.

But why is it always just us? Why doesn't anybody love us?

Eve pictures her mother, the last time she saw her, six years ago.

How about an ice cream? she says.

And this boy, he is not stupid. He knows a diversion when he hears one.

Yes please, he says.

And he pushes his question into his trouser pocket, saves it for later like a shell, a sticker, a stone for his mother's shoe.

His mother is teaching him to blow away the clocks.

Daniel loves it. He has never done this before, never plucked a dandelion from the grass and puffed its fine threads into the air. He grabs one after the other and blows. She laughs. You're full of beans today, she says. It's because I had two Weetabix, he says.

This morning they reached the two-Weetabix milestone. It made him feel grown up to eat as much as her for breakfast. He looked proud of himself, even though he wasn't crazy about Weetabix, preferred Coco Pops or waffles, neither of which was allowed. Afterwards, he told her he wouldn't be eating two again, maybe for a year or maybe forever, but at least he knew he could do it.

Over the last few days, Daniel's appetite seems to have changed. He is showing more interest in food, appears to enjoy his meals instead of pushing things around the plate with his fork. He has never been an easy child to feed. He is fussy, complaining, will go hours without eating a thing. But since they moved to Abigail Gardens, he has begun to sit with her in the kitchen, scribbling in his colouring book at the big wooden table while slowly eating everything on his plate. Is this really what has shifted his appetite? Surely it can't be as simple as having a kitchen table? Their last kitchen was tiny, there was no room to sit. It wasn't a place to stop and eat, not for Daniel anyway, who was too small to reach the worktops. Eve never minded the lack of space – she was happy to stand and listen to the radio while eating a meal – but he is clearly more affected by his environment than she is.

Really, Eve? Are you sure this is true?

Maybe it isn't, she thinks. Maybe she has hardened herself to the impact of her surroundings. How else would she have lived comfortably in all those places? The damp, leaks and mould, the music and yelling from above and below. The kids from the flat beneath them, always ringing the doorbell and running away. The couple across the street threatening to kill each other several times a week. Boarded-up windows, broken glass. And the ambush of unsocialised dogs, wandering loose without collar or care, their slow prowl, their loneliness.

Eve thinks about all this while Daniel blows away the clocks.

She thinks about growth spurts, wonders if Daniel is having one, if maybe *this* is what's affecting his appetite. Interesting that he would grow now when there is literally space to grow. It seems ridiculous, simplistic.

She glances at her own waist. Is she growing too? Are they both going to expand, change shape?

She feels excited, nervous, has no idea why.

I think that was the last clock, Daniel says, hunting around the garden.

Are you sure? she says.

Then they both jump. Eve puts her hand on her chest.

I'm so sorry, I didn't mean to startle you, a voice says.

There is a woman, standing in the garden next door, leaning over the fence. She is older than Eve, in her thirties maybe.

I've been meaning to say hello, she says.

Eve walks over to the fence, says hi, I'm Eve and this is Daniel.

I'm Sherry, the woman says.

Nice to meet you, Eve says. Sorry to scream like that, I was lost in my own thoughts.

Sherry waves her hand as if to say honestly, no need, I made you jump didn't I, no problem. And how old are you, Daniel? she says. You must be at least nineteen.

Daniel smiles. I'm six, he says.

Really? Not sixteen?

No.

Not sixty?

No, I'm the number six with no other numbers.

Well, I've got something for you, she says, hold on a sec.

Their new neighbour disappears. Eve is curious, Daniel looks anxious as usual. It's fine, she says, don't worry.

Then Sherry is back, holding a large chocolate cake covered in Smarties. I'm afraid I didn't make it myself, but it *is* home-made, she says. I got it from the market this morning. Welcome to Abigail Gardens.

Thank you, Eve says. That's so incredibly kind.

The thought of this woman deciding to buy her a welcome gift, deciding that she's *worthy* of a gift, then choosing one at the market and carrying it home, is something Eve can't take in. It feels like a foreign body, something to reject.

She has the urge to throw the cake in the air, as high as it will go.

We love chocolate cake, don't we, Daniel? she says.

He is silent.

How are you getting on? All unpacked? Sherry says.

90

Almost, Eve says. Stuff everywhere as yet, you know what it's like.

Awful, Sherry says. There's a reason why they say moving is up there with bereavement and divorce when it comes to stress.

Oh it's not too bad if you're organised, Eve says. We've had a lot of practice. I try and label every box.

That's very impressive, Sherry says.

They stand in silence, two women and a boy, separated by a rotten fence that will fold during a gale this coming winter, collapsing the boundary between two households. And no one will mind or bother to replace it. The broken panel will sit flummoxed on the grass like the messy aftermath of a glorious party – a symbol, a gateway, a joy. Eventually it will be thrown on a bonfire, where it will spit and float in the night-time air, red-hot and rising.

I like that Wendy house, Sherry says, looking around the garden.

It's mine, Daniel says.

Is it? I assumed it must be your mother's place, and that you live in the main house.

No this is *my* place, he says, stomping up to the Wendy house. And we're getting a rabbit too.

Are you now? Well that's very nice.

Eve grimaces, whispers something to Sherry that Daniel can't hear. *We're not, we're really not.*

What? he says.

Nothing darling, she says, sing-song.

This is the first time Eve Berry whispers to Sherry Marsh. The first time they share a secret.

They stand in their respective gardens, chatting about rabbits while a chocolate cake melts in the sun.

91

We should get together sometime, have a drink, Sherry says.

That would be really nice, Eve says.

The local store is called Pendle's. Walking through it now, the unfamiliar colour scheme and back-to-front layout, makes Eve feel like she is on holiday. Sad really, to feel like you're on holiday when you're only in Pendle's. But she enjoys it while it lasts, the sensation of not quite knowing where she is, the way it enhances her vision, brings small details into view. As she grows used to it, everything about this town will blur. She will no longer notice the daily change of books in the charity shop window, the musical sound of market stalls being set up first thing on a morning, the way someone always fly-tips in the corner of the car park: bin bags, shelving units, even a mattress once. All of it soon to blur.

Funny what familiarity does to a person, a brain, the senses.

Funny that fly-tipping is a term only applied to rubbish, when its usage could be far wider.

To throw things away on the fly, on the sly.

Don't we do that with human beings too? Discard them without care, as if they were trash that meant nothing to us?

She thinks of her parents, just for a minute.

I have fly-tipped my parents, she thinks.

And the fly-tipping of her parents, this too will blur all over again. It's happening right now as we speak. Like the graffiti on the wall that Eve will pass every day. See it now, blurring? Catch it while you can, before it –

Hazy, soft focus, world obscured. Until something makes you look again, look closely, or see in a way you've never seen before.

Crisis makes us look.

Art makes us look.

Science makes us look.

This is what Eve thinks now, and what she will say to Daniel when he is old enough to understand such things as crisis, art and science.

And he will say Mum, there are other things too you know.

Like what? she'll say.

Like love, he'll say.

And she will roll her eyes and say honestly, no need to get silly is there, when we're having a serious conversation.

Eve is thinking of applying for a job in Pendle's. She worked in a corner shop before, so this would be a step up, with big modern tills and a chair and –

A step up, how ridiculous. Nothing wrong with Pendle's itself, nothing wrong with working there. But, the trouble is. She had wanted to do A levels, maybe a degree, something scientific. She did all the sciences at O level, biology, chemistry and physics. She and the bump got an A for each one, plus an A for geography and history and Bs for everything else. He's my exam superpower, she said to her friend Robbie, while stroking circles on the bump. He's a top-grade baby, Robbie said.

Eve also had a flair for sewing, even though she had never been taught, had never seen another person sew on a button, let alone turn up trousers, make a toy dog from an old dress, embroider a perfect flower.

Oh well, she thinks. I'm doing things in a different order, that's all. When Daniel's schooling is done, mine will restart.

Which is why, while Daniel is sifting through illustrated stories in the public library, Eve always heads for the science books.

Why do you like them? he says, standing there with a book about Dave the dragon.

I find them interesting, she says.

What are they about?

You'll find out when you're a bit older, when you study sciences at school. It'll make you see everything differently. You'll learn loads of important things, like how solids turn to liquids and liquids turn to solids. You'll learn about sound and electricity and heat and chemical reactions and –

Mum?

Hmm.

I need the loo.

Okay.

Eve is in the spirits aisle now. Pendle's has a decent selection, she thinks. She moves past the whiskies and the bourbons, the vodkas and the gins, and arrives at the sherries.

She smiles at the thought of drinking sherry with her new neighbour.

What is Sherry like when she drinks sherry?

What is Sherry like when she isn't drinking sherry?

Maybe she could find a bottle with a pretty label, an unusual sort, not too expensive, tie a ribbon around it and give it to her neighbour as a gift. She pictures herself knocking on Sherry's front door and saying *so, how about that drink?* Sherry might find it funny and endearing, the bottle in Eve's hand. She might notice the unusual label, take it as a sign that Eve knows things about the world and how to live well in it. Yes, something like that.

She won't find what she wants in Pendle's. She needs to find a good off-licence, an independent sort of place.

She wanders through town, gazing into shops.

Is there an off-licence nearby? she says to a woman in a pinstriped suit.

Just down there, take a right then a left, weird little place, bit pricey, the woman says.

Weird I like, pricey not so much, Eve says.

Me too, the woman says. I like my weirdness to be cheap.

Eve is not a superstitious person, but she takes this stranger's friendliness as a good omen, a sign that moving here hasn't been a mistake. It's always so hard to know where to go. How do other people decide where to live? A new job probably, or wanting to be closer to family and friends, or maybe they simply love a place, feel it in their bones, the sense that they might actually belong. The bones know everything, according to Eve. Archaeology, excavation, maybe *this* is what she'll study when she's older.

Ever since Daniel was born, Eve has moved at least once a year. It's the safest thing to do. It's the *only* thing to do. She chooses each new town by standing in front of the map on her kitchen wall, the one she keeps Blu-Tacked to an old noticeboard. She closes her eyes and lets her hand move in a figure of eight, that's how this process always begins, and then she is off, her hand zigzagging this way and that way, going north and east, south and west – *does anyone really know where's best?* – and then, finally, the frantic tour stops. She sticks a pin in the map and opens her eyes. Okay, she says, that's the place.

But this time, she had tried something different. She lifted Daniel up onto a chair and handed him the pin. Close your eyes and stick this pin in the map, anywhere you like, she said, as if it was just a bit of fun, no more responsibility than pinning a tail on a donkey. Why? he said. It's a surprise, she said. He did what he was told, then he opened his eyes and looked at the pin, and Eve ruffled his hair and said excellent, job done, *that's* where we're moving to next.

It took the rest of the evening to calm him down. The power he had been given was too big for him to hold.

I'm sorry, Eve said, but we need to go.

Why do we? he said.

It's good to keep moving, she said. It keeps things fresh.

Fresh, he said, thinking of milk, thinking of ham, thinking of cress in a pot on the windowsill.

She told him she thought it was a nice idea, playing a game with the map, leaving it up to chance.

Trouble was, she hadn't left it up to chance. She had left it up to a six-year-old boy, who already hated that map on the wall. In some homes, a map would evoke an atmosphere of learning, open-mindedness; *let's be aware of the wider world, there are more places than home*. But for Daniel it triggered fear and a sense of transience; *always on the go, never know when*.

What if the next place is horrible and full of monsters? he said.

We've discussed monsters and what did I say?

You said they only exist in books.

97

That's right, in books and films and made-up worlds, Eve said.

But that's not true, Daniel said. You told me Granny and Grandad are monsters. So monsters do exist don't they.

They're not *actual* monsters, Eve said. It was just my way of saying they're not good people, that's all.

And there they were, Roger and Gail Berry, waxy skin and tatty jumpers. The little lace collar of her mother's blouse. House heated by bucketfuls of scorn.

Eve pictured Mr and Mrs Jenkins, who had turned up at her parents' house when she was seven months pregnant. Eve had answered the door, assumed they were Jehovah's Witnesses. They looked down at her belly. You must be Eve, they said. And then she knew. There were wolves at the door, the drabbest wolves you ever saw. Out came the special tea set. Earl Grey, garibaldis. They shuffled into the lounge. It's a win-win situation, Eve's mother said. Mr and Mrs Jenkins finally get a baby and you get your future back. Since when did I lose my future? Eve said. I don't remember being careless with time. Facetious girl, Eve's father said. That's my name, don't wear it out, Eve said. Her mother's sigh was a gust of ill wind. You can't keep it, Gail Berry said, you know you can't. For a moment, Eve was lost in a saggy armchair. Then, somehow, she found herself. She sat up straight, leaned forward and spoke with a calmness that surprised her. I can and I will, she said. These words marched around her like smart little soldiers, a defiant infantry of letters. She placed her hands on her belly: *Hush now, my soft watery boy. Don't worry, don't listen, it's all right, I've got you.*

Will it make you feel better if *I* stick a pin in the map instead? Eve said to Daniel.

Can't we just go somewhere nice? he said. No pin.

Okay, she said. No more pins.

She took a deep breath. No one had told her that being a mother would involve so many lies.

Well, she said, there is one nice place I'd thought of.

Is there?

But the thing is, she said. It's so nice I thought it might be too expensive, but maybe I should find out for sure, what do you think?

His eyes were fierce and bright blue.

Mummy, he said.

What.

Is it my fault we're moving?

Eve pictured two upside-down cups being shuffled around by a magician. Under one of these cups was the correct answer, the one a good mother would instinctively find. And where was Eve in this picture? Queueing outside, of course. Counting her change, trying to find enough money for a ticket to see this rare magician, the one with astounding pockets full of right and wrong answers.

Of course not, Eve said. The people who own our flat want to move back in, that's all.

Another lie.

Again, he began to cry, and she pulled him close, said this isn't something to be scared of, do you hear me, are you listening to what I'm saying.

He was imagining strangers coming into the flat and throwing them out. Then his bed and his toys, chucked onto the pavement outside. His toys kicked into the road, run over by cars. Teddies, dismembered. Lego people, beheaded.

Daniel, are you listening to what I'm saying?

Rain on my bed and ted has no head, he whispered to himself.

Eve placed her hand on his forehead and held it there. He closed his eyes. She stroked his eyebrows, ever so slowly.

His breathing deepened.

Will Auntie Fig be there? he said, opening his eyes again.

What's it got to do with Auntie Fig? she said.

I like Auntie Fig, he said.

He was talking about Anna Feigenbaum, who once told him that her surname meant fig tree in German. I love it, he said. Will you be my Auntie Fig? I'd be honoured, she said.

Anna was the one person they could rely on. Every month, along with something for Daniel, she sent Eve a cheque in the post.

She'll come and visit, Eve said. Now go and brush your teeth and get in your jim-jams. No more worrying. I'm going to find the very best place. All right, Danny Boy?

Later that night, Eve closed her eyes and stuck the pin back in the map: *Norfolk.*

Later that night, Daniel was sure that his bed was moving, that his whole room was swaying like a ship on the sea. He wanted to run to his mother, the captain of his ship, and warn her of the coming storm. *Take the wheel, Mummy, take the wheel.* He was her one-man crew, with wide eyes and a wet brow, doing his best. But the task was beyond him.

Daniel had sensed his mother's fear. A problem shared, a problem doubled.

And his mouth, always too full of questions. He knew they upset his mum, but he asked them just the same. Where's my daddy? Where are *your* mummy and daddy? he would say. And she would say Daniel, I've told you, can we just put this to bed. They're not interested in us, we're better off without them. I'm not sad about it. You're enough for anyone, darling. I'm so lucky to have you.

And he *had* put it to bed. The fact that they came from monsters. The fact that they were unwanted. In bed with him every night, beside his knitted horse and hot water bottle, these facts slept soundly while he dreamed of tall ships on rough seas and woke up feeling sick.

Years later, when Daniel wanders by chance into a gallery, stands for the first time in a room full of ships in a storm painted by Turner, he will feel like he has discovered an exhibition of his childhood, some kind of visual poem, all about him.

I hate paintings like this, Erica will say. They're so bleak and depressing don't you think?

Her words will come towards him like old plastic bottles, bobbing about on the curves of a silver sea. The room, so bright and fierce.

I really need some new trainers, she will say, as she looks down at her feet.

Eve peers through the window. This doesn't look like any off-licence she has been to before. It's a dark cavern, semi-lit with orange light, bouncing off dusty old bottles. In the corner, a man is playing something Spanish-sounding on a guitar.

Hello, he says as Eve walks in.

Hey, she says.

She moves from shelf to shelf, listening to the music, gazing at bottles of dark liquor, no idea what most of them are.

Clever, she thinks. How the space has been used to mimic the effect of what they're selling. It's an intoxicating experience, standing here with all the coloured glass, all the reds, oranges and yellows, the low light and the music and that sweet medicinal smell. It's going to her head. But then Eve has always been a lightweight, easily intoxicated.

She walks through an archway into the back of the shop, not completely sure it's open to customers.

More bottles, wine this time. But this is not all. The far wall is completely covered in paintings.

For you, a voice says from behind her, making her jump.

It's the guitar player. He is holding two tiny glasses and a bottle.

A little rum? he says. It's the best I've ever tasted. It has just the right amount of honey, vanilla and fruit, and heat too, plenty of heat.

Thank you, she says, why not.

He lifts his glass. To you, he says.

And they drink.

Christ on a bike, she says.

He laughs. The young lady likes the rum?

She does. I wouldn't call myself a lady though.

I'm Franklin, he says, holding out his hand.

Eve Berry, she says with a firm shake.

Would you like another? On the house, obviously. Something to drink while you browse, he says.

Really? she says.

He takes this as a yes, refills her glass.

Then he is gone, and she can hear the sound of his guitar again. She sips her rum and moves closer to the paintings. They are all for sale. Below each one is a postcard listing a title and a price. They are mainly landscapes – vineyards, mountains, yellow fields – apart from one, whose label says *Still Life with Sherry*. In this painting there is a kitchen with a wide window, dark blue cupboards, a long table draped with white cloth. On the table there is butter and cheese, a loaf of bread, a plate of peaches and pears, a jug, two glasses and a bottle of sherry. How funny, Eve whispers, as she studies the flamenco dancer on the label of the bottle, her swirling red and black dress. Funny how she feels seen by an object that can't possibly see her.

She is hungry now. She forgot to eat lunch. Her hand moves to her stomach and is about to rest there, in the way a hand instinctively does when a stomach growls, but it keeps on going until it lands on her chest.

In front of this painting, Eve's hunger is neither ordinary nor in its usual place.

She touches the canvas.

I just want someone to sit me down at this table, give me bread and cheese and fruit, look after me, she thinks.

As a rule, Eve won't let herself think about the fact that there is no one to take care of her. What good would it do? She made a decision to go it alone when Daniel was born. With Anna's help, she got out. There's no point feeling sorry for herself, longing for what she doesn't have. There is always a cost to freedom.

She finishes the last of the rum. Medicine for the soul, she thinks.

She glances at her watch. Daniel will be coming out of school in an hour. Better go, buy some mints, get rid of the boozy smell.

She steps back through the archway, sees Franklin serving a customer. She puts her glass on the counter and wanders over to the bottles of sherry. Some of the labels are quite striking, one in particular: a large ampersand on a cream background, no words at all. She runs her finger across it.

&

Isn't it lovely? Franklin says.

Very, Eve says.

I love ampersands, and that one is a stunning example, he says.

It looks like it was done by hand, by a calligrapher, she says.

Fancy you noticing that, he says, a man who loves detail, typography, the way things are put together.

Is it sherry? she says.

Franklin nods. If you like almonds, pears, fresh bread and sea air, you'll definitely like this one, he says.

This place makes me profoundly hungry, Eve says.

Shame we don't sell food then isn't it, he says.

You should, you definitely should. You could turn the back room into a cafe, something rustic. Those paintings on the wall would be so nice to look at while eating bread and cheese, she says.

Interesting, he says.

She asks if it's his place, if he owns it.

I'm afraid so, he says.

She tells him she likes it, it's sort of hypnotic, like being in a chemist and a bar and a gallery all at once, and also sort of like being in a church somehow, not that she's religious, not that she ever goes to church, but a tiny old church in France maybe, not that she's ever been to France.

He is laughing now. And she doesn't know what to make of this.

Anyway, he says, I haven't even asked what you're looking for.

Sorry?

You must have come in for something in particular.

Oh, she says, I think it's beyond my budget. I'm sorry, I shouldn't have drunk your rum if I wasn't going to buy anything.

Don't be silly, he says. So what *would* you have bought, if money were no object?

Money is always an object, she says.

But otherwise, he says. Go on, humour me.

A bottle of sherry, Eve says. For a friend. Well, a potential friend. Her name's Sherry you see, she's my new neighbour. We've only met once, over the garden fence. She gave me a chocolate cake, it was covered in Smarties.

And you wanted to give *her* a bottle of sherry, he says.

Well, that was the idea. I wanted one with a pretty label, something that looks a bit special, you know, like the one in the painting over there. I thought it would make her smile, Eve says. Then she pauses. Do you think lots of people will already have given her sherry? she says. I mean, do you think I'm being tacky and ridiculous, trying too hard? I've only just moved here, I don't have many friends, so –

Franklin is laughing again, soft and airy, his eyes half closed.

I think you're very interesting, he says, loudly, as if he is making an important announcement.

Pah, she says.

Most people politely decline my rum and leave without saying a thing, let alone about my paintings, he says.

You did them?

He takes one of the ampersand bottles off the shelf. For you, he says.

What?

It's a gift.

No, really.

Yes, really. For your potential friend, your friend with potential.

He looks cheeky now, she doesn't know why.

There's no need, honestly, I couldn't just –

Please, Franklin says. It'll make me happy.

She looks at the bottle, looks at him.

Pop in sometime, tell me if she liked it, he says. If you want to, obviously.

Eve is stubborn, silent, tempted.

If you don't take it I'll be offended, he says.

All right, she says. Thank you so much.

She stares at the label on the bottle.

I'm going to ask her if I can have this back when it's empty. Maybe I can steam it off and frame it, she says.

Why don't you just draw an ampersand? he says.

Oh I could never draw one like this. It's so full of verve and movement.

He wants her to stay all afternoon, talk like this all afternoon.

She looks at her watch. Oh God, I have to collect my son from school. Thank you so much, for the sherry and the rum.

No problem, he says, as the bell above the door rings.

Her leaving is a jingle and a jangle. He picks up his guitar, sits back on his stool, plays an old country song about friendship.

He pictures a young woman, knocking on a stranger's door with a bottle of sherry and an ampersand.

It's nothing big, or remarkable.

But it touches his weary heart, deeply.

Outside, Eve hurries back to the car park, only realising now that she shouldn't have drunk that rum, she'll be tipsy behind the wheel of her Mini with Daniel in the car, and she's usually so sensible, how could she have forgotten herself?

Think of the boy, how much better his life will be with people who can take proper care of him.

Everyone knows you're crazy. We could have you locked up.

Such a waste of money, the taxi she takes to school.

There is always a cost to freedom.

And Daniel looks so happy as he runs towards her at the gates.

She doesn't think she has ever seen him look this happy.

We made dinosaurs from papier-mâché, he says.

Did you? she says. That's very advanced.

Is it? he says, looking pleased.

Absolutely. What sort of dinosaur?

Mine's a Stegosaurus, I've called her Fig. She's not finished yet.

Oh Auntie Fig will love that. I used to own a Brontosaurus you know.

He looks up at her, amazed.

And a Diplodocus. They were sort of rubbery.

Do you know all the names? he says.

Not all, just some, she says. Triceratops, Brachiosaurus, Tyrannosaurus rex ...

As her list goes on, and they begin to walk home, he takes her hand.

It's nothing big, or remarkable.

But it touches her weary heart, deeply.

107

She has painted her fingernails milky blue.

She pushes hard on a white button, expects to hear a buzzing sound coming from inside the house, but no. The doorbell of 4 Abigail Gardens plays a tune and plays it loud: 'I Do Like to Be Beside the Seaside'.

Well that's different, Eve thinks.

She looks down at her flowery silk shirt and denim skirt, bought from a charity shop last week, hopes she looks all right.

Yesterday she cut the hem off an old dress, used it to make a ribbon for a bottle, tied a bow around an ampersand.

It's a sign that means *and*, she told Daniel when he asked about that thing on the side of the bottle, that dancing thing.

Dancing? she said.

It looks like it's dancing, he said. What is it?

It's an ampersand, she said, which is a type of conjunction.

What's a conjunction? he said.

It connects parts of a sentence. But the word *conjunction* has other meanings too. A conjunction can be a set of events all happening at once. It can also be used to describe planets coming into alignment, looking like they're close together when actually they're not.

Daniel looked up from his Lego, then away again.

Darling, I thought I put that T-shirt in the washing basket. Why are you wearing it again?

It's not smelly, he said.

It doesn't have to be smelly to be dirty, she said.

But there's no dirt on it, he said, looking down at his yellow T-shirt with Bryan the lion on the front.

She shrugged, carried on snipping the hem off a dress. Fine, she said. If you want to wear the same thing for days on end, knock yourself out.

Knock myself out? he said.

It's just a phrase, she said. It means do what you like, on your head be it.

On my head? he said.

Now they are at the front door of their neighbour's house, quietly waiting, hoping to deliver a gift before dashing back home to watch telly. They are in this together, it's a joint effort. Eve has told Daniel that this is what people do, and it's important, the making of new friends, being generous. What she hasn't told him is how nervous she is. The last thing he needs is to absorb *her* anxiety, have it rush into his like river into sea, an estuary of fear. So she is pretending to be fine, standing here in her flowery shirt with milky blue nails, bottle in one hand, boy in the other.

'I Do Like to Be Beside the Seaside' is still playing loudly, which must be annoying if you live at 4 Abigail Gardens. Eve is concerned about it going on forever. Is there a stop button somewhere? What if someone calls round and you're inside this house, hurt on the floor unable to move – would you potentially have to listen to this eerie muzak until your dying moment?

Dark, Eve.

Not really, she thinks. Practical, that's all. And Eve is a practical woman, wholeheartedly pragmatic.

I think their doorbell's malfunctioning, she says.

Why doesn't our door play music? Daniel says.

Because we have that brass door knocker. It's a fox, isn't it.

She turns to glance at the garden, which is so much bigger than the one at the front of their bungalow. There are three flamingos, standing in a row in the middle of the lawn. Decorative, obviously. And heavy-looking too, no chance of a drunken teenager running through town with one of these. To Eve they seem slightly sinister, rancorous even; scarlet-plumed guards ready to lunge. It looks like someone has spent a lot of time out here, planting hedges, trees and flowerbeds, making colourful little circles.

But it's not a real fox, Daniel says.

Well no, Eve says.

That would be disgusting and really mean, he says.

Yes it would, she says.

She looks down at him, her beautiful blameless impediment. In an ideal world she would have rung this doorbell mid-evening by herself, said she was wondering, she just happened to wonder if Sherry might fancy a drink. But there was no one to babysit, to keep an eye on Daniel. There is *never* anyone to keep an eye on Daniel.

But he is beautiful and blameless.

It's 5.30pm on a Tuesday and they are in this together.

What are those pink things? he says.

Have you only just noticed them? she says, as 'I Do Like to Be Beside the Seaside' finally thank goodness stops, and the front door opens, and Sherry Marsh is here, right here.

Eve's mouth is unbelievably dry.

Hello you two, Sherry says. I'm sorry it took me so long to answer. One of my daughters thought it would be *hilarious* to jump in the pond. You should see the state of her, she looks like a creature from the deep, all covered in slime. Anyway, come on in.

Oh, Eve says, no, we're just here to –

Before she has a chance to explain, to say they're just dropping off a gift, something she just happened to see while she was out shopping, Sherry has stepped backwards and fully opened the door and Daniel is moving towards her, shy little Daniel, stepping towards a stranger.

Sherry pats him on the head as he crosses the threshold.

Eve is frozen.

Daniel turns around.

Now he is with another mother. She is older and taller than Eve, with broad shoulders that look brave somehow. There's an excitability to her body, and a calmness too, she seems so at ease, it's confusing and attractive. Eve's own body is reedy and careful, this is how she sees it, how she judges herself. They are a straight line and a swirl, these two mothers, peering at each other from either side of a threshold.

But you haven't discovered the purpose of our visit, Eve thinks, protesting against the warm welcome, the come on in, with feet fixed to the floor.

Sherry doesn't care why they've rung her bell. She is pleased to see them, that's all. Hers is an open house, she loves the flow of people, the more noise the better.

Get a wiggle on then, she says.

And now Eve is inside too, and the door has closed, and all three of them are in the hallway when Eve says:

I like your flamboyance of flamingos.

111

My what? Sherry says.

Flamboyance, Eve says, blushing. It's the collective noun for a group of flamingos.

Is it really, Sherry says. A *flamboyance*. You know your collective nouns, do you?

Some of them, Eve says.

She is twenty-two, feels about eight.

So what's a group of owls? Sherry says.

That would be a wisdom or a parliament, Eve says.

And what's a group of swans?

I tend to think of that as a ballet.

Sherry is smiling, Eve thinks it's sarcasm at first, a kind of belittling, then Sherry touches her arm, says how wonderful, my Rae is going to *love* you. Come through, let's make some coffee, or is that something stronger you're holding there?

Oh this, Eve says as if she had forgotten all about it, didn't even realise she was clutching it at all.

(For dear life.)

(For any kind of life.)

I brought you a bottle of sherry, Eve says. It's from that little off-licence in town. Apparently it tastes of almonds, pears and sea air, that's what the guy told me. You suggested a drink, you see, so –

Eve pushes the bottle towards Sherry, a gesture more desperate than graceful.

Goodness, Sherry says. Let me take a proper look.

She flicks the light on in the hallway, even though it's perfectly bright.

And now they are illuminated.

Daniel looks up at the walls, covered in lilac flock wallpaper. He has never seen anything like it. The pattern is so weird, like golden feathers with alien eyes, it makes him think of *Doctor Who*, makes him feel like he's being watched by extraterrestrials living inside these walls.

Sherry is studying the bottle, but is distracted by Daniel's hands, both of them stroking the wallpaper.

Do you like it? she says. It's new. My husband finished it last week.

It looks like aliens, he says.

Aliens? she says. Ha, I see what you mean. No these are peacock feathers, see? That's what the pattern is based on. Have you ever seen a peacock?

No I haven't, Daniel says.

You touch it too, Sherry says to Eve.

Me? she says.

Go on, it's *so* luxurious, Sherry says.

Three sets of hands, stroking a velvety wall inside 4 Abigail Gardens.

Then a child rushes in. A girl covered in pondweed, dragging a huge yellow towel behind her.

Daniel slams against Eve's legs. She puts her hand on her son's shoulder, squeezes gently, *it's all right*.

And this is my very own creature from the deep, Sherry says. For goodness' sake, Pauline, look at the state of you. Come and say hello to Daniel. You're the same age, you two. You must have met at school?

Pauline stomps up to Daniel and curtsies in front of him.

He is terrified.

She is dripping all over the carpet.

Sherry is shaking her head.

Eve is thinking that maybe this was a terrible idea. She watches Sherry put the bottle down on the floor, pull the towel from Pauline's head and wrap it around her. Pauline squirms and giggles because Sherry is cuddling her, and it tickles, and they are sort of wrestling, and at the end

113

of this slimy hullabaloo Pauline is in her mother's arms, all wrapped up in yellow, soggy and happy because her mother has won this game, won her over.

Daniel looks up at Eve. She doesn't move, tries not to catch his eye. In this moment, she needs her separateness.

Come on, let's make some hot chocolate, Sherry says.

They all walk through to the kitchen, where there is another girl, sullen at the table, reading. This girl is older than her sister, perhaps by a couple of years. She is wearing a black polo neck and headphones.

Rae, meet our new neighbours, Sherry says.

The girl looks at them, briefly, then back at her book. She takes a crisp from a bowl and puts it in her mouth.

This is Eve and her son, Daniel, Sherry says. Eve knows all the collective nouns for things. Did you know that a group of flamingos is called a flamboyance, Rae?

Rae stares at Eve intensely.

What's the name for a group of peacocks? Sherry says.

Oh, I don't know that one, Eve says.

Never mind, Sherry says.

Later, Eve will chastise herself for this. She does know, she *does*. She has heard a group of peacocks called many things: a pride, a muster, an ostentation. But right now, her stomach is a rabble of butterflies and her mind is blank. No, that's a lie, it's not blank at all. It's an anticipation of ampersands, because the bottle has been left in the hallway by itself & it meant so much that stupid bloody thing & was it really worth it & what will happen next & why am I so dizzy & why is my face so hot & I don't know what I'm doing & look at her lovely shoulders I really like her shoulders & where has Daniel gone?

Mrs Sherry, he says, coming back into the room. You forgot this present from Mummy.

Oh, I'm so sorry, Sherry says. That was very rude of me. I didn't even say thank you, did I. Thank you so much for this, it's incredibly sweet of you.

It's fine, Eve says, waving her hand. No problem, so what, I forgot there even *was* a bottle, her hand says.

The label is really unusual, Sherry says. And I love this ribbon. May I open it now, would you mind, shall we have some? I think we should toast your arrival.

Why not, Eve says. We could have a little glass, couldn't we.

Sit yourself down, Sherry says. There's too much standing going on in here.

She makes three mugs of hot chocolate for the children, then pours sherry into two glasses. She grabs a stool, pulls it over to where Eve is sitting at the table, right beside her, close.

To you and Daniel, she says, looking Eve in the eye.

And they drink.

It's like one of those staring competitions that Eve plays with Daniel, first person to blink is a loser.

Well Eve is not going to lose this one, no chance, no way. She may *look* reedy, a little feeble, but –

Absolutely magnificent, Sherry says when her glass is empty.

My thoughts entirely, Eve says.

And they keep on staring, until Sherry blinks.

Eve grins.

They keep on looking.

They are both smiling now, looking into each other's eyes like it's a game, a competition, a fight.

A long weird hello.

Magnificent.

&

Eve bursts into the off-licence, making Franklin Jones and all his bottles jump.

Didn't expect to see you so soon, he says.

She is holding a bunch of dried cornflowers, royal blue, wrapped in brown paper.

I just popped in to say thank you, she says, handing him the flowers.

These are for me? he says. What a gorgeous colour. Thank you, Eve.

The sherry was a hit with my new friend, she says.

You drank it already?

Not all of it, obviously. But quite a lot.

Disgraceful, he says.

What's disgraceful? a man says. This man has appeared beside Franklin. Nice flowers, look at that blue, he says.

Peter, this is Eve Berry. Eve, this is Peter, Franklin says.

Ah, I heard about you, Peter says.

Really? Eve says.

Oh yes, Peter says. Then he turns back to Franklin. I'm sorry to rush off, I said I'd be there ten minutes ago.

Don't forget to collect my parcel will you, Franklin says.

Peter rolls his eyes. As if, he says. He kisses Franklin, picks up a set of keys. See you tonight, he says. Nice to meet you, Eve.

Where were we, Franklin says.

He looked so familiar, Eve says.

Which isn't actually true. It's just a reflex, that's all, something she instinctively says, a way to refer to Peter.

Otherwise he's only a kiss and a wave, such mischievous eyes, who was that?

Maybe you've seen him around, on his bike, Franklin says. Anyway, I was hoping you'd come back in.

Were you? Eve says.

I have a proposition, he says.

Oh God, she thinks. A proposition is usually a demand, and now she will have to wriggle under its netting to escape.

You've just moved here, he says.

That's right, she says.

So, do you have a job? I mean, are you looking for work, or –

I'm looking, she says.

Excellent, he says. I need some help in here. In fact, I'm desperate. I don't get time to paint any more.

Oh, Eve says. But you don't even know me.

I know what I need to. I'm sure it's beneath you, and not really what you're looking for, but in case you need something to tide you over.

I'm in, Eve says.

Really?

Yep.

That's fantastic, Franklin says. And now we've got that out of the way, this new friend of yours, tell me everything.

Eve smiles. Apparently, she was conceived after her mother drank half a bottle of Harveys Bristol Cream. Hence the name, she says.

How funny. What's she like?

I don't know really, we only just met.

Well if I were to paint your first impressions.

Eve thinks about this.

117

You'd paint a carnival, she says, a jamboree, a colourful procession moving through a city on a sunny day, a day that's hazy with heat.

Nice, he says.

Yes, she says.

Daniel is in the bath, watching a wind-up boat whizz across a wild and frothy sea, its tiny engine whirring. As he moves in the water the boat begins to sway. Don't rock the boat, he says. His voice is gentle and silly. Today has already been a boatful of happiness and it's only 6.30am, still dark outside, but all the lights in all the windows of the houses are on, and the Roberts radio in the kitchen is on, and the oven, on, everything that can be on or off is right now on, it's up and about and merry and on high, for it's a day to push the boat out, to put on your best jumper, to look at shiny things and eat as much as you like.

Daniel's outfit has been laid out on his bed by his mum, his black corduroy trousers and red jumper positioned as if an invisible flat boy is already wearing them, is lying there waiting, ready to say look at me, Dan, can you see me in your outfit, my name's Flat Boy, I slide in and out of other boys' clothes, boys with real bodies and proper dimensions, and happy Christmas Daniel, happy Christmas.

From the bath, Daniel can hear his mum singing along to 'Like a Virgin', which is a song by a woman called Madonna. He knows this song because it's on the radio all the time, and he also knows that a virgin is like snow that no one has walked on yet, this is what his mum told him when he asked, just think of snow, she said. So every time

119

he hears this song he imagines boots stepping into snow, and this image makes him feel good and relaxed, so he sings along, lets his voice go high and squeaky then very low, and his mum always laughs, and all of this means that he really loves Madonna.

The song ends and another begins. This one is sung by lots of different singers to raise money for people in Ethiopia who don't even know it's Christmas. How can they not know it's Christmas? was another thing he had asked his mum. Because they're living in poverty, she said. They have nothing to eat, it's called a famine, and every time someone buys this record the money goes to help them. Daniel imagined coins and notes flying through the skies, all the way to Africa. He was halfway through a Mars bar and felt bad as he wasn't hungry, didn't need it, had only taken it for the fun of eating a Mars bar. His mum had bought the single about people not knowing it's Christmas, even though they didn't have a record player, only a portable radio that she carried from room to room.

You all right in there? she shouts from along the hallway.

Yes thanks, he shouts back.

His mum has made a dress to wear today. She has been making it for ages. She can't decide if it's deep purple, which is also the name of a band, or Cadbury purple, which is the colour of a bar of chocolate. Apparently there are lots of shades of purple, and deep purple is not the same as Cadbury purple, and purple is a colour that she associates with opulence, which is what? he said, which is splendour, a touch of glory, she said.

This dress for Christmas Day has involved a great deal of conversation between Daniel and his mother. *Is it still too loose, do you like this stitching, shall I take it in at the waist?* Thankfully, he now has a train set to entertain him while they talk, which the boy down the road didn't want any more. There was a knock at the door and a woman was there with a giant teddy and a train in a box, saying Eve, I was just having a clear-out and I thought of your Daniel, I really hope you don't mind, please say if this is annoying, but I wondered if he might like these at all?

Eve was delighted. The woman rushed in for tea and Battenberg cake, said she'd washed the teddy in her machine and it had come out so lovely, and her son, well he'd never really taken to the train set, more into cowboys and guns, he's always been a bit well boisterous you know, doesn't have the patience to sit and watch small vehicles move around a track.

Daniel spent all day playing with the train set, but decided to leave the bear by the back door. When he looked into its eyes, all he could see was its previous owner, a boy who had once held a toy gun up to Daniel's head and shouted BAM!

Now he is in the bath, and the whole bungalow smells of biscuits baking in the oven, and this morning there was a pillowcase with the letter D sewn onto it, just beside the Christmas tree, and his mother was already there when he jumped out of bed and ran down the hallway, she was in her dressing gown, thick socks and woolly hat, knitting in her armchair under a tall lamp, and the lights on the tree were on, and the gas fire was on, and when he stepped into the room she literally dropped what she was doing as she moved towards him and picked him up, all six years of him, her lips on his hair his forehead his face.

He thinks of this now, lives it all over again, how light he feels when she picks him up.

Happy Christmas darling, she says, putting him back down on the floor.

Happy Christmas Mummy, he says.

Then she is quiet and still, and he notices her hands by her side, her fingers curled, how she is clutching the cuffs of her pink quilted dressing gown, taking a deep breath and blowing air from her mouth.

Little girl lost.

He watches her, and she is a mystery, a Christmas morning puzzle in the shape of a woman.

But today he has more important matters to attend to than deciphering his mother's code. Like the pillowcase with the letter D on the front, which he knows will contain a tangerine and a net of gold coins like it always does, but what else what else what else?

Eve's eyes tell him to grab it, go on, hurry up, *let's go.*

They sit in front of the fire, facing each other.

Slowly, carefully, he dips his hand into the pillowcase, lifts out a present, then another.

A robot pencil sharpener.

A Matchbox car.

A tangerine.

A wind-up boat.

Two comics.

A tub of hair wax.

A bag of chocolate coins.

A knitted pirate.

A knitted tank top.

And then, he can't believe it, wasn't expecting anything like this: a *watch.*

The watch has a brown leather strap and a gold face and looks like a watch that a man would wear.

Do you like it? she says.

Daniel is an open mouth, breathless.

Let me put it on for you, she says.

He holds out his left wrist, then his right wrist, can't decide which. As this goes on, he looks like he is practising some kind of martial art.

Either's fine, she says, it doesn't matter.

This one then, he says.

She fiddles with the watch strap and buckle, makes it too tight then too loose then perfect.

He looks down at his left arm. He pulls up the sleeve of his dressing gown, so it doesn't obstruct the brilliance of his watch.

Wow, he says.

And she kisses him again.

He stands up and runs out of the room, leaving Eve alone and confused.

She stares at the gas fire, ugly, grey, glowing beside her.

Until her son returns with a big box, all wrapped up in Christmassy paper and red ribbon.

By the time he has placed it on her lap, she is pale. He has never given her a Christmas present before. A card made at school, yes. But not a gift. And she has never expected him to.

Why do you look scared? he says.

I don't, she says, becoming aware that her palms are pressed hard against her cheeks.

It's a shock, receiving a Christmas present after all this time. She has grown used to being someone who doesn't, and it's fine, no it's more than fine, it's autonomous and mature and politically impressive, it's anti-commercial, part of who she is.

123

How had he bought this, wrapped it, hidden it from her? And what the hell is it?

He is a mystery, a Christmas morning puzzle in the shape of a boy.

He sits down with a thud, one sleeve up, one sleeve down.

Look at all these Father Christmases, she says, studying the paper her gift is wrapped in. What would be a good name for a group of Father Christmases?

Just open it, Mummy, he says.

So she does. And her instinct is to go slow, avoid tearing the paper, but something else takes over, some other desire, and she rips it open with a squeal.

Beneath all the Father Christmases is a cardboard box. And inside the cardboard box there is another cardboard box. And so on.

She imagines opening box after box until she comes to a little box full of nothing, a sort of joke, clumsy and weird but also fine. She prepares herself for this, and doesn't mind, in fact it's almost pleasing, like a glimpse of familiar territory, the promise of solid ground.

Her hunch is right and wrong.

Finally, six boxes in, she arrives at her gift: the most beautiful wooden box full of nothing. Eve opens it, looks at all the compartments inside, lined with velvet.

Opulence, Daniel says.

And despite all her efforts not to – the grimace, gritted teeth and frantic blinking – Eve starts to cry. Not a rolling tear to quickly wipe away, but convulsions, coughs, the whole damn thing. She is a sopping wet mess, what a sight what a fright for a boy on Christmas morning.

Deary me, she says.

She tells him how much she loves her present, tries to explain as clearly as she can that there are many types of tears, and those just now were tears of joy, and she's a silly old thing, honestly what a wally, and he says yep, you're a big wally, Mum.

Oh am I, she says. Well you're a nincompoop.

You're made of rabbit poo, he says.

You're this knitted pirate's bottom, she says.

No I'm not, he says. You're a table cloth.

A table cloth? You're the kitchen bin then.

You're a dirty puddle.

That's a good one, she says. You're a dirty dishcloth.

You're a muppet, he says, and smiles, because muppet is actually a good thing to be called, they both love watching *The Muppet Show* on telly, and there isn't a rubbish muppet among all the muppets, so he has lost this game.

He takes the knitted pirate from her hand. I like him, he says.

Do you? she says. That's good. But he is actually a she.

Oh, he says, I was going to call him Jimmy, but now I can't.

Of course you can. A girl can be called Jimmy.

No, I don't like it, he says. She doesn't look like a Jimmy. I'm going to call her Madonna.

Eve laughs. So where did you find my lovely present? she says.

Mrs Sherry got it for me, he says. But it's from me not her.

Of course, Eve says.

Now they are marching past the flamingos and ringing a bell on a door.

125

Can I ring it? Daniel says.

Go on then, Eve says.

Leslie Marsh had banished 'I Do Like to Be Beside the Seaside', called it nightmarish and unseasonal, so now Eve and Daniel and their arms full of festive things are greeted by 'We Wish You a Merry Christmas', a wordless version, slow, electronic, off-key.

Daniel is wearing his black cords, but instead of the red jumper he has chosen a shirt, brushed cotton and brown check, with his new tank top. His hair is slicked back with his new wax, which makes him look like Elvis, in his mind at least.

Eve is in her new dress, which is more purplish blue than purple, this is what she decided as they were leaving the house. Over the dress is a black cardigan with a belt and her favourite green coat. She is holding two bags and a large Tupperware full of cinnamon biscuits shaped like Christmas trees.

When Leslie opens the door, Daniel rolls up his sleeve and holds out his arm. Look, he says to a man who seems very old, even though he is forty-six, which apparently is not old at all according to his mum, who had explained that some people look older than they are, maybe due to lack of sleep or the wrong clothes or getting upset a lot, and Leslie Marsh is one of them.

It's half past eleven, Daniel says.

So it is, Leslie says. I assume Santa brought you that handsome watch?

No, Mum did. Santa got me a cactus.

A cactus?

It's what he wanted, Eve says. He collects them.

Right, well happy Christmas, Leslie says. Come on in.

As they step inside, Leslie shakes Daniel's hand and kisses Eve on the cheek. He is wearing a suit, and his tie has reindeer all over it.

Daniel wonders if he should also be wearing a tie, if this is what men do when they spend time with other families on Christmas Day.

The smell, he says to Leslie.

Smell?

Of your house.

Does it smell bad?

Oh no not bad, Daniel says.

He has no words to describe the amazing smell as they approach the kitchen, as Leslie wanders off and Mrs Sherry turns around, all dangly earrings and frilly pinny, and says well look at you, Daniel, don't you look smart with your hair and your tank top, cute as a button, come here and give me a kiss.

To Eve's surprise, Daniel doesn't just walk up to Sherry and let her kiss him. He runs.

This kitchen is the most chaotic thing Eve has ever seen, and she has witnessed her fair share of chaos. Bowls of peelings, screwed-up wrapping paper strewn about, half-empty champagne glasses, packets of food, jobs begun and abandoned. If this were her kitchen, she would have a nervous breakdown. If this were her kitchen, she would be the luckiest woman alive.

Can I do anything? she says, placing her bags and Tupperware on the table beside the Quality Street, mince pies and After Eights, the bottles of wine, rum, sloe gin and champagne.

Happy Christmas, Sherry says, putting her arms around Eve.

Oh, happy Christmas to you too, Eve says.

Sherry is laughing as usual, Eve has no idea why.

No help required, Sherry says, we're bang on schedule.

You have a schedule? Eve says.

Leslie did it, even got it laminated. He has a thing for lamination.

What's lamination? Daniel says.

It's this, Sherry says, flapping something about, close to his face, a flimsy sheet of paper made solid.

He stands there with his eyes closed, leaning into it, enjoying the warm air and the funny sound and the fact that it's just for him. It sounds like the quietest helicopter in the world, hovering right beside him in this kitchen with overflowing cupboards and steamed-up windows.

I'm fanning you with my laminated list, Sherry says.

It's nice, Daniel says, smiling as the wind blows, as the woman in the frilly pinny makes weather.

Eve rolls her eyes. He is so easy when he's here.

Then Leslie reappears. Sorry about that, too much Guinness last night, he says.

Leslie, Sherry says. No need to overshare. Where are the girls?

Playing upstairs, he says. Not together, obviously. How's the turkey looking? Are we all on schedule?

I don't know, Leslie, are we? Sherry says. A little shared responsibility would be nice, it's 1984 not 1954.

He laughs, seems to like this. He is smart and sparkly, this is what Eve thinks as she stands there looking at his suit, too big and too pale but sweet on him nevertheless.

Eve, you're still wearing your coat, Sherry says. For crying out loud, Les, why didn't you take her coat?

They just rushed through to see you, he says to Eve, and winks. Here, let me take that.

He helps her take off her coat, and Sherry is pouring champagne into a glass when she stops and says wow.

What, Eve says.

You, Sherry says.

Me?

Yes you. You in that dress.

It's very nice, is it new? Leslie says.

I made it, Eve says.

You didn't, Leslie says. Well that's impressive isn't it, Sherry.

His wife doesn't answer. She fills three glasses with champagne and takes one over to Eve.

It's a beautiful dress, she says quietly, her face unusually serious.

Thanks, Eve says.

They all drink champagne, apart from Daniel, who says Merry Christmas with Vimto in Leslie's favourite glass, it's heavy and has a handle, he has never drunk squash from a glass like this before.

What a day, he says. This blushing boy in an argyle tank top, with slicked-back hair and a pint glass, standing beside his mum. Why's that funny? he says, looking from Eve to Leslie to Sherry.

It just is, Eve says.

Would you like a present? Leslie says.

Shouldn't we open them all together later? Sherry says.

Nah, Leslie says.

Because there is something about Daniel that melts him, every time he sees him.

And the look on his face when he opens his box of Lego. The shock, innocence and gratitude.

Somehow it makes Leslie fear for the boy, and love him.

*

Like any Christmas Day, this one has its ups and downs.

Rae Marsh spent most of the day playing Operation by herself. She was focused, intense, highly committed to the task at hand, as though her patient were a real person who would die if she made a wrong move. Sitting there in the lounge in gold cords and a yellow sweatshirt, she burned like a flame.

Pauline Marsh, mad as her long ponytail held in place with a fluorescent sock, poured herself some rum, then a bit more rum, and was sick in the garden pond.

She's six years old, how can this possibly be happening? Leslie said from the patio. And why's she so obsessed with that bloody pond? I swear I'm going to fill it in, build a shed, you know I've always wanted a shed.

Daniel Berry ate like a king, like Elvis himself, seated at the end of the table in the dining room, placed there at two o'clock on the dot by Leslie, man on a schedule, who said right then, Daniel, you can sit opposite me, head of the table, what d'ya think?

Head of the table, *honestly*, Sherry said.

I want to sit next to Eve, Rae said, pushing Pauline out of the way.

And then there were six. Three adults, three children, a feast at a long table.

There were tall candles, some red, some gold. There was mistletoe, holly, a tree in the corner so full and proud, so bright and perfectly dressed, all those miniature wooden decorations, the chocolates dangling in coloured foil, the tinsel and stars and even an R2-D2, which Pauline had tied with string and hung from a branch.

There was turkey, bacon, stuffing. Roast potatoes, red cabbage, parsnips and carrots. Sprouts, peas, bread sauce, cranberry sauce, gravy.

I love sprouts, Daniel said.

Since when, Eve said.

Since now, Daniel said. These taste different to yours.

I finished them off in a pan with some butter, bacon and chestnuts, Sherry said.

That's so inventive, Eve said.

They pulled crackers, told jokes, groaned at the jokes, put paper hats on their heads and admired mini nail clippers, mini screwdrivers, a mini comb.

Then there was Christmas pudding, which Leslie poured brandy over and set fire to.

Oh my *God*, Daniel shouted.

And chocolate log, ice cream, pavlova.

Leslie scrunched a torn-up cracker into a ball and threw it at Daniel.

Hey, Daniel said. He picked it up and threw it back, and while he was doing this, Leslie searched the table for something else to scrunch up, make throwable.

But Pauline beat him to it, tossed a leftover sprout.

No, not food, Sherry said, as half a roast carrot flew through the air and hit her in the face.

Eve was shocked. The mess, the waste of food.

But now they were all throwing things, everyone still seated apart from mad Pauline, who was running towards the Christmas tree, her grubby hands reaching for anything she could pull down and throw at her dad.

Pauline, *no*, Sherry said.

Pauline!

The tree wobbled, it shook, needles were liberated from branches.

Then the whole thing came down. The angel at the top, landing with a bounce on the cream carpet, long and plush and soft as grass. R2-D2, the little wooden soldiers, the stars and tinsel and gigantic baubles, all of them on the floor.

Eve wanted to run. She braced herself for the shouting, the rage. Time had stopped, it was like a paused video, she looked at Daniel, couldn't work out the expression on his face, it was almost neutral as if nothing had happened, no paper, plastic and cardboard thrown across the room, no tree shaken and tipped over by a girl. Any second now, that girl would be slapped and sent upstairs and the day would be over and she and Daniel would have to leave.

The silence was agony. Two seconds felt like sixty. This is what fear does, it plays with time.

Sherry's hand was over her mouth.

Rae was looking at her mum then her dad then her mum.

Leslie raised his glass of red wine, said ho ho ho in a deep voice.

And Sherry burst out laughing.

Merry Christmas, ho ho ho, Leslie said again.

You're such a clumsy bugger, Pauline, Sherry said.

Daniel found this hysterical. He got out of his chair and went over to Pauline, stood beside her, assessed the damage. Clumsy bugger, he said, and nudged her with his elbow.

Pauline smiled at him. It was the first time she had really acknowledged his presence, despite being in the same room many times, being in the same class at school.

Sleepy and red-faced and woozy from laughing, they piled into the lounge for Guess Who? and TV, closing the door on the mayhem that was now the dining room.

Does your person have glasses? Daniel said.

132

Does yours wear a hat? Pauline said.

The house was hot, their stomachs were full, Leslie fell asleep in his recliner.

Oh my goodness, Eve said. Your presents, I forgot all about them. I left them in the kitchen.

She disappeared for what seemed like a long time, then returned with two plastic bags.

For Sherry and Leslie: knitted socks, a pair each, and a bottle of Scotch.

For Pauline: a patchwork toy dog and a selection pack.

For Rae: a giant Toblerone and a pencil case full of coloured pencils, which seemed to change her mood entirely, make her lighter for a while, less intense. She inspected the pencils one by one, said they were excellent quality.

Did you make these yourself? Sherry said, looking at the dog and the pencil case, turning them over and over.

Eve nodded.

Well I never, Sherry said.

Eve snuggled further down into the sofa.

Here, Sherry said, lifting her feet off a pink floor cushion, kicking it along so that Eve could share it. Put your feet up. Do you like my new poofy?

Your what? Eve said.

I think it's called a pouffe, Leslie said, opening his eyes for a moment, then promptly falling asleep again.

Oh no, Sherry said, it's a poofy.

Whatever it was, Eve put her feet on it.

They were watching telly now, Mary Poppins with her magical bag, her spoonful of sugar.

I love Julie Andrews, Sherry said, over the sound of Leslie snoring. *Some Like It Hot*'s on tonight, quite late though, have you seen it?

Eve said she hadn't but she'd like to.

Or *The Nutcracker*'s on at teatime, if that's more your thing, Sherry said. I've never been to a ballet, have you?

Never, Eve said, but I'd like to.

Is there anything you *wouldn't* like to do? Sherry said.

Eve blushed. Because right now, with Sherry, there wasn't. She would probably say yes to anything, just to spend time with this woman. She was a yes in a home-made dress, a dress that had made Sherry say wow.

She glanced at Daniel, deep in a brown beanbag, watching *Mary Poppins*.

Sherry, Eve said. Thank you so much for the wooden box.

You're welcome, Sherry said. Would you like your present from me now?

Oh I don't need a present. All of this is enough, honestly, the food, the drink, the –

Don't be *silly*, Sherry said.

She pulled herself up off the sofa, went over to the Christmas tree in the corner, which was nothing like the one Pauline had uprooted in the dining room. This was small and fake, more a light than a tree, its branches turning pink then white then blue.

Here we are, Sherry said. Rae helped me choose it, didn't you, Rae.

Rae was lost in a comic, didn't look up.

Eve began to unwrap her gift as slowly as possible. Thank you so much, she said.

You haven't even looked at it yet, Sherry said, back on the sofa now, staring at Eve.

It was deeply exposing. Eve was tense, shy, grateful for the champagne, wine and rum in her system. Imagine doing this sober, she just couldn't, wouldn't, she'd have to save the gift for later.

It was a silver brooch, containing two pieces of painted glass, one blue, one orange.

It's a kingfisher in flight, Sherry said.

I love it, Eve said to her generous new friend, the woman she had only met this summer, who kept inviting them round, spoiling them.

You spoil me, she said.

Someone has to, Sherry said.

And that was it. The moment when the fence came down. All day it had blown a gale, there had been warnings on the news but no one cared, it was Christmas Day after all, everyone expects some turbulence, a little wind.

What was that? Leslie said, waking up, sitting forward, kicking his recliner back into a regular chair.

I think the old fence finally caved in, Sherry said, over by the window now with a husband in a crumpled suit. Oh dear, and our neighbour that side is so crabby, what's she going to say?

She's going to be a nightmare, Leslie said.

Later they eat leftovers, sausage rolls, ham, cheese, quiche and pickled onions, piling it high on their plates and taking them back to the lounge.

They eat Christmas cake and After Eights and Eve's cinnamon biscuits.

And finally, despite Sherry's attempts to make them all stay up and watch *Some Like It Hot*, it's time for Eve to take Daniel home.

The street is ablaze with luminous creatures.

What's the collective noun for a group of fluorescent reindeer, Eve? Sherry says.

Well I would usually call lots of reindeer a herd, Eve says, but in this case I'd call them a twinkle. Did you know that a group of otters is called a romp?

I did not, Sherry says.

Well it is, Eve says.

They step into the driveway to get a better look at all the lights, and Daniel leans against Eve's legs, half asleep.

I love it when all the trees are lit up like this, Sherry says.

It's pretty, Eve says.

Talking of pretty, Sherry says, fiddling with the collar of Eve's coat. She pushes the coat open. Look at you, she says, in your Cadbury purple.

It's actually purplish blue, Eve says.

Then Sherry moves closer, whispers something in Eve's ear.

That dress makes me want to unwrap you like a chocolate, she says.

And the effect on Eve's body, from only those words from only that whisper.

You're drunk, she says.

I am not, Sherry says.

Eve gets out of bed, peers through the curtains at the street down below.

Elbows on the windowsill, chin on her hands, she watches Abigail Gardens.

It's not a dramatic sight, something to take your breath. But it is.

This clear night, full moon, suburban wonderland. The scene is electric, majestic, this is what Eve thinks as she stands alone in her bedroom in the early hours of Boxing Day, gazing at all the fluorescent reindeer, the waving snowmen, the radiant penguins.

Where Eve grew up, people switched their Christmas decorations off when they went to bed, but not here. Her parents would have called it wasteful, ostentatious, having them on all night like this, having them at all.

She sees a black cat eyeing a neon Santa, creeping around it, a feline performance of suspicion. The pets of Abigail Gardens must wonder what's going on when Christmas arrives, when an eerie menagerie steps into their territory, stands bright and strange and petrified.

Eve's front garden is the only one in darkness. Her purse can't play these festive games. She told Daniel they were tacky, garish, honestly darling we don't need all these silly decorations, please don't ask me again.

Oh my God, she thinks now. I'm just like my parents.

And then she sees two women, standing in the driveway of 4 Abigail Gardens. There is a child leaning against one of them, boy in a tank top, boy on the verge of sleep.

Funny how she can hear their voices from all the way up here.

And how she will always hear their voices.

I love it when all the trees are lit up like this, one of the women says.

It's pretty, the other says.

Then something about a dress, what kind of purple it is.

That dress makes me want to unwrap you like a chocolate.

This scene is repeated over and over again. Eve feels like she is watching actors rehearsing a play, she's in her own private theatre, has a dress circle all to herself.

She turns to face her bedroom now, to face the dress hanging on her wardrobe, not ready to be put away. Will it ever be ready? This dress is a talisman, a good omen, a turner of tides. And she made it herself. Which means that she, Eve Berry, has more control over her future than she thought.

Along the hallway, Daniel is asleep under a sky of glow-in-the-dark stars. She creeps past his bedroom, past the band of light beneath his door, emanating from his nightlight, a ceramic mushroom with windows and a spotted roof, bought last year to help him feel safe.

Now she takes a cup of tea into the lounge, sits in the dark with her portable radio on her lap. She plugs in a pair of headphones, listens to a local station: Tears For Fears, Wham!, Paul Young.

Then Frankie Goes to Hollywood, 'The Power of Love'. She turns it up.

She is a cartwheel, she is nauseous.

She wants to open all the windows, open her arms and let the night air wash over her.

She is wearing her summer nightie, diaphanous pink. It didn't feel right, stepping into the brushed-cotton pyjamas that were waiting for her when she got home last night, folded under her pillow.

And now Eve is see-through, translucent.

She is impishly unseasonable.

She is the urge to smoke.

She is candlelight and Nina Simone, the back row of a cinema, a dirty weekend in a rainy city, a slow dance on a sticky floor.

She thinks about buying a suede jacket and some body spray.

By morning, coffee on two hours' sleep makes her dizzy. She feels reckless and sensible, standing here in the kitchen in her summer nightie in the middle of winter, when Daniel walks in, says hello Mummy. She sees his little bare feet on the cold tiles. Where are your slippers? she says. Where's *your* dressing gown? he says. They march to their bedrooms then meet once again in the kitchen, both suitably dressed this time in pyjamas and dressing gowns and slippers.

Cooked breakfast? she says.

Yes please, he says. Can we eat in front of the telly?

But it's a special occasion.

I thought that was yesterday.

He has a point. They have no plans for Boxing Day, may as well enjoy being lazy.

They watch *Bugs Bunny*, a double bill.

Are we going next door again? he says.

Not today, she says.

Why not?

We can't go *every* day.

Why not?

They need some time to themselves, as a family, she says.

They eat in silence. Eggs, bacon, fried bread.

There is tension in the air, as if they have fallen out, which they haven't.

They are miserable and twitchy. This boy and young woman, seemingly bored but not bored at all, bewildered in their own home, wanting to be here and elsewhere, confused by life's new rhythm of riotous then quiet, wonderful then empty, feverishly quick then weirdly slow, like emerging from a dream somehow, like being exhausted, like wanting the dream again.

Being with and without their neighbours is infinitely complicated.

They are fun and exciting and incredibly warm.

They are a crowd, an intrusion, something to recover from.

Eve swings her legs over the side of the armchair, stares out of the window, watches a robin hop about. Maybe this year I'll buy a sofa, she thinks, as if 1985 has already arrived, as if a new phase of life has already begun. They have always had a chair each, one for her and one for Daniel, which felt right, reassuring, sort of funny. But this morning, as she glances from the garden to the other empty chair, their furniture strikes her as embarrassing and anti-social. She doesn't understand how it could have made her smile, the sight of two old chairs from the charity shop, and no sofa, no coffee table, no bunch of flowers, no photographs on the wall.

Daniel is on the floor, examining his Lego. Nothing can compete with these interlocking pieces, with the deep satisfaction of building this and building that, then taking it apart, putting it away, starting all over again.

He picks up a smiley astronaut, pulls its head from its torso and throws it at his mum.

Hey, she says. What was that for?

He doesn't really know, says nothing.

She wants to tell him off, give him a lecture about not throwing his toys, can't be bothered.

Where did it go? he says.

How should I know? she says, rummaging around, feeling for a tiny plastic head.

They jump at the sound of someone knocking at the door.

Who's that? he says.

No idea, she says.

The knocking comes again, rhythmical this time, like the beat of a song, insistent.

Eve rises and leaves the room, leaving Daniel holding a headless spaceman. She can see a familiar shape through the mottled glass of the front door. This shape makes her nervous. She braces herself for awkwardness, over-politeness, the subtle undoing of what was said the night before. Which must be the purpose of this visit, surely. Unless they've run out of milk.

Hello again, Sherry says.

Good morning, Eve says.

Sorry, were you still in bed?

No, we were just watching telly. Would you like to come in?

I won't actually, Sherry says.

And there it is. The start of the undoing. The keeping her distance now.

141

It's just a quick thing really, Sherry says. We were wondering if you'd seen *Ghostbusters*?

We haven't, Daniel says, appearing beside his mother's legs.

Hey you, Sherry says.

Hey, he says.

Sherry smiles. Look at the two of you in your matching outfits, she says.

Eve blushes. We're not matching, she says. And I wouldn't call them outfits.

Daniel looks up at his mum, then back at Sherry. Have *you* seen *Ghostbusters*? he says.

No, but there's a special Boxing Day showing at the cinema this afternoon.

Is it suitable for children? Eve says.

Oh I'm sure it's fine, Sherry says. We thought we could all go, if you're interested, but no pressure obviously. You may have Boxing Day traditions. We only thought of it this morning.

Can we? Daniel says.

Are you sure you don't mind us coming with you? Eve says.

Sherry rolls her eyes. Come over at two, she says. We'll drive.

But won't there be six of us? Eve says.

Yep.

We won't all fit in your car.

It'll be fun, Sherry says. You don't mind sitting on your mum's lap do you, Daniel?

Can I sit on *your* lap? he says.

Hmm, I'm not sure about that. Are you heavy? Let me see.

Sherry steps into the house, puts her arms around Daniel's waist and picks him up.

Oh my God, she says, you're as heavy as a *horse*.

I am not.

You're as heavy as a pig then.

I am *not*, he says, giggling.

She puts him back down, right beside his mother.

You two should be on a calendar, she says.

What? Eve says.

Sherry says she'll see them later, then she is gone.

And the Berrys get lively.

The telly goes off, a bath is run, a head is found and returned to a body, dishes are washed, clothes come out of wardrobes and go back in, get swapped for better clothes, more *impressive* clothes.

Daniel gets nervous, says maybe they should play Lego instead.

Don't you want to go? she says.

I do, he says, but –

But what?

Will we be all right? he says.

Of course, she says.

Now they are inside a Vauxhall Cavalier.

The driver is Leslie Marsh, dressed in slacks, white shirt and a blazer. His wife called him dapper as they left the house, but mainly he looks nautical, retired.

Pauline is beside him in the passenger seat. I have to sit in the front or I'll be really really sick, she says.

Unusually, she is telling the truth.

There is a discussion about the remaining four, how they will position themselves in the back. Daniel wants to

143

sit on Sherry, Rae wants to sit next to Eve but also by the window, Eve doesn't mind where she sits.

We're going to miss the film at this rate, Leslie says.

All sorted now, Sherry says, with her arms around Daniel for the second time today.

He looks down at his mum, beside him in the middle of the back seat, legs awkwardly placed.

I'm the king of the castle, he says.

I'm the dirty rascal, she says.

You're not supposed to call *yourself* that, he says.

Why not?

I get to say it.

Who says.

I do.

All right you two, Sherry says. Try to play nicely.

And Eve is mortified.

(But happy.)

At the cinema, Leslie buys them all popcorn and soft drinks.

The drinks are so big, Daniel is worried about needing the toilet during the film.

If you do, I'll take you, Sherry says.

Okay, he says, then sucks through a straw.

There is another kerfuffle about who will sit where. Rae wants to sit by Eve again, but so does Pauline now, mainly to annoy Rae, and Daniel wants to sit between Leslie and Sherry.

So here they are from left to right, in the formation they will opt for many times over the next three years: Leslie, Daniel, Sherry, Pauline, Eve and Rae.

The cinema is loud and surprisingly full, and this would

144

normally unnerve Daniel, fill his mind with rhyme, but this afternoon it doesn't. Because he is flanked by guards, by people who own a big car and make a lot of noise, and no one will mess with them, no one.

Afterwards there is pizza, all kinds of pizza.

I've never had pepperoni before, Daniel says. And what's this?

That's garlic bread, Rae says.

He takes a slice, sniffs it, then nibbles the crust. I like it, he says.

Daniel, you've had garlic bread before, Eve says.

It's pleasing to see her son so relaxed, so amiable, but must he behave like an alien who has just landed on Earth?

He looks at her, briefly, moving only his eyes.

She tries to smile, to detract from the unexpected harshness of her voice just now. What kind of mother snaps at her son when he is revelling in the simple joy of garlic bread? Especially when that boy is not usually a reveller.

In the background, all through the meal, Pauline hums the music from *Ghostbusters*. She jigs about while eating her pizza, obviously used to doing her own thing, being fiercely independent in the presence of others.

Rae is quiet, but her expression is lighter, less pensive than usual. Maybe it's this food, Eve thinks. Or the distinct combination of movie and pizza. She hadn't really thought of this before, how a child might enjoy these things one after the other. Her parents never took her to the cinema, let alone out for pizza. This kind of afternoon is as new to her as it is to Daniel. Maybe she will bring him again, on his birthday. They could bring their own drinks and sweets, try to make it cheaper.

Eve doesn't realise that Leslie and Sherry will pay for all this, that they would never accept her money. So she drinks water instead of wine, says no to a dessert, watches them all eat cheesecake with a rising sense of dread.

When the bill finally comes, Sherry throws a bunch of crumpled notes on top of it while Eve opens her purse.

Put that away, Sherry says.

No really, Eve says. I can't let you pay for all this.

It's our treat, Leslie says. We're just glad to have your company, that's enough isn't it, Sherry.

Absolutely, Sherry says.

And there is a look, which contains a hint, and makes Eve sweat, and isn't noticed by anyone else.

Was that a *flirtatious* look? Eve thinks.

Her question is answered when the day is done.

Sherry lingers in the driveway as Daniel ambles to his front door and the others march to theirs.

Eve, she says, beside the Vauxhall Cavalier.

Yes? Eve says, assuming she must have left something in the car.

Do you fancy going out sometime, just the two of us? Sherry says.

That would be nice, Eve says, but what about Daniel?

He can spend an evening with Leslie and the girls.

Oh, Eve says.

Sherry is disappointed. She thinks Eve's face is a story of coolness, lack of interest, but it isn't.

Eve is panicking. Saying yes to this invitation isn't as easy as it should be. How can she tell Sherry that Daniel has never been left with someone else? That apart from when he's at school she has never gone out without him, never left him with a babysitter, a friend, a family member. She doesn't know how he would react.

The trouble is, she says. He's a bit nervy, as you know.

They both look over at Daniel, whose forehead is pressed against the glass of the front door.

I think he'd be fine at our place, Sherry says. Ask him later if you like. Leslie could teach him how to play chess.

I'll ask him, Eve says.

Okay, Sherry says. How about we go out on Friday?

This Friday? As in the day after tomorrow?

Sherry's voice turns serious. Please? she says. If you want to, that is.

Six years into motherhood, Eve feels guilty for this thought, but bloody hell, she is *free*.

She is going out for the evening, not as a mother, but simply as herself.

When she ran the idea by Daniel, floated the notion of an evening next door while she and Sherry went out, his response was unusually enthusiastic.

Okay, he said. Why not. I like Leslie.

Rae and Pauline will be there as well, she said.

He nodded.

Leslie wondered if you'd like to learn how to play chess.

I would, he said.

She thought he looked proud, even a little defiant – a look of *you have plans, well I have plans too*.

He asked her if *she* knew how to play chess.

I don't, she said.

He seemed pleased with this answer.

Three days before the close of 1984, they go to a student bar.

Neither of them is a student.

It's Sherry's idea.

I've always wanted to come here, she says.

Really? Eve says. Why?

Curious I suppose, Sherry says. About what these places are like. And what the *brainiacs* are like.

Eve laughs. Brainiacs? she says.

Intellectuals then. I thought it'd be quiet in here, I thought they'd all have gone home for the Christmas break, but it's heaving isn't it, Sherry says, looking around. Then she leans forward, lowers her voice. Do I look like someone's mother? she says.

You *are* someone's mother.

Well so are you, but you're also the same age as everyone here.

Hardly, Eve says, I'm twenty-two.

Exactly, Sherry says.

Well how old are you? Eve says.

You know how old I am.

I don't actually.

How old do you think?

Let's not play that game.

I'm thirty-one.

Are you? You don't look it. Anyway, it's not your age that makes you stand out in here, it's your, well –

My what?

Your glamour, Eve says.

You think *I'm* glamorous?

Well you don't exactly have a second-hand vibe.

Is that your definition of glamorous, Sherry says.

Probably, Eve says.

They laugh and drink cheap cider.

Sherry buys two raffle tickets, one for her and one for Eve. First prize a bottle of whisky, second prize two pints and two bags of crisps, and so on.

148

They are deep in conversation about Eve's parents when a voice at a microphone interrupts them. He announces the winning number of third prize, then second prize.

Oh well, Eve says, head close to Sherry's, peering at the ticket as if it's impossible to remember three digits.

And the winner of a bottle of whisky is 133! the barman says.

Oh my God, Sherry says. It's me, it's me.

Eve watches her move through the pub in her silk blouse and A-line skirt. To the barman's surprise, Sherry hugs him, kisses him on the cheek, holds her whisky in the air like a trophy.

There is a round of applause from the students. Then the music starts again and Sherry is back in her chair.

I've never won anything in my life, she says. I love it in here.

Clearly, Eve says. I thought you'd want to go to some spangly bar where all the women drink white wine and wear court shoes.

Sherry sticks her foot out, waggles it close to Eve: a court shoe.

Oh, Eve says.

Now I'm offended, Sherry says.

Are you? Shit. I just meant –

Not *really*, Sherry says. It takes a lot to offend me.

I actually think your shoes are nice, Eve says.

Later that evening, before heading home, Sherry suggests a walk around town.

Really? Eve says.

I like to walk, Sherry says.

Well I didn't expect that, Eve says. Not in those shoes, anyway.

And just outside the bar there is a wall. Sherry takes
Eve by the hand and pulls her towards it, pulls her close.

And did you expect this, she says.

Or this, she says.

There are wheels beneath him, moving towards a destination that's definite, planned, attached to a schedule.

He looks at his watch, follows the progress of his journey.

A woman wants to know if he would like to buy something from her trolley. He tells her he would and buys a cup of tea, a KitKat, a bottle of water.

As he counts out his change, he wonders if the stench of him offends her. She seems unfazed but maybe she has a cold, no sense of smell, who knows.

His bag is on a rack above his head.

His body, on a soft seat.

A week ago, he wouldn't have thought of this as a soft seat.

A week ago, he hadn't slept on a bench or in a doorway, and his definition of what is soft and what is not was naive, unsophisticated.

Define *soft*, he thinks. Define *naive*, define *journey*, define *hope*.

This is quite possibly the best cup of tea of his life.

Also, he had forgotten how good a KitKat tastes.

Three days into 1985, instead of going straight home after work, Eve returns to the wall.

She stomps all the way, heavy in her duffel coat and Doc Martens.

Was this graffiti here before? Too dark to see, probably. Not that she would have noticed.

WE WERE REAL, WE WERE AMAZING
PLEASE DON'T SAY IT ISN'T TRUE

is what the graffiti says.

Eve stares at the words. She wonders who wrote them, and what it must feel like to be that person, with a can of spray paint and a fearful heart.

She thinks about what's true and what isn't and who decides.

And talking of real and amazing. Sherry isn't working on Monday, and she has asked Eve to take the day off work, to spend the whole day together while the kids are at school.

She leans against the wall, in the exact spot where she stood last week in the foggy night when Sherry kissed her and unbuttoned her coat.

Now she looks up at the sky. When Eve has a decision to make, she always turns to the birds for an answer. How they soar when it's blowing a gale, how they hop from branch to branch, miraculous, ordinary and effortless. Somehow it's easier to know herself when she is looking up at the birds.

She pulls a small bottle of gin and tonic from her pocket. She has never tried pre-mixed G&T before. Franklin rolled his eyes when she picked it up at the end of her shift, said seriously you're going to drink *this*? Don't be such a snob, Peter said, she can drink whatever she likes. She tried to pay but they wouldn't take it. Go, Franklin said, waving her off with a smile. See you tomorrow, Eve Berry. And don't forget you're coming to ours for dinner tomorrow night. I won't, she said, hugging them one after the other.

She pictures Franklin's disapproval as the bottle hisses open, but it tastes surprisingly good, out here in the cold air as young people walk past on their way to lunch, glancing in her direction as if she is simply one of them, just hanging around, enjoying a taste of freedom.

Eve imagines freedom being sold all over the world as a fizzy drink in a bottle. And the political implications of this. And what would happen if it was given to animals, especially those in a zoo. And what would happen if you drank too much. And since we're all constrained in unique ways, being drunk on freedom would look different on everyone. Take prisoners, for example. Or those held captive by their own fears. Or whoever painted the words on this wall. Or a teenager whose parents want to give away her baby. Or a woman in love with her neighbour.

Yes, let's focus on *her*.

That's what we're here for, isn't it? That's why you walked all the way here today, back to a first kiss, a second and a third. To make your decision: yes to Monday or no to Monday?

A life can be defined by a yes or a no.

And Eve watches the birds, the dazzle of their feathers, the dazzle of their song.

There's no decision to make, there never was, she says to the birds.

Which is in other words a yes.

As long as I protect Daniel, I'm free to do whatever I like.

Before walking away, she searches her handbag for a pen.

Her words are tiny, ridiculous, compared to the bold gesture of gigantic lettering above them. And all she has in her bag is a pink biro. But better to make a mark than no mark at all.

Her pen hovers as she thinks.

She closes her eyes, and what she immediately sees is this: the painting on the wall at work in the back room of the off-licence, the painting of a long table in a dark kitchen, a table draped with cloth, and on this table there is bread and cheese, a plate of fruit and a bottle of sherry. On the bottle, a woman is dancing. Every day, Eve watches her dance.

She opens her eyes, scratches the title of the painting into brick:

STILL LIFE WITH SHERRY

It's a funny kind of graffiti, not really graffiti at all, no more street art than a girl scratching a name into bark, leaving it on a tree to be found weeks later, this proof that she exists, this proof that she is real.

What is it about Sherry? she thinks. What's going on, what's got into me.

154

It's as if –

What, she thinks. Come on, give me something solid, scientific, to go on.

She is part of the fabric of my being. Which isn't at all scientific. In fact, it's just woolly.

The fabric of your being?

Yes, she thinks, enjoying the buzz of G&T on an empty stomach and having just written on a wall; these small acts of defiance, fun-size rebellion. She has been so good since Daniel was born, so virtuous and careful, as if one wrong move will make him disappear.

She looks down at the brooch pinned to her coat, a kingfisher in flight.

Her mother had been wrong when she called out her goodbye: *We'll find you, you can't do this on your own.*

And what Eve says yes to is this:

Sherry Marsh, on a Monday unlike any other Monday.

In fact, Mondays will never be the same.

And Eve Berry, she will never be the same.

They are upstairs in Sherry's spare bedroom.

I never liked that lamp anyway, Sherry says when Eve knocks it over.

They are bright planets. Everything else that exists right now is revolving around them.

So this is what it's all about, Eve finally says.

Sherry smiles. I'm hungry, she says.

She begins to get dressed.

Not yet, Eve says.

She is surprised by her own confidence, by who she is when she is naked with Sherry Marsh.

You are so beautiful, Eve thinks. I wish I'd met you before Leslie met you. This is the best I have ever felt in my

155

sorry life. I want this every day. I want you to be mine. You have reduced me to nothing but happy cliché. The thought of waking up to this every morning, to your face on the pillow next to mine every morning. Let's go on holiday. Let's go travelling. Let's get our own place, a cottage by the sea. Do you have any idea how beautiful you are?

What? Sherry says.

Nothing, Eve says. Just looking, that's all.

Downstairs, they eat mushroom quiche and salad at the kitchen table.

They carry large mugs of tea into the lounge and sit on the sofa, no longer the people who sat in this room on Christmas Day.

Sherry puts on a record, says she bought it at the weekend. Just listen to this, she says, jumping up from the sofa. You'll know it already, it's in the charts.

She lifts the needle, places it gently on the twelve-inch, turns up the volume.

The song begins as she sits back down. Foreigner, 'I Want to Know What Love Is'.

They sit and listen.

Do you like this one? Sherry says. She looks shy, possibly nervous, for the first time today.

I do, Eve says. It sounds sort of spiritual doesn't it. I'd like to hear it sung by a gospel choir.

My earnest girl, Sherry says.

Do you like 'The Power of Love' by Frankie Goes to Hollywood? Eve says.

Oh I have that too, Sherry says. Shall I put it on?

Yes please.

So she does.

And they listen with great seriousness.

And they think about what just happened upstairs.

And they wonder if they have time for it to happen again.

It's a really great time for music right now isn't it, Eve says.

And Sherry laughs.

Which makes Eve laugh too.

And now they are hysterical.

I feel like a fucking teenager, Sherry says, wiping tears from her eyes.

It's brilliant isn't it, Eve says. Let's listen to Foreigner again now, but louder this time.

This loud enough for you? Sherry shouts.

Definitely, Eve shouts back.

Outside the lounge window, a cat is striding across the grass when it hears the song. It turns to look: *what the hell is that infernal noise?* And a chaffinch on a branch, it too turns its head towards the sound: *my goodness, what a terrible racket.* And a dog in a house nearby begins to bark. And a woman walking past puts her shopping on the floor and just stands there listening.

It's as if Foreigner themselves are playing live inside 4 Abigail Gardens.

And Eve and Sherry have never cared less about being heard or being cool.

Sherry gets up and asks Eve if she would like to dance. She looks like she's joking, but she isn't. Which is how Sherry looks most of the time.

They laugh as they dance ever so slowly pressed together like it's all daft like it's all silly, which it is and most definitely isn't.

I feel it in my bones, Eve thinks. And by the way, I love the bones of you, do you know that, she thinks.

Eve in her pink shirt and old jeans.

Sherry in her gold blouse and white trousers.

(I say shirt, you say blouse.)

They are bright planets. And later they will light up their children with their annoying chirpiness, then their homes, and the street itself, and the whole bloody town, why not, they're unstoppable. The music is loud, their hearts are loud, everything inside this room is loud.

Until it isn't.

Well, thank you for a lovely day, Sherry says, before opening the front door.

Thank you for the quiche, Eve says.

They smile.

They are dishevelled, rosy, Eve's shirt is buttoned up wrong.

Bye for now then, she says.

Bye for now, Sherry says.

It's August and everyone is buzzing. The weather is good. The telly is good. All the books from the library are also good. Films, all of them, are somehow good. Food, actually, is much better than good. Clothes feel fantastically good on the skin. Showers, baths, oh so good. Rae and Eve playing badminton against Pauline and Sherry: unbelievably good. In the pool nearby, on Saturday mornings and days off work, Leslie teaching Daniel how to swim is implausibly good, both men in armbands, the little man and the older man, messing about in the shallow end: *that's it, son, I'm letting go now, you won't sink I promise.* Neither family has the money for a holiday this summer, which on the surface is not so good, but their resilient response – trips to the beach, the cinema, the park, the library and the sports centre, plus all the lazing and reading and board games and crafting – is, you have to admit it, pretty damn good. So, holiday or not, ask Rae Marsh what this summer is like and she will say, after a while, in her nonchalant way, yeah it's okay. Which is her way of saying it's astoundingly good.

And where is all the goodness coming from?

Now there's a question.

Oh my God is that Wonder Woman? Rae says.

It is, Eve says.

159

I don't believe it, Rae says through her fingers, which have just gone over her mouth in shock and awe and some other kind of feeling that makes her want to whoop and cry and punch the air, to spin around and touch the ground, why not, what the hell, she's a winner she's a spinner, this moment is pure glory it is nothing else.

What has just happened?

Eve Berry has made the most super impressive thing, that's what.

And Rae hadn't even imagined this thing, let alone asked for it.

Eve just thought of it all by herself.

Conjured it from thin air by needle and by thread.

The best gift *ever*.

The most moving human gesture.

A patch over a tear on the knee of a pair of trousers.

That's all, that's it, sometimes that's all it takes.

Rae tries to contain her excitement, play it down. Because she is Rae Marsh, and it's her way, to play things down; she is naturally reserved, understated, or so it seems. Her mother, who expresses every emotion with intense theatricality, who takes up all the space, calls her eldest daughter the quiet one, as if this quietness is a kind of fragility – not a powerful act of disobedience and unruliness.

Rae Marsh jumps to her feet and throws her arms around Eve Berry, who once heard the girl say that her favourite cords had a tear in the knee, were ruined, over, done; who once heard the girl say that she loved Wonder Woman in a really big way. And in secret, Eve Berry took those cords from the pile of mending that Sherry Marsh would never get round to. She opened one of her son's comics, put Wonder Woman in front of her and began to embroider the superhero onto a square patch of material.

Rae imagines her doing this – artfully, with great care. And this is what blows her away about Eve, how artful she is, how caring, how she pays attention to detail and remembers the things you say, the things you like and don't like, which sounds like nothing at all but is *everything*.

You blow me away, Eve, she wants to say, here and now in the summer of 1985, in a kitchen full of sunlight, confusion and awe. You make everything good, Eve. You take the dregs of life and make them pretty.

It's a beautiful day to hear good news, she thinks. It's a beautiful day to be sitting in this kitchen, stroking a pair of jumbo cords, the same but different.

Rae's head is crammed with thoughts like these. Her usual monotone voice is all girly and breathy and high.

And what's also not helping is this:

Just as Eve gives Rae the cords, the song from *Flashdance*, 'What a Feeling', starts playing on the radio. This is the one and only song that destabilises Rae, threatens her equilibrium, makes her unable to hold it all in. It really is the most exciting song, according to her wriggly shoulders, her tapping feet, the words in her mouth that won't come out because Rae Marsh doesn't sing, not ever no way you must be joking.

Now Rae's mother enters the kitchen.

She walks right up to the woman who is not Rae's mother.

(And the fact that she is not makes Rae's fingers curl into fists. *It's not fair, it's not FAIR.*)

What are you two up to? Sherry says.

Before Rae or Eve can answer, before either of them has a chance to say *Wonder* or *Woman* or *patch* or *knee*, Sherry begins to sing along to 'What a Feeling'.

Rae can still smell Eve's perfume from the hug they just had. But even this is being overpowered by her mother's voice, laying itself on top of Irene Cara's, squeezing the life out of it.

How DARE you interrupt us!

She dies inside, this girl, who for a moment was ablaze with life.

Some parents extinguish their children, simply by being themselves.

Sherry Marsh is one of these parents.

But Eve Berry is still here.

There's life in this nine-year-old yet.

Try them on, Eve says, trying to reach the girl across Sherry's singing.

Shall I? Rae says.

Go on, Eve says.

And so Rae hops off the kitchen stool and runs into the privacy of the hallway, where she steps out of her shorts and into her cords.

Now she is back, holding up her left knee with pride.

Oh yes, Eve says with a big smile, Rae is sure it's the biggest smile she has ever seen on Eve.

Thank you so much, she says. I'd like to save them really, they're so nice now, but I also want to wear them, what do you think?

So how's Franklin doing? Sherry says.

He seems a bit brighter now, Eve says. He thinks it was the flu. Peter's been waiting on him, he's *so* nice.

Rae is in the doorway, out in the cold. She listens as they chat and she is lost. Yet again, her mother has stolen Eve. They seem to have their own secret place, complex and walled, full of dark corridors and sharp corners.

She watches the way they touch hands.

Her jealousy is mountainous.

Isn't it a bit hot for cords? her mother says.

Both mothers look over at Rae, who is flushed and sulky.

It's never too hot for cords, Rae says.

I agree, Eve says.

Sherry tuts. You two, honestly, she says.

What's that bird in the tree, right at the end of the garden? Eve says.

Daniel doesn't really care for this game, mainly he joins in for his mum, but what he does like is this:

Sitting beside her now, how different she seems.

Even the air around her has changed.

I like you at the moment, he says to his mum.

Thank you, I think, she says to her son.

Darling, Eve says, one morning.

Yes? Rae says.

Shall we alphabetise your books?

Oh dear God.

On Monday, at Eve's suggestion, they had taken a long walk through a forest – Sherry, Eve, Daniel, Rae and Pauline. As they walked, Eve named all the trees and flowers and birds. When they got home, she and Rae made biscuits in the kitchen while the others collapsed in the lounge. It was the best day of Rae's life. Even better than the day she was given her Wonder Woman cords.

And now Eve wants to alphabetise her books.

Unbelievable!

This truly is the summer of love.

Rae is dizzy. She is sitting on the step that leads into the garden, drinking Orangina, wearing aviator sunglasses, a rainbow T-shirt, a pair of baggy shorts.

You really want to sort out my books? she says.

It'll be fun, Eve says.

Rae doesn't doubt that for a second.

And so they pull books down from the shelves, spread them out on the floor, dust the shelves, dust the books, organise them into piles, passing As and Bs and Cs to each other, then Ds and Es and Fs, and the morning goes on this way, they pause for a drink and a Jammie Dodger from Sherry's secret tin, before putting the books back and admiring their orderly creation, their wonderful A to Z of Rae Marsh's literary pleasures.

Now you can find a book really easily, Eve says.

It's spectacular, Rae says.

Which makes Eve laugh.

This girl, she thinks. Who couldn't love this girl.

Later, while Sherry is out buying Pauline a dress, and Leslie is at the pool with Daniel, Rae and Eve sit quietly in the garden.

That island you go to, Eve says. The one you told me about.

Petula? Rae says.

Hmm, Eve says. Will you take me there?

How? Rae says.

Describe it to me, while I close my eyes. It'll be fun.

Does Eve find *everything* fun? Rae thinks.

She is feeling very shy.

I'd love to see it, Eve says.

You want me to describe Petula?

Only if you want to.

This is a moment that demands great bravery. Rae doesn't know if she can do it. Yes or no, am I in or am I out? She looks at Eve, whose eyes are already shut.

All right, she thinks.

She sits up straight, takes a deep breath.

First we must get on a boat, she says. Our own private boat.

Lovely, Eve says. And are you driving or am I?

I'll drive, Rae says. It's not easy to find, this island.

Is it not.

Oh no. That's the point.

Ah, of course.

We'll know we're there when we see the lighthouse, Rae says.

And they travel together, miles and miles.

And when they reach Petula it's more beautiful than ever. Rae sighs. She breathes in the cleanest air, looks at all the rocks and the woodland and her cottage over there in the distance.

This is heaven, Eve says, stepping out of the little boat.

I know, Rae says. It really is.

And here is Anna Feigenbaum, Auntie Fig.

She is, this summer, being dragged around the bungalow by Daniel.

And this is our new settee, he says, it's gold velvet with brown spots. And also, he says, there's a girl next door called Rae who loves the colour gold so she *really* loves our settee.

I know it's a bit icky, Eve says, but we like it.

I wouldn't call it *icky*, Anna says. It's –

Daniel dives headfirst onto the sofa. It's ace, he says.

Yes, that's the word I was looking for, Anna says.

It's from a charity shop, he says. But it wouldn't go through the front door, it got stuck.

Eve shrugs. I didn't think to measure it, she says.

She remembers the delivery men, trying to manoeuvre it this way and that. There was no other way in, the windows were too small, there was no access to the back garden. Then Leslie appeared, said how about we carry it through our house instead, out into the garden? The fence has collapsed, you see. Then we can lift it straight into Eve's lounge through the patio doors. What do you think?

Talk about going round the houses, one of the delivery men said.

It worked.

Good job I never put up a new fence, isn't it? Leslie said.

Please don't put one up, Daniel said. I like scaring you at the window when you're watching telly.

Little monster, Leslie said.

Which cast a dark shadow over the boy's face.

Only joking, Leslie said. You know I'm only joking. And I'll never put a fence up I promise, all right?

Daniel jumps off the sofa, grabs his aunt's hand and takes her on a high-speed tour of the two bedrooms, the bathroom, the kitchen, the garden and Wendy house.

I love it, Anna says, back in the kitchen now. It's very different to your other places. More homely, I suppose.

Well it costs money to be homely, Eve says. Did I tell you I've been sewing in the evenings? I mend people's clothes, turn up trousers, that kind of thing. Sherry from next door, she knows everyone around here, she's been spreading the word. You won't believe this, but people even pay me to do their ironing. What a waste of money, honestly.

You can't have much free time, with that and the off-licence, Anna says.

I have plenty of free time. Anyway, now we can have things like this, Eve says, nodding towards a bowl of straw-berries on the table. I could never afford fruit before. Daniel loves it. He finished off all the raspberries this morning.

You do both seem happy, Anna says.

I feel like I'm finally thriving, Eve says. And you've helped, obviously. I don't know where I'd be without you, I really don't.

To say that Anna had helped was an understatement. Once, Eve asked her why. What do you mean, why? Anna said. Why are you so kind to me? Eve said. Anna thought for a long time, said it was hard to explain. When I was fifteen my parents kicked me out, she said. But someone helped me. And if I can help you, why not? Eve kissed her on the cheek. You're more of a mother to me than Gail Berry ever was, she said. Which made Anna cry. Maybe I'll adopt you, she said. I think you already have, haven't you? Eve said to her champion, her surprise, her sheltering wing.

They sit quietly, eat strawberries, listen to the sound of the TV coming from the lounge. *Road Runner*, Eve thinks. Or maybe it's *Danger Mouse*.

Are you sure you don't mind going out tonight? she says.

It'll be nice, Anna says. It's not like we have to go far, is it. It's kind of them to invite us to their barbecue.

Eve laughs.

Why's that funny? Anna says.

I don't know, Eve says.

*

Leslie opens the front door. He is holding a pair of giant tongs. Instead of saying hello, he clicks them in the air as if they are a musical instrument.

Daniel steps into the house, turns to face his mother and his aunt. This is Auntie Fig, he says to Leslie. Her real name is Feigenbaum, which is German and means fig tree.

I see, Leslie says.

And she is a teacher of science, Daniel says.

I'm Anna, she says.

Very nice to meet you, Auntie Anna Fig Feigenbaum, Leslie says.

And this is Leslie, who has a girl's name but is not a girl, Daniel says.

How do you know I'm not a girl? Leslie says.

Daniel looks at him blankly, then looks back at his aunt. Leslie is teaching me how to swim and play cards, he says.

Anna shakes Leslie's hand. The boy's confidence has brought a lump to her throat. She has seen him in sad states, coughing up broken verse, wheezing with anxiety. Eve has been telling her on the phone how much better he is, but it's hard to believe, even now.

And this is Daniel, Leslie says to Anna. He lives partly in his own home and partly here, don't you, son?

Yep, he says. I have two houses. And who is *this*? he says, pointing at his mum.

It's rude to point, Eve says, bursting the bubble of his game.

They walk through the house, out into the garden.

Goodness, Anna says, what a lively space.

By lively, she means it's a mess.

Here's Pauline, running up and down with an aeroplane, making aeroplane noises, entirely immersed in her own flight of fancy.

And there is another girl, lying in a hammock between two apple trees, reading a book.

Smoke is rising from the barbecue, but not in a good way. Something is burning.

Anna scans the rest of the garden. There's a tent with an awning, a climbing frame, a swing. And who is this, marching towards her now, making her way past the paddling pool, saying you must be Anna, I've heard so much about you, come here and give me a hug.

Oh, Anna says, as she is engulfed by Sherry Marsh in her black vest and long flowery skirt, smelling of coconut, her body hot against the science teacher's skin.

Sherry pulls back, takes hold of Anna's shoulders. You're a saint, she says.

I'm definitely not, Anna says, glancing nervously at Daniel, who is close enough to hear. She wonders if Eve has told them the full story.

You're wearing the skirt, Eve says. Do you like it, is it all right?

It's more than all right, Sherry says. It's my new favourite.

Anna is perplexed. She studies the skirt, its red and black flowers.

I made it, Eve says.

Did you? Goodness. Where did you learn such things? Not from your –

There is silence now.

Don't say it, don't say it, please don't –

The word *mother* does not fall from Anna's mouth and land on Daniel. Of course it doesn't. Because Anna is solid as a rock, that's what Eve once called her. You're a true solid, she said. Unmeltable, unerodable, that's what you are. Thank you, I *think*, Anna said.

169

Leslie reappears now, holding a ghetto blaster and a plate of uncooked burgers.

Oh *no*, the sausages, he says. Sherry, you were supposed to be keeping an eye on them.

The girl on the hammock looks over, shakes her head in a weary kind of way as if she has seen it all before, the shambles, the disarray.

White wine or a G&T? Sherry says.

Wine would be lovely, thank you, Anna says as she steps on a squeaky toy, then a paper plate, then a crayon.

Excuse the mess. We're having summer at home, you see.

Sherry says this as if it explains something, sheds light on the objects scattered all over the lawn, which it doesn't.

What about you, darling? G&T with lemon?

Please, Eve says.

Then the hammock sways and the girl is out and now she is right here, leaning against Eve, staring at Anna. She is wearing a straw hat, a black polo neck and cords. Anna likes her straight away, senses something kindred, nerdy, repressed.

This is my girl, Rae, Eve says. And Rae, this is my Anna.

No, it's my Auntie Fig, Daniel says.

You can call me either, Anna says.

Eve grabs the hat from Rae's head, puts it on.

Hey, Rae says, deeply flattered.

By the end of the evening, as the light fades, Anna can see the appeal of this family. They're too glaring for her, too slapdash and eager, but what's obvious is their kindness. They make Eve and Daniel feel welcome, not only with them but in a more general way, a way that bolsters a person, builds them up, makes them feel accepted, welcome in the world.

Also, what's the word? Come on, think, it's on the tip of her tipsy tongue.

Ah yes. *Rambunctious*. That's what they are. These people are truly rambunctious, clumsily exuberant.

But when it comes to Eve and Daniel, Anna is wholly protective. Her protectiveness makes her ache, makes her worry. They may not be her flesh and blood but they are true kith and kin, the kind of bond you know and sense, the fact of its unbreakable ongoingness. So forgive me if I don't take you at face value, she thinks, as she watches Sherry smile at Eve, watches Daniel at the barbecue, wobbling about on a pile of encyclopaedias, flipping burgers beside Leslie.

The garden is full of the Beatles, 'Can't Buy Me Love', 'Love Me Do', 'All You Need is Love'.

Rae Marsh is back on the hammock, reading her book by torchlight.

Sherry Marsh is dancing, not for the first time this evening, while eating corn on the cob.

And the little girl with long black hair – Anna tries to remember her name – she too is dancing all by herself at the other side of the garden. She is waving a chicken leg in the air, making figures of eight as if it were a sparkler in the dark.

These people certainly know how to enjoy themselves, Anna says.

They do, Eve says, staring ahead of her, her eyes fixed on the woman in the swirling skirt, who is teaching her what it means to feel giddy, lustful, happy, which is a dangerous thing to be taught.

The view from the window is straightforward, uncomplicated. There are cows and sheep and horses, all standing still, all speeding by, it's unbearably beautiful.

Inside the train, a convolution of humans.

Good collective noun, Daniel.

He watches them step on and step off.

The sound of the doors opening and closing makes him picture an elephant's tail happily swishing.

Will passengers please mind the parade of elephants currently boarding the train.

He dozes through a rumble of hours, keeps waking up and falling asleep, sees himself reflected in the window each time: *you are still here.*

But what if they're not? he thinks. It hadn't even crossed his mind that they might have moved away.

Sometimes I am the definition of stupid, he thinks.

Aren't we all, Daniel? a voice says.

Well, not a voice exactly.

It's the view from the window, gentle and forgiving, saying something now about the wider world, all the lives being lived, the mistakes being made, but there are fields and flowers and ancient trees, there are badgers and butterflies, and there is nothing as fertile as foolishness, and there is always the tender sky.

Leslie has been promoted. He has been wanting this promotion for years, didn't think he'd ever get it.

This is such a great year, he says to his wife as he stands in his new Pringle jumper, an argyle V-neck, burgundy with cream and grey diamonds.

What do you think, do you like it? she says.

Like it? he says. I love it. It's very smart.

Well exactly, she says. And it makes you look like a golfer.

Is that a good thing? he says.

Of course, she says.

He kisses her on the cheek. Thank you, darling, he says.

Just wanted to say well done, she says. I bought steak too, for tonight.

Perfect. And you remembered to invite Eve and Daniel?

Of course. Are you still going to the pool?

I assume so, he says. Why wouldn't we.

It's what they always do, Leslie and Daniel, on a Saturday afternoon. Not only because they love to swim, but because they are the kind of people who thrive on routine. This is about more than security, sense of purpose, the usual things we associate with pattern and habit. It reflects their playfulness. To them, a good routine feels like having a board game waiting in another room, always something ongoing, always something to return to.

Daniel and Leslie never stop playing. They are seriously recreational, easy to amuse. This forty-nine-year-old man and ten-year-old boy, they talk about music, films, bikes and trees. They share observations about everyday life, are exceptionally interested in each other's likes and dislikes, opinions and thoughts. They play cards, chess, hangman, noughts and crosses, snakes and ladders. And on a Saturday afternoon they go to the pool.

Leslie would never admit this, but he liked it best when Daniel was seven years old and unable to swim, when he floated in armbands, paid careful attention to every instruction he was given. Soon they began to swim together, doggy-paddle for Daniel and breaststroke for Leslie. It was slow, companionable, until Daniel grew in confidence, abandoned his float and mastered his breathing. His favourite stroke now is the front crawl – determined, quick, antisocial. He will emerge at the end of five lengths, steamy goggles, smiling, looking around for Leslie. He is proud of himself, and it's a good sight, but it's also a kind of leaving behind.

Shall I teach *you* the front crawl? Daniel says this afternoon in the pool.

I've told you, it's not for me, Leslie says. I like to see where I'm going, admire the view.

What view? Daniel says.

There's always a view, Leslie says. Also, I can't be doing with all that moving your head from side to side. That's not my idea of fun.

Daniel laughs. But it's really fast, he says.

Speed isn't everything, Leslie says.

If you say so, Dad, Daniel says.

Then his face alters.

As he realises what he just said.

A three-letter word the size of a whale.

Or maybe a shark, zigzagging between them now.

Is a word shark like a card shark? A proficient rogue, ready to undo you, ready to stitch you up.

Fancy finding a shark in an indoor pool.

Fancy calling Leslie *Dad*.

Sometimes the only thing to do is keep perfectly still.

This is what they both obviously think.

Daniel's face, pink as a red snapper.

Leslie watches this reddening face. What to do, what to say? Make a joke, make light, pretend nothing was even said. Or, he could say what he thinks. That hearing Daniel call him Dad felt right and fitting and true. *Yes*, is what he wants to say. To his sort-of son, his son of sorts, to the water, the pool itself and all the other swimmers. *Yes, that's me.*

Crap, Daniel says. Don't know why I said that. Called you that. Stupid or what.

He smiles, then he is gone.

His arms propelling him through the water.

A kind of leaving behind.

On the journey home they listen to the radio, as they always do.

Daniel eats a Mars bar that Leslie bought him from the vending machine, which is what he always does.

Nothing has changed, but it has.

All sentences are a kind of music. They can be sung and heard in boundless ways.

If you say so, Dad is a song of trust.

I love you is what this sentence sings.

As Leslie's car pulls into the driveway, they see a bright banner, taped above the doorway of the house.

CONGRATULATIONS! the banner says.

Bless her. My wife doesn't do things by halves, Leslie says. See you and your mum at six?

Daniel nods.

He crosses the front garden with his duffel bag, his damp rolled-up towel, his feeling that he has done something wrong and embarrassing and good.

He walks through the hallway, drops his bag on the kitchen table.

Nice swim? his mum says.

He wonders whether to tell her. It was only a three-letter word. Leslie probably didn't even notice.

But he knows that he did. Leslie is always polite, considerate, but this afternoon he was overly so. What's that phrase, the one about gloves? Daniel frowns, looks down. Kid gloves, he thinks. That's it. After I called him Dad, he went all weird and *super* polite, treated me with kid gloves like I was new or ill or much younger than I am.

It was quite busy today, he says. There was a group of women doing an exercise class in the water.

Really? That sounds fun. Maybe I should come with you sometime.

If you want, he says.

Eve watches him open a cupboard and take out a bag of crisps. She watches him sit and eat them while staring into space.

What's the matter? she says.

Nothing, he says.

176

Okay, she says.

She turns her back on him, fills up the kettle, knows that pushing never works with Daniel. What works is asking lightly, then giving him space, letting him be alone while she is nearby. Even better if she puts on the radio, whistles, seems distracted.

She makes two mugs of hot chocolate, sits in front of him, opens a magazine.

Mum, he says.

Hmm, she says.

I called Leslie something weird.

Did you?

I called him Dad.

Dad?

Yeah. It was an accident.

Why would you call him that?

I don't know.

He's not your father.

I know that.

And what did he say?

Nothing. He probably didn't notice.

Oh he'll have noticed. You are *not* to call him that again, do you hear me?

I'm sorry, it just came out. I don't, I mean, I –

He is *not* your dad, Eve says. She paces up and down the kitchen, throws her mug into the sink.

Daniel can feel a lump in his throat. He is shaking. He stands up, attempts to match her somehow, if only in height. He is short for his age, but for a second he feels as tall as Leslie.

Did you even like my real dad? he says.

I beg your pardon, Eve says.

Did you? he says.

177

What do you mean, your *real* dad? she says. There is no dad, real or otherwise.

The dad from the disco, he says. Disco Dad.

Don't call him that. He isn't your dad. He's the reason why teenagers shouldn't drink cider, that's all. And do you know what? I barely remember him.

Daniel takes a sharp breath in. Who *is* this woman? How can she not remember his father? Hate surges through him, he is quick with hurt.

I want to live with Leslie and Sherry, he says. I want them to adopt me.

Eve turns away.

She pictures Leslie standing at his front door with Sherry and Daniel behind him.

Bastard.

She is a howl.

She is sandpaper.

She begins to retch, her head over the sink.

Mum, what the hell, Daniel says.

Mum, stop it.

He runs out of the room.

Daniel rings the musical doorbell and waits.

He is fidgety and fast.

He is a tremble, a twitch, a wound.

No one answers.

He walks up to one of three flamingos on the front lawn, strokes its head, sits on the grass, presses the side of his face against its cool body.

He remembers his mum explaining the origins of the word *flamingo*. Something to do with Spain, flamenco dancing, flames.

He remembers the flamenco party she had in the garden

178

last summer, how there had been brightly coloured lanterns, tiny plates of food, dancing with castanets. Uncle Franklin played a song on his guitar, Uncle Peter read a poem, Leslie unveiled the minigolf course he had spent hours making for the occasion.

He wonders why it's all right to call Franklin and Peter Uncle when they aren't his real uncles, but it's not all right to call Leslie Dad when he isn't his real dad. And also, what about Auntie Fig – she isn't a real aunt, is she?

His confusion about what's real and isn't is overwhelming.

Sherry is in the kitchen, making a trifle, listening to Queen's greatest hits. She is thinking about Freddie Mercury, what a marvel he is, how she'd love to meet him for afternoon tea, share their darkest thoughts over Battenberg.

Her husband is upstairs in the shower.

Rae has bribed Pauline to hold a cardboard box very still while she paints a cat on it.

Just a typical afternoon.

They don't hear the musical doorbell, then the young fist thumping on the door.

So Daniel sits with the flamingos for a while, and even though they are not real, they seem to understand him. He can feel them, taking his hurt.

They have known each other a long time now, Daniel and the flamingos. He has often told them his stories, and what he likes about these birds is how clever they are with their listening, how he can hum, say the odd word or no words at all, and they get it, straight away, everything he is and isn't in a damp grassy moment. His entire message, always received.

*

179

Cold and hungry, Daniel gets up and goes home, moves silently through the bungalow, lies on his bed and reads the *Beano*.

His mother, she too moves silently. She keeps her distance, her apology forming, not yet ready.

We promised to go next door for tea, she says, stepping into his bedroom. Her voice is quiet, slow. Do you still want to?

He shrugs. Do you? he says.

Well, it's steak and chips, she says. Onion rings as well, probably. If we cancel and stay in, it's beans on toast. We could just think of it that way, couldn't we. As just about the food. And leave the rest here?

Fine, he says.

Leslie is wearing his new jumper, he tells Eve and Daniel it's a present, a woolly pat on the back from Sherry.

Very posh, Eve says. But it's not really patting you, is it. It's just sitting on your back.

Well, he says. It was just a silly play on words, wasn't supposed to be accurate.

Congratulations, she says, and smiles.

This is a new one, Leslie thinks. He has seen this kind of fake smile on his wife's face many times, but never on Eve's. If Eve doesn't feel like smiling, she doesn't. It's part of her charm, how consistently honest she is.

Thanks, he says.

I was going to buy you a tie, but they were all a bit garish so I didn't. But I did bring this, Eve says, holding up a bottle of wine.

Well this looks fabulous, he says, thank you. And don't worry, I have plenty of ties.

I wasn't worried, she says.

Daniel stands beside her, hands in his pockets.

So, can I get you a beer, young man? Leslie says to him, and winks.

Have you got any cider? Daniel says, glancing sideways at his mum.

How about a Vimto as usual, she says.

See, I told you there'd be onion rings, Eve says when they are all at the table in the dining room.

I love 'em, Pauline says, grabbing two from the plate.

Pauline, Sherry says. Calm down. And use the tongs, not your hands.

The Marsh family are heavily into tongs. There are three pairs on this table, for serving onion rings, pineapple slices and breaded mushrooms. Everything else is already on six individual plates: steak, chips, tomatoes.

Rae, take off your bobble hat, Leslie says.

Why? Rae says.

Because it's rude.

I know, but why is it? Rae says. It's odd that wearing wool on your head is rude but wearing wool on the rest of your body isn't. Like, why isn't it rude for you to be wearing that jumper?

In some countries that jumper *would* be considered rude, Eve says.

Like where? Leslie says.

Just take the hat off, all right? Sherry says.

Rae pulls it from her head, folds it in two, places it neatly on the table.

Leslie pours wine into Eve's glass, then his own.

You still not drinking? Eve says, looking at Sherry's glass.

Sticking to the lemonade, Sherry says, with a sad smile that's all about the migraines she has been having lately.

Probably best, Eve says.

Good job you're not drinking cider, Daniel says. Cider gets you pregnant, doesn't it.

Sherry and Eve both blush.

Daniel, Eve says. *Please.*

You told him? Sherry says to her husband.

Of course not, he says.

You told Leslie? Eve says. Sherry, I asked you not to. I told you about that night in confidence.

What are you talking about? Sherry says.

My dad, Daniel says. Disco Dad. There was too much cider and then there was me.

Enough, Eve says. This is not the place.

I'm not sure what's going on, Leslie says.

Pauline's chubby hand reaches out for more onion rings.

Rae cuts all her chips in half, chews slowly while looking from her mum to her dad, from Daniel to Eve, afraid of the tension, excited by the tension.

Now there is silence. A group of minds, trying to work out what just happened. Collective noun: an agitation, a bewilderment.

Eve is squinting at Sherry as she replays the last few minutes. You can't be, she thinks. If you were, you would've told me. So you can't be. Unless. Have you been lying about the migraines?

Oh my God, she says. Are you pregnant?

What? Rae says.

Yuck, Pauline shrieks.

You're too *old*, Rae says. It's disgusting.

Leslie stands up. Look, he says, this isn't how we planned to share this wonderful news, but –

Wonderful news? Eve says.

Well yes, he says. We're expecting. I'm going to be a dad again.

Expecting the unexpected, Eve thinks. You smug fucker.

Leslie is still speaking, saying something firmly to Rae and Pauline, but Eve can't make out the words.

What she hears is deep water.

The kind of sound you might hear from the ocean floor.

As you try to rise back up.

And now, the taste of blood.

She has bitten her own mouth.

And Daniel has gone, his chair is empty.

How can she have missed his leaving?

He has left her alone with an expanding family, of which she is not a part.

She looks for him in the lounge, in the kitchen, upstairs.

Daniel where are you, where have you gone?

Then Sherry's hands are on her shoulders.

We were *so* drunk, she says. It was an accident. It was New Year's Eve, we'd all been drinking.

New Year's Eve? I was with you for most of the day. We kissed in here, do you remember. Then you went off and fucked *him*.

It didn't mean anything, Sherry says, honestly it didn't.

Didn't mean anything? You're such a cliché. You're pregnant for God's sake. You began the year by screwing someone else.

He's hardly someone else, he's my husband.

You said you never have sex.

We don't. Not very often, anyway.

You told me you didn't want any more children. Was that a lie too, like the migraines?

This wasn't planned, darling, it was a stupid drunken accident.

Stop saying that. I don't know what to believe. Why didn't you tell me? I had to hear it in front of everyone.

I've been trying. But it's only early, these things can go wrong, disappear.

And then what, you wouldn't have told me at all?

Eve, calm down, they'll hear you. There's no need to go crazy.

You're calling me crazy? Eve says. Seriously?

Sherry reaches for Eve's hands. Let's talk properly tomorrow, she says. I'm so sorry. But this doesn't need to change anything, honestly it doesn't.

Eve is shaking her head, muttering, calling herself an idiot. So what are you, about ten weeks? she says.

Roughly, yes.

You've been lying to me for ten weeks.

I didn't know for a while, I didn't realise.

I thought you were brave, Eve says. But you're not are you? All those plans we made, you've just been stringing me along. You're never going to tell Leslie about me.

Don't say that, Sherry says.

Well he's not having Daniel as well, Eve says.

What?

He's *my* son, you're not taking him.

Eve, wait. What on earth do you mean? Eve?

Daniel is back with the flamingos, cross-legged in the dark.

He is thinking of Leslie with a new child.

A baby boy, maybe.

184

Who might enjoy the swimming pool.

The cradle of his father's arms as he looks in fear at all the sparkling water.

Then his father, speaking ever so softly:

Here we go, little one. It's all right, I've got you. Nothing to be scared of, see? I've got you.

They are all fired up, unable to sleep, turning over and over, smouldering.

If frantic thoughts were trails of smoke, the air tonight above 3 and 4 Abigail Gardens would be catastrophic.

Ablaze, emergency, help.

But no one comes.

Because when it comes to human beings, there is no smoke where there is fire.

We burn alone, invisibly.

Three weeks later, they are leaving.

Leslie, Sherry and Rae watch from their dining room window as two men carry Eve and Daniel's belongings into a van.

His and hers armchairs, the old spotty sofa.

On the side of the van it says KARL'S HOUSE CLEAR-ANCE.

Leslie can't bear to watch, but he does. I just don't understand why she's getting rid of it all, he says. It's madness. Are they going travelling, going abroad, why won't she speak to us? I know you had a row, but this is ridiculous.

She's clearly unwell, Sherry says. No one reacts to an argument like this. She's not who we thought she was.

He turns to face her. Really? he says.

Then he turns back to the window, and his boy is finally

there, marching across the grass towards the van. He leaps into it, grabs a cardboard box, jumps back out.

Daniel does this again and again until the pavement is covered in boxes.

Oh my God, Rae says. What's he doing?

He's grabbing his stuff, Sherry says.

The men are perplexed, annoyed, their palms face the sky.

This is hideous, Leslie says.

The boxes go back in as Daniel cries and shouts, kicks the wheel of the van.

Then his protest is over, the pavement is clear, the doors of the van shut with a bang.

All around, people shudder as this sound moves through them.

What was that noise? Can't have been a door closing, too loud and horrible for that. Sounded like a bang, a shock, like someone has just been hurt.

I feel like I'm watching a hearse, Leslie thinks, as the van pulls slowly away.

Daniel is sitting on the ground, his head buried in his hands.

Eve sits beside him, pulls him close.

He won't cope with this, Leslie says. They've moved too many times. He'll twitch and rhyme all the way.

All the way to where? Rae says, fighting the desire to pack a bag and run outside and go wherever they are going.

Later that day, Anna arrives.

They watch as she fills her old VW with boxes.

Now what's going on? Leslie says. I'm going out to speak to them.

No, Sherry says. You can't interfere, it's her choice.

186

They stand in silence, he takes her hand, she holds it for a while then lets it go.

It's all right, Anna says to Eve. You're both going to be all right.

They carry boxes full of Lego, toys and books into Anna's car, then the old map pinned to a noticeboard that Eve insists on keeping.

Are you sure this is okay? Eve says. There's a bit more than I thought.

It's fine, Anna says. There's plenty of room in my loft. There's not much here, not really.

Next, Franklin and Peter. They park behind Anna's car. They are holding flasks and some kind of gift.

Leslie watches them all go inside.

You can't stand here all day, Sherry says. Come and eat something will you?

In a bit, he says.

He is about to step away when Eve's front door opens again. Franklin and Peter come out first, then Anna and Daniel, followed by Eve.

There are hugs, tears, Daniel is shaking Franklin's hand.

Peter ruffles the boy's hair, bends down to give him a hug.

Then Anna and Eve, their long embrace.

Anna's hands are on Eve's face, she is talking to her in a serious way, lowering her head slightly to catch Eve's eyes.

Two engines start. Hands are raised.

Then Eve and Daniel are alone.

And Daniel runs.

Shit, Leslie says.

*

He runs and she follows.

Around the corner, one street after the other.

Was that Eve Berry chasing her son? a voice in a driveway says.

Eve shouts Daniel's name until she manages to catch him up.

I won't go, you can't make me.

I'm so sorry, we just have to.

Tell me why.

It's really complicated.

Tell me why.

It's not that easy.

I hate you. I'm not going I'm really not. You go on your own, go on. I'll stay here. I'll stay with Leslie and Sherry.

Eve falls to her knees.

The way she cries, here on the pavement, he doesn't know what to do.

The way she cries, it makes him angry and frightened and sad.

He gently pats the top of her head, like a boy testing an animal, will you or won't you bite.

She looks up, and she has changed, all her fight seems to have gone. She has been stomping for days from room to room, making lists, making things happen. All the cleaning and scrubbing. Her furious face.

Daniel pictures a pink Duracell bunny, banging a drum until finally it slows and topples to the ground.

Okay, he says.

What, she says.

I'll come with you, he says.

Somehow, then, he is waiting in the back of their car. How he gets there is a blur, he will never be able to remember. He glances at Leslie, Sherry and Rae, all at their dining room window.

Leslie waves, but maybe Daniel hasn't seen him.

Eve walks over to her car and opens the door. Whatever she says to Daniel makes him get back out.

They've gone inside again, Rae says. What's happening?

I really don't know, Leslie says. Oh, hold on.

What's that? Rae says.

I think it's her painting, Leslie says.

As Eve and Daniel carry it to the Marshes' front door.

There is a sealed envelope, taped to the top of the painting. Eve's handwriting, blue ink: *FAO Sherry Marsh*.

Franklin had given this painting to Eve last year on her birthday. She was so excited to have it that she invited them all round for dinner. They had laughed at the title, *Still Life with Sherry*, called it *such a funny coincidence*, called it *meant to be*. I just can't believe you've given this to me, Eve said, hugging Franklin again. I love it more than anything, apart from my Daniel, obviously. She stood in the middle of Franklin and Peter, their arms around her, and the sight of Eve like this – how solid she looked, older somehow, strong and happy and beautiful – made Sherry feel so much, it was terrifying. That evening she made herself a promise: *I'll never let Eve go, no matter how awful it gets.*

I'm going to see her, Leslie says.

Because she is just there, right outside the window, she is –

No, Sherry says, grabbing his arm, holding him back. Please, she says.

He pulls away from her, and is about to go outside, to say what on earth, Eve, isn't this all a bit extreme? But he catches his wife's eye. And her fear stops him. She never looks afraid, not Sherry. This row between her and Eve must have shaken her badly.

There is a piece of cloth, stuffed into the mouth of his desperation.

Eve's driving away is imminent, obvious, they all know it's about to happen.

But all three of them gasp, just the same.

What's going on? Pauline says, stumbling into the room wearing Rae's bobble hat.

There are no words to answer her question.

That night, unable to sleep, Rae sits on the edge of her bed and stares at her alphabetised books.

In the kitchen at 3am, Sherry stares at the painting leaning against the wall. The letter that came with it, still unopened.

Leslie stares at his bedroom ceiling. Why the hell didn't I stop this? he thinks. I just let her drive away with him. How will he ever forgive me.

Daniel's bed in the motel is creaky and hard. He dreams of a ship caught in a terrible storm. When he wakes up, all he can see is mess that will never stop; it will rise and rise until he is buried in his mother's mistakes, forever lost, forever on the move.

Eve doesn't dream at all that night, because she doesn't sleep. She is on the floor below the window, staring at a book that she forgot to return to the library. She is sitting cross-legged, gripping the book tight, her tears tapping out the code of how lost she is on its matt paper, on a drawing of a compass jellyfish, its radial shapes like a geometric parachute gliding through the sea. Beware the soft medusa and its sting.

Tonight these people are nothing but aerials, desperately transmitting messages of ache and no and please and want.

Their messages go out through the airwaves.

And they wait.

Send again.

And they wait.

Send again.

Two weeks later, Leslie turns fifty.

To cheer him up, or maybe herself, Sherry throws a party.

He says the idea is sweet, but really, he doesn't want it.

Don't be silly, she says. I'll invite the neighbours, shall I?

No, he says.

The day before his birthday, he goes into town to buy a jigsaw. A picture he can restore, make whole. Something he can put back together.

On the way home, he drinks four pints of ale in the pub.

You all right, Daniel? he says aloud.

And the space where an answer should be.

He falls into it.

And stays there for another hour.

Drinks himself silly in it.

And after a while, it sort of feels like Daniel is there too.

Somehow, it's nice.

So maybe he'll do this every week, every Saturday afternoon.

Yes, good idea.

They should have games in here, something on the go to return to.

He'll suggest this as he leaves.

And when he gets up the next day, he is fifty.

There is a party that isn't a party.

It's a sham, and they drink to it, to him, with Babycham.

A few neighbours, a guy from work he doesn't like.

But not the new neighbours. The ones who have moved in next door.

I don't even want to meet them, Sherry says.

And late evening, sober as a tree, she does the oddest thing.

Which Leslie can only put down to stress.

Or maybe the fact that she is pregnant.

To be honest, he still can't believe it.

Anyway, here she is.

About to do the oddest thing.

They are all in the lounge, talking about something and nothing.

When she stands up and rings that bell of hers.

Her town crier's bell.

Says she has a special gift for her husband on his fiftieth.

Dear God, he says.

And then it begins.

She starts to sing.

All by herself, no music.

'I Want to Know What Love Is'.

Their guests are bemused, embarrassed.

As the song goes on.

Her version is long, angry, intense.

It changes as it goes, her eyes fill with tears.

It's a painful and confusing kind of birthday present.

Like witnessing an intimate performance of anguish and rage.

But he thanks her, gives her a kiss, says goodness that was really something.

And Sherry is never quite the same after that.

Hard to say how or why.

The freight of forty years, all on a single seat.

The train slows, pulls closer to a crowd on a platform.

The jostle of passengers as the doors open.

Their immense seriousness.

Daniel holds his breath, out of fear, indecision.

Go back.

Keep going.

He steps off the train, and the air is lively and warm, it smells of hot doughnuts and fir trees, a complicated hello.

extraterrestrial

Leslie Marsh is at his jigsaw again. This is how he has spent his evenings lately, hunched over the dining table, head under a reading light, trying to solve the visual mystery Rae bought him for his eightieth birthday.

His wife objects to his use of the word *mystery*. You know what it's going to be from the photo on the box, so where's the mystery? she says.

The mystery's all in the process, he says, holding up a piece. Do you have any idea what this is? Me neither. It's a mystery.

I feel like I'm in an old people's home, she says.

Sherry, people of all ages do jigsaws, he says.

But Leonardo da Vinci? she says. It's like a bad omen, giving a man *The Last Supper* for his eightieth. It makes me feel horribly superstitious. You have to finish it, Leslie, then get it out of here.

I'm trying, he says.

She stands there for a while, watching her husband. The fifteen years between them used to feel irrelevant, but lately, every now and then, it shocks her. It's as if this ongoing fact of their lives, this difference between them, has gained an electrical charge.

Now here's a mystery for you, Leslie: how can something

that a person has always been aware of only now reveal itself? Solve that conundrum, dear.

Leslie is a puzzle fanatic. All the word searches, crosswords, sudoku. His brain likes to be teased. And yes these puzzles exercise his brain, but what about his body? He is too inactive, habitual, this is what Sherry thinks.

Which is why, for his eightieth birthday, along with her special performance of 'I Want to Know What Love Is' by Foreigner, she gave him running shoes, a tracksuit and a Fitbit. And now every evening they go speed-walking together. Which, in reality, means Sherry striding ahead while Leslie loiters behind.

Why are you loitering? she says.

I'm just looking at this new fence. The quality is so impressive, he says.

Seriously? she says.

You have to admire this wood, this craftsmanship, he says.

If you were to ask this couple to perform one of the main differences between them, to perform it in a theatrical way, this is what you might see:

A woman with her hands on her hips, sighing.

A man crouched down, happily appreciating the fine details of a garden fence.

Here is an entire marriage, encapsulated in a single moment on a balmy springtime evening.

There's so much to stop and look at, Leslie thinks. In the neighbouring streets there are new camper vans, gardening projects, extensions; renovation and renewal, a spot of topiary.

He catches up with his wife, who has been jogging on the spot.

In her mind she labels him as slow and befuddled. Why

is he just standing there with a blank look on his face? She feels sorry for him, and also irritated.

But he is neither slow nor befuddled. He is busy devising a sentence, a way to tell his wife how much he dislikes speed-walking, dislikes walking with her in general. Ideally, by the end of this conversation, she will end up feeling closer to him, even though he has just pushed her away.

Like so many people who are seen as mild-mannered or extremely polite, Leslie has a hidden talent for damage limitation. His placid exterior conceals a feverish degree of hard work. If only his wife could recognise his communicational prowess, his artfulness.

Darling, he says, after pausing to ruffle the curls of an Old English sheepdog being walked by a neighbour.

What is it? she says.

You're an amazing wife, he says.

Oh, she says. She wasn't expecting *that*.

And I'm sure you'd rather not have to drag me around the streets every evening. I'm cramping your style. I know you're trying to help, he says, holding up his wrist, but this whole Fibbit thing.

It's a *Fitbit*, she says.

Whatever, he says. I don't like it. I feel like Big Brother is monitoring me. It makes me feel stressed.

Really? she says.

Hmm, he says. Doesn't yours?

No, it makes me feel motivated.

Well it was a lovely gift, but I'd like to give it to Rae, he says. Speed-walking isn't for me. I want you to *enjoy* your exercise, not be held back. Why don't I take you out for dinner tomorrow night instead? We could try that new Italian place. You deserve a lovely meal.

Do I? she says.

Of course you do, he says. You have to live with me, don't you.

True, she says.

How easy this is. How quickly she is flattered and defused. For a moment it makes him feel tired. Where's the challenge, the puzzle, the mystery? And at the same time, he enjoys it. Who wouldn't? All these small victories, this still being able to win her over. She is vivacious, spirited, he has seen how other men look at her.

She kisses him on the cheek. And it's lovely. And he is lonely. And he sees himself as a fortunate man.

Truth be told, he'd love to take an evening walk, to stroll around here at regular speed, admiring fences, chatting to neighbours and their dogs. But not with Sherry. It's ironic really. She wants him to be healthier, but her impatience stresses him out, gives him palpitations.

You'll be the death of me, he thinks.

Don't leave me, he thinks.

They decide to walk home a different way, along the path by the river.

Under a bridge, Leslie stops. He leans forward, his hands on his thighs. He wheezes and coughs for a long time.

She strokes his back and waits.

All these small humiliations.

You all right? she says when he is upright again, red in the face.

Peachy, he says, just peachy.

It's what he always says when he is fine and not fine.

You're my peach, she says.

Which is how she always responds.

Every relationship has its own language, shorthand, code.

When Sherry feels low, they discuss it at length.

When Leslie feels low, they speak briefly and mainly of fruit.

Daniel stands outside the house, takes off his trainers.

His feet hurt from walking.

New windows, he thinks. And a garage now. And look at that stunning cherry tree.

He glances at his watch, almost 8pm.

There are no words for the breadth of his tiredness.

He feels extraterrestrial. Like ET in the basket of a boy's bike.

Now he takes off his socks.

Leaves them on top of his rucksack.

Rolls up his trousers as if he's about to wade into water.

Or something that might soak him.

Across the grass, to 4 Abigail Gardens.

He's looking for a musical doorbell, wonders if they still have one.

It's highly unlikely.

There are no words for how good it would be if they did.

Or, for why it would matter.

(The most precious things, formidably inarticulate.)

Please, should anything be constant, let it be this.

Let them still be here.

Let them still be here.

He is full of hope and devoid of hope, as a person always is.

He sees a little white box and presses it.

It works, it works.

'Hello, Goodbye'.

It's the Beatles, well sort of, a version of.

Musical bloody doorbell!

And he waits.

And no one comes.

And he waits.

And no one comes.

Down by the river, bridge overhead, he opens his rucksack for a Cornish pasty and a can of gin and tonic.

What's one more night? he thinks.

It's a song by Phil Collins, he thinks. Which is a song he didn't originally like, but now, as it plays in his mind, it's quite pleasing.

Is it just him, or were people less afraid of being seen as sentimental in the 1980s?

Maybe it's just him.

And the breadth of his tiredness.

He imagines it as a bird with the wingspan of a church.

There is music coming from the church, someone is playing the cello.

Soft soporific lullaby.

The bird flaps its wings, closes Daniel's eyes with a breeze.

This is strange, this is lovely.

What I would really like, he thinks, is to bring Erica here in 1984. But would Erica be who she is now or Erica from 1984?

Well that's a lumpy question to sleep on.

What was Erica like in 1984? What is she like *now*?

This thought kills the mood, alters the shape of his tiredness.

He dreams of an ugly troll, sleeping under a bridge.

Erica Yu, stamping on its bones.

There is a man, sitting at a dining table.

It's not a dramatic sight, a life-changing moment, something to take your breath.

But it is.

Daniel stops in the driveway. He needs a moment to take this in. The rush of affection he feels for this man. A sort of giddiness laced with fear.

Calm down, he thinks. It may not even be him. And even if it is, it doesn't mean she is there too.

But it does.

This woman walking through the dining room, putting something down on the table, a cup of tea maybe, yes probably a cup of tea.

It's unmistakably her.

He moves straight to the doorbell, lifts his finger to the button.

Hears the Beatles again.

And he waits.

And there are footsteps.

And he hasn't seen her for thirty years.

Hello, she says, sharp and suspicious and perfectly correct.

He is a filthy fright. She *should* be suspicious.

But then he speaks.

Mrs Sherry, he says.

He is the only person to have called her this.

She squints, tries to find the boy she once knew in this stranger. It's like a Magic Eye puzzle: can you see the child, hidden in this pattern of a man?

There is another voice. Everything all right? it says.

And here they are after all this time. Both of them, still alive, still here.

Bloody hell.

Daniel grins.

And *there* he is, the boy smiling through the years, through his wear and tear, a shabby smelly fucker of a man, but definitely Daniel Berry.

Oh my God, Sherry says. Leslie, look who this is.

Leslie pouts with confusion, takes off his reading glasses, scrunches up his nose. Who are you, son? he says.

We all have words that will melt us.

When we didn't even know we were frozen.

For Daniel, one of these words is *son*, spoken by this man.

And now he has lost the capacity to speak.

Tenderness is all that remains.

Darling, Sherry says. This is Daniel Berry.

Leslie's mouth falls open.

Eve's boy? he says.

Eve's boy, Daniel says.

We all have sights that will melt us.

When we didn't even know we were frozen.

Sherry Marsh is a flood, a shock, a woman making tea for a stranger.

My God, just look at him. He's so much like his mother, she thinks.

The stranger is a matryoshka doll, man of many parts.

There is a woman, nesting inside this man.

And there is a boy, nesting inside the woman.

A spectre, a hint, a ghost, a flash.

The past inside the present, nothing ever separate.

Eve had bought Sherry a set of Russian dolls. It was 1986, she was in the charity shop as usual, sifting through wicker baskets, looking for something fun or pretty or useful.

For you, she said later that day.

Sherry held it up, admired the doll's cheery paintwork, her red headscarf and yellow apron, the cartoonish pink dots on her cheeks. Babushka, she said.

Matryoshka, Eve said. I think that's what they're called. Not babushka. Open her up, lift her lid, go on.

And so she did. And there were six dolls inside.

I'll keep her beside my bed, always, Sherry said.

Will you? Eve said, wondering if Sherry's bed would in time become hers too, if these bright dolls would be something she picked up when she cleaned and dusted the home they had made together, when she threw open the windows and turned to face Sherry's cluttered bedside table and felt shocked by her own good fortune all over again.

I will, Sherry said.

They stood in silence, looking at all the dolls lined up on the worktop.

I've got that Kate Bush song in my head now, Sherry said.

Me too, Eve said.

And Sherry began to sing 'Babooshka'. She swirled around the kitchen, made a song and dance for Eve.

Eve laughed. That's actually quite good, she said.

Sherry ignored her. She already knew it was quite good. Her eyes were wild and dramatic as she sang the tale of a woman incognito, a wife hidden inside a mistress.

That moment happened right here in this kitchen.

Her stomach in knots, room full of dancing dolls, Sherry makes a pot of tea, opens a packet of Jammie Dodgers and arranges them on a plate.

Why is Daniel here? she thinks. *Is she dead is she dead* is all she wants to say. It would explain his bloodshot eyes, his frayed edges. That boy adored his mother.

She replays her own thoughts, realises how crazy they are. He was probably just passing by, she thinks. Yes, that's it.

And couldn't Leslie have cancelled his osteopath appointment and stayed home instead? Just because this man used to be little Daniel Berry doesn't mean he isn't dangerous.

Do sit down, Daniel, she says.

I'm a bit muddy, he says, glancing at his trousers.

It's fine.

I'm sorry I'm in such a state. I must smell a bit too.

Don't you worry, she says, watching him take a seat at the table.

I slept by the river last night, he says, in the tone a person would use to say they went to the cinema or saw a play.

You did what? she says.

I've been sleeping rough for the past week, so please forgive how I look.

Daniel, she says. What's happened to you?

She moves towards him, reaches out to touch his hair.

She takes his face in her hands, the whole grubby weight of it.

They look into each other's eyes.

Well you're here now, she says.

His eyes are full of tears.

It's all right, she says. A cup of strong tea and a long hot bath, that's what you need.

He nods.

And we can have a chat, if you feel like it, she says.

He nods again. Don't ever let go of my face, he thinks.

Sherry lets his words settle, the fact of him sleeping rough, and why, what this means, why he didn't stay with his mother.

Is she dead is she dead is all she wants to say.

The sun is streaming into the kitchen now.

He smells of a garden pond, strangely aquatic, to be honest she doesn't mind it.

She forms a plan. She will give him some of Leslie's clothes, something bright and cosy, maybe the turquoise fleece and his new tracksuit bottoms. She will roast a chicken, call Rae, see if she'd like to join them for dinner tonight. She's bound to be free, is always free. But she won't invite Pauline, she's too loud, too much. And she won't mention his mother until he does. Yes, that's the best approach. Saying the word *Eve* could unearth all kinds of trouble.

Where are you, Eve?

This is a lovely cup of tea, he says, holding the mug tight with both hands.

Are you homeless, Daniel? she says, sitting beside him now, dipping a biscuit into her tea.

I don't know what I am, he says.

Okay, she says, pushing the plate towards him.

Beneath the biscuits, Daniel can see the Beatles, all four of them peering out.

Sherry thinks carefully about what to say next. It's difficult, knowing where to tread, and how softly. She imagines him as a boy, sitting here smelly and cold.

Tell me anything, she says.

Anything? he says.

Whatever comes to mind, she says.

She watches him turn this over, his eyes closing ever so slightly.

Erica, he says.

Erica? she says.

My girlfriend, she left me, he says.

I'm sorry, Sherry says.

She leans back in her chair, tries not to rush in with questions. She knows she can be careless, heavy-handed. Her husband is the one with a gentle touch. He is the great solver of puzzles, immensely patient, more adept at going slowly than she is. Softly, softly, catchee monkey is one of his favourite phrases.

210

You must be exhausted, she says.

I am, he says. I was sick in a cafe, all over the table.

Oh dear, she says.

Do you remember how I used to rhyme when I was little? he says. I used to come out with all this weird nonsensical rhyme.

I do. But it got better, didn't it? It stopped happening.

It got better for a while. But when we moved away from here it started again.

Her face reddens.

I learned to manage it, pretty much, he says. But now it's back. It happened really badly this week, in the cafe, that's what made me throw up. And afterwards there was a sort of peacefulness, like stepping into a warm breeze on an empty beach. Being sick in that cafe, in there of all places, was one of the lowest points of my life.

Well, it could've been worse, Sherry says.

Could it?

Definitely.

Have *you* ever vomited in public?

Daniel, do I look like a woman whose life has been so small that she's never thrown up in public? Now drink your tea, have one of these Jammie Dodgers and tell me more about this fuckwit called Erica.

She's really not a fuckwit, he says.

Because a word against her feels like a word against him. He is a crushed man, fists swinging to defend his crush. And the energy it takes, even for this.

When did you break up? Sherry says.

A few weeks ago, he says.

And the look on his face, well there are many ways to describe it. Later, when Sherry gives Leslie an update, tells him what she discovered while he was out, she will choose the word *broken*. I haven't discovered much really, she'll say. Not so far. His girlfriend of six years left him, and he seems, well, *broken*.

I messed everything up, Daniel says. *I'm* the fuckwit, not Erica.

Maybe we're all fuckwits, Sherry says, putting her hand on his.

Yeah, he says, and smiles.

His smile is quick, sad, she tries to catch it.

It's all a load of fucking bollocks, she says.

Which makes him laugh, how she is still as sweary as ever.

What is, he says.

Love, obviously, she says.

Erica

1.

A life can be defined by a yes or a no.

How will you come to your answer? By heart or by gut? Pros in one hand, cons in the other?

Don't take too long, don't overthink it. A question can undo itself you know.

2.

Erica Yu's answer is yes.

She says it quickly, casually, as if he has only suggested coffee, a walk in the park.

Really? Daniel says. You'd like to move in?

Why not, she says. Yes.

3.

Five weeks later, a man with a van pulls up outside the cottage.

How can I be this lucky? Daniel thinks. It's unbelievable, a joke surely.

He has bought champagne. Never bought it before, hopes it's a nice one.

He has cleaned from top to bottom – the kind of deep clean where you move all the furniture, wipe all the paintwork. The fridge is full of food, he's put flowers in a pretty jug, a bowl of fruit on the table. Yesterday he bought fairy lights, draped them over mirrors and pictures, and although it isn't yet dark, isn't even close to dark, he has switched them all on.

Erica parks behind the van, her car full of boxes and plants and photographs.

Daniel helps them carry things inside, boxes so full they're splitting, banana boxes from the supermarket, useless, what was she thinking. Next, all the boxes he had bought her: double wall, stackable, different sizes. You're so sensible, she said when he turned up with these boxes, plus two rolls of bubble wrap, parcel tape, scissors. And she meant this in a good way, she was glad that he was sensible.

Jesus I'm knackered, she says to him now.

He makes tea for the man with a van, says thanks so much, took no time at all really did it, well less time than I thought it would anyway.

How long have you two been together? the man says.

Six months, Daniel says.

It's only five months, actually, Erica says.

4.

That evening, even though it's December, they drink champagne in the garden.

I could get used to this, she says.

He wants to grab, eat, swallow the sight of her: that cheesy grin, Nordic jumper and bobble hat, those dusty jeans and red trainers.

Yes, all of that.

Look at how excited she is, how perfect.

He feels a bit monstrous, greedy, overwhelmed. And it's odd, disconcerting. Why this sense of himself as greedy? For a moment he feels ashamed.

It's human dynamics, Daniel. The unfathomable sensations of intimacy. And also, what you're sensing, let me tell it like it is. This is a flourish of low self-worth. And I'm sorry, but since you ask. This is what it feels like, every now and then, to be with someone who doesn't love you in the way you love her. Can you hear me, Daniel? Are you listening to your intuition?

Daniel, hello, are you still with me?

He takes a deep breath, sits up straight.

They are fizzy and new and untouchable, this is their truth.

They are rapacious, hot-headed.

Mouths full of champagne, new beginnings.

She wants to grab at him too, pull his clothes.

They are ferociously happy.

This moment in their lives, as hopeful and clear as a freshwater lake.

Only a fool wouldn't want to jump right in, to skinny-dip in this.

We need a Christmas tree, she says, glancing at the cottage.

We do, he says. A really tall one.

Or maybe just a small one, she says. We don't want to be garish do we.

Good point, he says.

5.

He says he could look at her all day, do nothing else but look. This is a lie. A person cannot be sustained by the act of looking, but right now, at this moment, he is delirious, feverish, blinkered; an embarrassment of bliss. And sometimes such madness makes a person taller. And sometimes such madness makes a person smaller.

217

6.

He comes home from work every day, overalls covered in paint.

She asks him to pick up more champagne, says they should celebrate *everything*.

Really? he says, because he would happily celebrate with an evening walk, an ice cream, a chapter of a good book.

Oh, you got prosecco, she says when he gets home.

They drink in front of the telly, a documentary about trees, littered with commercials for cold remedies, sofas, sensitive toothpaste.

Then, the John Lewis Christmas ad.

Oh look, Erica says, as she watches a snowman travel for miles to buy his love a gift.

She starts to cry, and she rarely cries, she is not what you'd call sentimental.

It's so moving, she says. And isn't the music lovely?

It's eerily sad, he says.

Really? she says. It's romantic, I think.

He is confused. The documentary about trees, now *that* was romantic, he has often given his heart to an old oak tree.

She downloads the song, Gabrielle Aplin's cover of 'The Power of Love' by Frankie Goes to Hollywood, plays it constantly for weeks.

I love our life, she says.

That's good, he says.

7.

They go to the wedding of one of her friends.

In the evening there is a disco.

It's not a *disco*, she says. It's a DJ.

They are sitting at a table, watching people dance.

Erica says look at that couple, they dance so well together don't they, and something inside him curls like metal under a blowtorch, and the curling hurts.

And so, when she asks if he'd like to dance, he barks his answer, says *no* as if she has said the most preposterous thing. She is wounded, then angry.

And now her chair is empty.

Look at her, so beautiful and free on the dance floor.

He is full of jealousy, desire and self-disgust as he watches her dance with a group of friends, one of them her ex.

He glances around the room, thinks how sad is this, being one of these people left behind at tables, staring at the dance floor.

He moves to get up and join her. But he is paralysed.

Erica, come over here, help me up, make this stop.

His shyness is pathetic, revolting, he knows it is.

Later, she will be distant.

Later, he will be distant.

And what he doesn't know tonight is how this moment will be stored in his Hall of Shame, that place in his mind that likes to taunt him, take him by surprise with a random despicable memory.

His beloved, simply asking him to dance.

Him, barking *no* like a weird little boy.

8.

Seasons come and go, Christmases, birthdays. They make cards for each other, think carefully about what to write with their favourite ink pens. They talk about children, she says let's have two, he says why not three. They watch *Winterwatch* on telly and worry about the plight of hedgehogs. They buy each other books, socks, practical things and daft things. He buys her a rainbow umbrella, she buys him better shampoo, no parabens, says she doesn't want him to get cancer, not ever. Their kisses are long, he never used to love kissing, never felt drugged by kissing before. He says it's surprising, he's never found it easy to be attracted to a person, which is weird for a bloke, he knows. She shrugs, looks pleased, says nothing. They wash and get dirty and wash. They get dirty a lot, fast and slow, through sweaty afternoons, misty mornings. The weather is wild and boring and melancholy and fantastic. He loves to watch how she uses her hands, the way she folds things and chops things and makes the bed. They watch *Springwatch* on telly. He grows flowers, talks about the wonderful simplicity of flowers. They talk about the world, how it's going down the pan. Then one of them hums a theme tune from an old TV show, says what am I humming, funny how I can't remember. And this is the general pace of their years: important, trivial, everything at once. Their voices fluctuate like perturbed symphonies, sometimes Erica's is so thin and cross. He begins to listen for her contrariness, those little vocal slaps, and his listening makes him feel tense, self-conscious, boring. You're very *tidy*, aren't you, Dan, she says in a way that isn't kind. Then she buys him a painting of a man diving into a swimming pool and a woman lazing beside it, says it reminded her of David Hockney and she knows how much he loves Hockney, says maybe the man is him and the woman is her, and we can look at it when we're in bed, do you like it, what do you think? It's amazing, thank you, I don't know what to say, he says, moved to tears. The following day they argue about her parents, who never imagined their daughter with a man who makes his living from decorating houses. There is a moment of giving up and a moment of deciding not to, and Erica tells him that *not giving up* is always better than *making a fresh start*, which is an abstract and foolish concept, an act of high pressure, that's what she says. Daniel isn't sure about this, he likes fresh starts, the fresh start of January especially, a brand new calendar, but maybe she has a point. There are thousands of small pleasures, which seem quite ordinary, but if you put them all together you'll see how they shine, even in the dark, even in midwinter, even when it seems that all hope is lost. Like, for example, a text message that says *Still thinking of last night, shall I pick something up for tea*. Like, for example, the smell of summer rain through their window while she reads to him in bed. And his old T-shirt, scruffy and soft, which she wears around the house. And her orange woolly scarf, which smells of honey and goes surprisingly well with his coat. Money is earned and spent, he buys her a little toy camper van, puts it on the windowsill, calls it *future symbolic, future fantastic*. They are delicate and sturdy like everyone else. They are childish and fragile and tough. They are more innocent than they know. They are around 60% water. They play host to millions of bacteria. Their cells divide and multiply, their skin regenerates, they are dermatologically miraculous, all of the time. They do the laundry, hoover, make dust. When it snows they walk like penguins, because someone on the radio said to do this. Fog comes down, snakes its way into the cottage, hangs all over them, snakes its way out. She helps him to improve, be a better man in all kinds of ways. She tells him what he is like, in case he doesn't know. She is deeply interested in his self-improvement. Thank you so much, he often says, confused and disarmed by criticism dressed as kindness. She says he could be a bit chattier, make more of an effort with her friends, and she's only trying to help by telling him this. He comes to believe that he is everything she says, that Erica alone harbours his truth, paints the truest picture of who he is. You could be a bit less *sensible*, she says. They drink wine in the garden under a full moon, talk about wanting to get away to the craggy coastline, swim in the sea. We should buy a camper van, a real one, he says, which makes her excited, makes her open another bottle.

9.
They do not buy a camper van.

10.
They have already survived five Februarys, crossed them easily in big jumpers and heavy boots.

But their sixth is hazardous terrain, catastrophic.

Daniel says they'll be fine, Erica says they won't.

She changes her mind, keeps waking him in the night. It reminds him of when they first got together, all the things she wanted in the early hours of morning. Their wordless fucking had always been loving and cold; it was the place where he felt like she knew him, in a way that no one else could. And when they surfaced, the transition was never easy. Speaking seemed strange and pointless, like circling an animal you can never understand until it bites you.

11.
Treacherous February begins with a kick in the stomach, ends with a punch in the mouth.

There is a woman, standing at their front door, soaked from the rain.

Does Daniel Berry live here? this woman says.

He does, Erica says.

She is invited in. They drink tea at the table, then Daniel throws her out, says enough of this, you need to leave.

He slams the front door and stands in the shock of everything this stranger told him.

Why did you have to be so rude to her, Erica says.

That's how you respond to what just happened? he says. Not *Jesus, Daniel, this must be such a shock*. Not *are you all right, darling*. Instead you criticise my behaviour?

I'm entitled to my opinion, Dan. I'm not a robot, she says.

I feel like I've just been kicked in the stomach, he says. I don't need you to kick me as well.

Oh don't be so dramatic, she says. Do you always have to be so metaphorical?

Metaphorical? he says.

If you were a bit more literal, you might be less emotional, she says.

Oh my God, he says.

Some arguments fade, are ruined by a kiss, gone by morning. But this one, no. It seems to energise Erica, she runs with it for days, he has no idea why she refuses to stop.

Why have you leapt on this? he says. I'm trying to deal with all this new stuff, all this horrible stuff, and all you're doing is criticising.

Well the way you're responding, she says. It's just so *you*.

12.
Deep into February she seems to change. Her hands inside his T-shirt. I'm sorry, she says. I feel like I've given you a rough time.

Well yes, he thinks, because you *actually have*.

223

It's all right, he says. It's good that you told me all those things. I had no idea you'd been so unhappy.

It just came out, she says. Once we started arguing, it just came out.

He imagines a puppet springing from her mouth with SURPRISE, I'M MISERABLE! written on the front of its stiff little blazer.

And for two days, they make an effort. They clean the cottage, go to the tip, go out for noodles, wander through town hand in hand, buy baklava and books. He is bruised and they are quiet, she tells him that sex will help, and it does, it does, it always does.

They are still asleep when the landlord knocks on the front door.

Saturday morning, 10am, they had bought croissants for breakfast and will forget to eat them.

Daniel grabs the nearest thing, Erica's dressing gown, and runs downstairs.

Oh, sorry to disturb you, the landlord says, I thought you'd be up and about. I've got some news.

13.
There is good news and bad news and fake news and sick news and welcome news and old news and *in-your-face BAM! I-will-never-get-over-you* news.

14.
Daniel is back in the bedroom with two mugs of coffee.

Who was it? Erica says.

She takes his pillow and puts it under hers, makes herself comfortable.

Why does everything have to happen at once, he says.

I mean, it's a rule isn't it, how bad things arrive in clusters. Why is that, do you think?

What's happened? she says.

That, my love, was our landlord, he says.

What did he want?

He wants to put our home on Airbnb.

Airbnb?

Yep. Reckons he'll make more that way. Said to tell you how sorry he is, and how brilliant we've been.

What?

We've got until the end of April to find somewhere else, he says.

And he remembers the exact words the landlord used: *Don't panic, you've got two whole months.*

He had said the word *whole* slowly and loudly, given it extra emphasis, as if he was describing a HUGE cat or a MASSIVE crowd, as if these two particular months would be special somehow, more *whole* than other months, and Daniel should be grateful for that.

He's evicting us? she says.

Oh no, Daniel says, he made a point of telling me this wasn't an eviction, he would never evict anyone apparently. He's *politely asking us to leave*, that's all. And guess what.

What.

He brought us a little gift too. A crate of artisan ale.

Bloody hell, Erica says.

She sips her coffee and watches him from over the cup as he frets and rants.

Funny how all of a sudden he seems very far away.

15.

Sometimes you have to congratulate a person for making a quick decision.

Look at her go! The spontaneity, the instinct, no dilly-dallying here!

Erica has made her decision by lunchtime.

I don't want to do it, she says.

What, he says.

Get another place together. Live with you again. I don't want to, she says.

But we just had sex, he says.

Which will strike him later as a strange thing to have said.

That was our last time, she says.

He grimaces at the condescending tone, sickly sweet and disturbingly parental, like a mother giving a child bad news.

And just now in the bathroom, when she had joined him in the shower – was that a calculated move, did she already know?

What a horrible thought.

He closes his eyes.

I'm sorry, she says.

16.
Fuck every single fucking February. He will never again welcome or enjoy that savage stretch of time between January and March.

17.
He tells her he doesn't understand. How can this, how can she.

I'm sorry, but it's what I want, she says.

It can't be, he says.

Look, Dan, she says. You can shake this tree as much as you like, you won't get any fruit.

What? he says.

18.

She stays for a month, he follows her around, spring is here and the flowers are beginning to bloom.

19.

Mainly he cries, is desperate and hysterical, embarrasses them both, he can't help it.

20.

Their future hangs in the air, so vibrant and real, prettier than any flower he has ever seen.

Why can't you see it? he says. It's right here, it's amazing, don't you see.

Nothing has felt more urgent than making her see.

No, she says.

Then she goes out for lunch with a friend, says this friend is going through a difficult time.

And you're not? he thinks. You're just fine?

21.

Relationships are *ridiculous*, he says to a bottle of wine and the dark of night. They're like vast buildings, complex constructions that can be dismantled with just one sentence. How can a thing that takes years to build take only a second to break?

22.

This month has been awful, let's not have another, Erica says. It's best if I go, then you can have the place to yourself, use April to sort your head out.

She says this as if it's a favour, a gift.

She says this as if the month of April has magical healing properties.

She hasn't even asked him where he's going to live.

I won't take much, she says.

Why not? he says.

Well, most of all this is yours really isn't it.

No it isn't, he says. You made me replace most of my stuff, so it's mainly all ours, surely?

Well you can have it, she says. I'll just take what I brought with me.

The way she dresses her guilt as kindness is repulsive.

23.

She drives to the local hardware shop to buy a few flat-packed boxes.

Don't waste your money on those, the owner says. I've got some out the back, you can have them for free if you like.

When she gets home, she tells him the story of what happened. How lucky was that? she says.

He will never forget how pleased she looked, how light and happy with all the boxes she would use for leaving.

Also, she had bought daffodils.

24.

He watches her move from room to room, gathering her belongings.

You can have this, she says, holding up a vase he once gave her.

Now she picks up a cactus from the windowsill. This is so cute, she says. I'll take this.

He grits his teeth. She was never interested in the cactuses before. They're cacti, she once said, not cactuses, and I don't know why you like them, they're so spiky and stern.

How is it, he thinks, that finishing with me has already

changed the way you see even a simple thing like a cactus. Does life look better to you now, Erica?

Here in the kitchen as she puts down the cactus and opens a bottle of wine, says would you like one of these chocolates I got for my birthday, I don't know why I've been saving these. Here in the kitchen with the posh chocolates and the cute cactus and her soft smile, he does something stupid (again):

Do you remember when we first met, he says.

Dan, she says, biting into a champagne truffle. Don't.

Rufus Wainwright, he says, do you remember?

Of course I remember, she says.

I'd already noticed you, he says. You were sitting outside on the steps in your Pixies T-shirt and Levi's, drinking a bottle of beer. I smiled at you on my way in.

She sighs. She doesn't want to hear this, doesn't want to remember how she had noticed him too, how she had smiled back. She saw him again after the support act, standing at the bar. She walked over and leaned against him as if they were already lovers. His unfazed smile, his beard back then, his black T-shirt and denim jacket.

Whisky? was the first thing he said to her.

Go on then, was the first thing she said back. With Coke, she said.

Their glasses clinked.

Are you here with someone? she said.

She couldn't make it, he said. What about you?

Just me, she said.

That night, as he walked her home, she pulled him close and kissed him under a street lamp, and up in a flat nearby a woman wolf-whistled from an open window, and when they stopped kissing they waved to this woman, and their waving was exuberant and silly.

25.

She has gone and he is alone and she wouldn't say where she was going.

It's best if you don't know, she said. You'll only want to turn up, send me intense letters, try and change my mind, I know you.

But what about your post? he said.

I've set up forwarding.

That was very organised of you, but what about all the closing bills, all the practical shit?

Text me the amounts and I'll transfer them, she said.

Then she kissed him.

Their kiss was long, he could taste her tears.

26.

April does not clear his head.

27.

Fuck dancing, Daniel thinks. Fuck camper vans, fuck the sea, fuck our favourite B&B. Fuck artisan bread, fuck the holiday postcard she left by the bed, fuck this lavender hand soap, fuck this scented candle, fuck fennel toothpaste, fuck Christmas and New Year, fuck our favourite cafe, fuck our favourite cinema, fuck the dangerous notion of shared favourite things. Fuck that song she used to sing in the shower, fuck that little Italian restaurant, fuck avocados, fuck champagne, fuck this orange scarf, fuck sex, fuck sex forever if not with her, fuck this bed, fuck this duvet cover, fuck this blanket, fuck I can still see her dozing on this sofa, fuck her handwriting in these books, fuck country music, fuck love, fuck these letters and cards, fuck anyone ever accepting me, fuck buying a house, fuck houses, fuck arguing in Ikea, fuck the smell of her on this unwashed pillow, fuck ever washing this pillow, fuck this lovely swimming pool painting, fuck all these ink pens, fuck this stomach ache, fuck clambering over the shock of every morning, fuck getting out of bed, fuck taking a shower, fuck my tidiness, fuck painting other people's happy homes, fuck the future, fuck *everything*. Well, apart from bees, obviously. Apart from puffins and hawks. Apart from hares and otters, and all animals in general actually, and all flowers and trees, all the oceans, rivers, ponds and streams. Oh for God's sake fuck this too, *my undefeatable hope*. Fuck how you could throw me face down in a ditch and I'd end up admiring a beetle, see it scuttling past my wide eyes, its hard shell lifting to reveal a second pair of wings – soft, translucent, open to the world.

28.
There is a voice that sounds like his, speaking on the phone.

He has no memory of finding a number or making a decision.

I have a house full of stuff, do you want it? the voice says. Thing is, it'll have to be this week.

29.
He says goodbye to the pink woodshed, the flowers and plants and all the empty rooms.

Then he locks the door, posts the keys through the letterbox.

It's over.

He is a walking bruise with a rucksack on its back.

After only a few steps he turns around and walks back to the cottage.

He peers through the front window, looks through the letterbox.

What am I doing.

He sits on the front step and falls asleep in the sun.

Forgot your key, Daniel? a neighbour says.

That's right, he says.

You got long to wait until Erica gets home? You can come in if you like.

That's okay, he says. I'm just heading out for a walk actually.

The neighbour looks bemused, he wanders up to his house and gets out his keys. Daniel can hear him calling *hello* as he steps inside and closes the door.

So where now, Daniel?

30.

This place, honestly, it's something else. Aubrey's is no ordinary charity shop. It's like a shifting work of art, a museum, a theatre set; it's inexpensive, properly useful, you really should pay a visit. He and Erica used to come here a lot, searching for second-hand gems, although she preferred brand new. The staff here, mainly volunteers, are brilliant. He has often watched them clean and dust donations before thoughtfully placing them in living rooms and bedrooms that no one will ever use. It's fun just seeing the latest arrivals – all the glassware, the pictures, the retro sideboards. And there's a sadness here too, because someone has often died, and here are the objects they lived with every day – a toaster barely used, a precious memento, a retirement clock.

What is this, a bloody sales pitch, Daniel? One minute you're suicidal, then you're asleep, now you're having good feelings of admiration for a hospice charity project. Your head is strange weather.

He wanders around, picks things up and puts them

down. If someone had told him this would comfort him, he wouldn't have believed them.

Then, he stops.

Erica, look. That's our sofa, our armchair, our coffee table.

He sits on their sofa and waits.

31.

He thinks for a long time about everything they did on this sofa.

And Erica feels so close.

She is almost right here.

32.

Before he leaves Aubrey's, something on a bookcase catches his eye. It's something they once bought together. A stupid ornament, that's all. A small ceramic sheep, on sale for £2.50.

He buys it.

Afterwards he marches up a steep hill and sits at the top with the sheep beside him on the grass.

Well this is a bit of a palaver, the sheep says.

And the wind gets up.

And Daniel stands, lifts his arms and stretches them sideways, his hands flat, palms down. He pictures himself being lifted off the ground and blown through the air like a tree uprooted by a storm.

He lowers his arms, and for some reason now he thinks of Antony Gormley's *Another Place*, all those cast-iron figures on Crosby Beach, copies of the artist's own body facing out to sea. He and Erica went to see them, and the sight of them late evening as the light began to fade had made him tearful.

They look so alone out there, so vulnerable, he said. The tide comes and goes, and they can't walk away. It's like watching men contemplate suicide.

That's so depressing, she said, her voice higher and thinner than usual.

He turned to look at her.

I don't think it's meant to be *upsetting*, she said. They wouldn't have installed it here would they, if they thought it was going to upset people.

Well, we all bring something of ourselves to art don't we, he said.

Exactly, she said.

Now he looks down at the ceramic sheep.

You gave me away, the sheep says.

I know, I'm so sorry, Daniel says. I shouldn't have done that. But I got you back again, didn't I.

They sit in silence for a while, shock-slow, companionable.

So it's just you and me now? the sheep finally says.

That's right, Daniel says.

I wish we could just go home, eat a mushroom pie and listen to some Amy Winehouse, the sheep says.

Me too, Daniel says. Me too.

Ella Fitzgerald

A song is playing inside the pocket of Rae's denim skirt.

What's that? a woman says.

Sorry, it's my phone, Rae says.

Is that the Beatles?

Uh huh. 'I'm Only Sleeping'. It's my mother's ringtone, so I know when to ignore it.

Why that song?

It's one of her favourites. Anyway, where were we? Rae says.

They are in Angie's, a cafe not far from SOM. 'Brilliant Mind' is playing in the background. Whenever they sip from their mochas, a trace of dark chocolate smile gets left behind. They are oblivious to these cocoa curves, intensifying as they drink, betraying their pensiveness.

Rae is interviewing a potential Stranger, asking why this, why now, what can Jelly bring to the role.

And yes, her name is Jelly. They have covered this topic already, how Jelly's parents were, how can Jelly put this, well, basically loopy. Not loopy as in mad, Jelly was keen to explain at the start of her interview. But loopy with contentment, you know? Like, silly with joy. Anyway, I prefer to be called Jenny, she said.

So why SOM? Rae says.

Well, it's the most fascinating job isn't it, meeting new people all the time, going to different places. And Sally Canto is a rock star, Jenny says.

A rock star?

Absolutely.

Why do you say that?

Jenny shrugs. It's her vibe, she says. I think she's going to reshape the zeitgeist. She was actually the subject of my MA dissertation. Not Sally herself as such, but her philosophy, her writings, a sort of sociological perspective.

Really? You didn't put that in your application.

I didn't want to appear sycophantic.

Interesting.

What is.

Rae sits back in her chair. Wouldn't it have made you look informed, passionate, well suited? she says. But instead you chose to preserve your aloofness. Such a curious decision.

The song playing now is 'Nothing's Gonna Hurt You Baby'. Rae knows this track from the office Spotify playlist, it's by Cigarettes After Sex. This is one of the surprising aspects of her new job, all the music she's being introduced to. Another surprising aspect is how much she enjoys mornings like this: drinking coffee and interviewing potential Strangers. Demand is soaring and there are never enough. The candidates so far have been much better than today's, and less intimidatingly hip, less edgy – look at her sitting there in her crumpled khaki jacket, all those badges with cryptic slogans, all that choppy hair. It takes a certain maturity to be a Stranger of Mine, and this one doesn't have it.

Preserve my aloofness? Jenny says. I like that.

Do you? Rae says.

Yeah, Jenny says, looking super intense now, even more intense than before.

So what's your biggest weakness? Rae says.

Before her interviewee can answer, her phone rings again.

It's your mother, Jenny says.

For God's sake, Rae says.

The screen of her iPhone tells her she's had two missed calls, two iMessages and a WhatsApp, all from Sherry Marsh.

Something might be wrong, Jenny says.

It won't be.

How do you know?

Never is. She's overdramatic.

But what if this time something *is* wrong?

Rae lays her phone face down on the table. This is actually a useful moment, she says, then pauses. She looks out of the window.

How is it useful? Jenny says.

So, Rae says, imagine you're sitting with a client whose phone keeps ringing. What would you do?

I'd ask if they want to answer it, Jenny says.

See, that's not the ideal response.

Why not?

It's intrusive. If they want to answer it, they will. You can't pass comment or judgement like you did with me.

I wasn't judging you.

I think maybe you were.

No, Rae Marsh, I really wasn't.

Rae is slightly thrown by this use of her full name, which must be some kind of psychological technique.

First you asked why I have that song as my mother's ringtone, then you implied that I was neglectful for not answering my phone, she says. I'm interviewing *you* here, there's a particular dynamic to adhere to. And that's the very essence of working for SOM: adhering to a particular dynamic.

Jenny crosses her arms. You're smart, she says.

Which throws Rae again. That wasn't what she expected.

I could learn a lot from you, Jenny says.

Well, Rae says. While that is of course true –

Jenny laughs. Yes? she says.

Rae can't finish her sentence. She is easily destabilised by flattery, which is what often happens when you haven't had much of it. And it's nice, being destabilised by flattery, like being set loose on a marvellous new bike and taking your hands off the handlebars and lifting them in the air and feeling on top of this wonderful world.

Snap out of it, Rae. These waves of happiness are not yours to surf.

But why not, she thinks. Why shouldn't I feel happy in a real, unimagined world, like other people sometimes do?

Shall I get us both another drink, Jenny says. Another mocha?

Rae can't help but be impressed by her nonchalance, by her deft manoeuvres, by the confidence of this woman called Jelly who prefers to be called Jenny, whose parents were loopy with contentment.

Maybe she *would* fit in well at SOM, Rae thinks.

Witness the transfer of power.

Witness Rae Marsh having fun.

Yes, *fun*.

On her way back to the office, Rae walks along with her jacket over her shoulder, her finger through its tag. This is a first, a novelty, an original moment in the life of Rae Marsh, who would normally drape her jacket over the strap of her bag and carry it that way. Quite often, a sleeve would drag along the floor, get dirty. Strolling like this today, she feels false and conspicuous, like she is playing a part, drawing attention to herself. Which she isn't. People are too absorbed in their own lives to notice her. Mostly, the people walking towards her look like they are talking to themselves, thanks to hidden wireless headphones. Rae can't get used to how this looks, and refuses to wear the SOM earbuds given to her by Sally. If you're in conversation with another person, she said, you should not appear to be talking to yourself – it's disrespectful to people who hear voices, who've been unfairly stigmatised. Sally thought about this for a long time. Would you be willing to write an article on that? she said. No, Rae said, not *everything* can be turned into an article, Sally. Which made Sally laugh. Are you aware that the word you say most is *no*? she said. And you never explain, apologise, try to soften your no. It's blunt and simple. I find that very endearing. You're a winsome creature.

Rae remembers this now as she walks in the sun. She had never been called endearing before, let alone winsome. She didn't actually know what winsome meant. You win some you lose some, she said, to deflect attention from the mysterious word and her inadequate vocabulary. Which made Sally laugh again. So far, this was *their* particular dynamic: Sally making demands, Rae pushing back; Sally finding Rae either fascinating or funny, Rae quite oblivious to both.

As she approaches SOM HQ, and sees Pam sitting at the reception desk, Rae remembers her phone, her mother's calls and texts.

iMessage: *You free to talk, Rae? xXx*

Second iMessage: *Hellooooooooooooo? xxx*

WhatsApp: *Guess who's upstairs in our bath!*

Rae squints at her iPhone, wonders if she can face a conversation with her mother. Who is in her parents' bath? She doesn't want to know. She does want to know. Her mother evokes uncertainty like no one else.

Pam is waving. She is enthusiasm personified, queen of the warm welcome, perfectly suited to her job. Rae waves back. She holds her phone to the window and points at it, to justify why she is remaining outside. Pam looks confused, but no less enthusiastic.

And Rae calls her mother.

Darling, Sherry says.

Just returning your call, Rae says. Everything all right?

Of course, Sherry says. How are things with you?

Fine, Rae says. So who's in your bath?

Try and guess.

Guess?

You used to love playing Guess Who? didn't you.

You're thinking of Pauline, not me. And I'm at work, Mum.

I keep forgetting you now have a job.

I had a job before.

If you're working in pyjamas are you really working? Sherry says. Anyway just try, try and guess, go on.

All right, Rae says. Is it a man?

Yes it is.

And is this a man you know?

Sort of, in a way.

Rae sighs. This is ridiculous. But also slightly enjoyable. When did she and her mother last play a silly game? The answer is never.

And he needed to use your bath, Rae says. So has this man had some kind of accident?

No.

Is his electricity off?

Sort of.

So he has no power.

That's very perceptive actually.

Is this man one of your neighbours?

Oh you're good, darling. He was, a long time ago.

Rae is no longer interested. An ex-neighbour, one of her parents' old friends – how disappointing. She makes a mental note to never call her mother during the working day.

Mum, I'm really busy, just tell me will you? I really haven't memorised all your neighbours from over the years.

It's little Daniel Berry, her mother says.

And Sherry's voice is different when she says his name.

And Rae's voice is different when she says his name.

Little Daniel Berry? she says.

Her mother doesn't answer. Because the boy is with her now, he must have come into the room, all clean and dressed after his bath. Rae expects to hear a small voice, quiet and a bit nervous, but the voice in the background is deep and warm.

You'll never guess who I'm talking to, her mother says to Daniel. Go on, see if you can guess.

Daniel takes a long hot bath, and the room is hazy with steam, and the bottle of bubble bath has John Lennon's face on it, and it feels from this bath that something geographical is happening, or maybe geological, something along the lines of tectonic plates shifting, and he imagines this bath perched on top of a tall mountain, and then it begins to snow, and everything falls soft and quiet, and the bath slides gleefully down the side of this mountain, slides through fields, villages and cities, he is tobogganing in bubbly bathwater, his mind has no borders, it's a strange and soapy ride, and he remembers his mum and Sherry always laughing in the kitchen downstairs, and how Leslie once taught him how to paint a garden shed, and all of them one winter night throwing snowballs at each other, and he wonders how many Beatles songs have the word *love* in their title, it must be a big number, and it really is nice, just being in this bath.

There is a pile of Leslie's clothes on the chair in the corner.

These clothes smell exceptionally good.

He smells them for a long time before putting them on.

Then he wanders quickly through the house, peers around the door of each room.

He can hear Sherry on her phone in the kitchen as he steps into the lounge.

Everything looks different, except for one thing.

Hello old friend, he says to Franklin's painting.

He moves closer to the peaches, oranges and pears, to all the bread and cheese, the bottle of sherry, then the dancer on the label of the bottle.

His mum had loved this painting. Does something of a person's love stay with an object long after the person has gone?

I thought they would've given you away, he says. But all this time, they kept you.

The painting doesn't reply.

Its silence as majestic as a mountain covered with snow.

Rae doesn't usually say yes when her mother invites her for dinner, let alone at short notice. But this time, it isn't technically her mother she has said yes to. Her yes is for little Daniel Berry, the boy who has reappeared after thirty years.

Rae can remember them leaving. She had been watching through the dining room window when Eve drove away like a boy racer, loud and fast, *gone*. He won't cope with this, her father said. He'll twitch and rhyme all the way. All the way to where? Rae said, floppy as a rag doll, all the life in her gone with Eve. She felt sorry for herself, and for her dad too, he looked so pale and weary, not himself at all. The state of him clearly upset her mother, or maybe she was worried about Daniel, either way she took to her bed and slept all afternoon.

Their house fell solemn and silent. Even Pauline stopped making her usual noises, all that babbling and mysterious grunting.

Then, shockingly, their father took up bowling.

You can't, you're only just fifty, Rae heard her mother say.

I need a new focus, he said. Now the boy has gone.

Honey, you do have children of your own. Isn't that focus enough?

*

246

The boy is back.

Here he is at the dining room table, eating roast chicken.

And look at her father now, soft and giddy for the boy.

This boy is forty years old. And fancy that. Seems odd to think of him ageing at the same rate as everyone else.

But maybe he didn't. Age is complicated isn't it, multiple, shifting, concealed. We are all the ages we have ever been, all the time and none of the time.

And so, Daniel, what the hell's going on? Rae thinks. Why are you sitting here like an uprooted plant, wearing Dad's fleece and tracksuit bottoms? And where exactly is your mum? *Tell me right now.*

Her father has put on one of his Ella Fitzgerald records, which he always does when he is in a good mood.

Right now, 'It's Only a Paper Moon' is playing.

More chicken, Daniel? Sherry says. Mashed potato, veg, gravy?

Yes please, he says.

Tall candles, yet to be lit. Red wine, sitting warm inside a shiny padded coat, the one Leslie puts in the microwave whenever they have red wine.

Thanks so much for dinner, it's really lovely, Daniel says.

Not at all, Leslie says.

The Marshes are full of questions, each of them poised with a different set, wanting to shine a light on Daniel, interrogate until he breaks.

But the boy is already broken. This much is obvious solely from his eyes. He is like a deer poised in a dark lane, just standing there waiting, half petrified of the oncoming car, half resigned to its fate.

No one has mentioned Eve, and the longer this goes on, the harder it becomes to speak her name. They are colluding in her absence, which is growing more conspicuous, poignant, by the minute.

So where do you work? Daniel says to Rae. I mean, what do you do?

She's the newly appointed *head of process*, Sherry says.

Rae rolls her eyes. I work for SOM, she says. Stranger of Mine. I don't know if you've heard of it.

No, sorry.

It's a bit *out there*, Leslie says.

Not really, Dad, Rae says.

She's practically the CEO, Sherry says. Only started a few weeks ago. Head hunted, weren't you. Which sounds funny doesn't it, the idea of someone out hunting for heads.

SOM is an anti-familiarity project, Rae says.

Okay, Daniel says.

Did she say anti-inflammatory? he thinks.

The idea is, it's good for our brains when we socialise with strangers, spend time with people who aren't like us, she says. And also, sometimes we just want some company without all the pressures of making new attachments or being with people we know.

He thinks you work for a contemporary brothel, Sherry says.

No he doesn't, Rae says. Do you?

I don't know, Daniel says. I mean, I haven't heard that phrase before, contemporary brothel. It's sort of catchy.

It's not a brothel, Rae says. It's completely non-sexual.

The perfect place for you to work, darling, Sherry says.

Mother, please, Rae says. She looks back at Daniel. Clients can hire one of our Strangers to accompany them on walks, to the cinema, or just to have a chat with over coffee, she says. Did you know that thousands of people regularly type the words *help me* into Google? It's a fact. So instead of doing that, they can use our app on their phones to hire someone non-judgemental.

Rae stops talking. She has exhausted herself with that long description. Coming here is always exhausting. Her parents have the same physical impact on her as a long-haul flight. She drinks her wine and waits for Daniel's response. He is obviously digesting what he has heard, his face looks busy.

So, he says, it's sort of like therapy, without all the boundaries.

Not really, Rae says. The Strangers aren't therapists.

It's for people with too much disposable income and no friends, Leslie says. But they're heavily involved in dementia research, so that's good.

Rae sighs. This isn't the first time she has found herself wishing she hadn't told her parents about SOM. She should have let them think she was still a copywriter.

It sounds really interesting, Daniel says. And very modern.

Modern? Rae thinks. Forty going on eighty, this one. Honestly, I thought *I* was behind the times.

She remembers how he hugged her when she walked in this evening. How unexpected and touching that was.

What about you? she says, wondering how to formulate the second part of her question, how to ask about his life in general. How do you, um, spend your days?

They all turn to face him.

Ooh well done, Sherry thinks. Now we can get some proper information. I knew it was a good idea to invite you.

Well, he says. I'm in a bit of a weird place right now, a bit of a hole. But generally, I'm a painter and decorator.

Oh heck, Leslie says. We haven't decorated this place for years. Try not to look too closely, especially at the hallway.

Daniel smiles. I love that wallpaper, always did. It's lasted well hasn't it?

It's peeling off, Rae says. Anyway, you said you're in a *hole*?

That's right, he says, pushing a large slice of chicken onto his fork, then into his mouth.

Leslie's foot touches Rae's under the table. Leave it, the foot says. Don't rush him.

So, Sherry thinks. All we know so far is this: he looks like his mother, he's been sleeping rough, he decorates houses, his girlfriend left him, he likes roast chicken, he is reserved, polite, and he still illuminates my husband. And this is something else she knows, that some people just brighten us, they are light to our shade no matter what.

I'm so glad you turned up, she says. It's wonderful to be able to use our dining table again.

Sorry? Daniel says.

I had my jigsaw on it, Leslie says.

Oh no, you needn't have put it away for me. I would happily have eaten on my lap. What was it?

The Last Supper, Leslie says.

Leonardo da Vinci, Daniel says. What an excellent choice of jigsaw.

I bought it for him last month, for his eightieth, Rae says.

You're never eighty, Leslie. You can't be.

Only on paper. You like jigsaws, do you?

Of course, who doesn't?

Well we should do some later, before bed. You can sleep in Rae's old room.

250

Really? Rae thinks.

No, honestly, that's not necessary, Daniel says. I just wanted to see you, to see if you were still here. I didn't expect you to take me in, I don't want to impose.

Don't be silly, Leslie says. You can stay with us for as long as you like. We have plenty of room, just take your time.

He makes this offer before discussing it with his wife, doesn't care if she minds.

Daniel's shoulders drop. He hadn't realised how high they had been, how the words *take your time* would unhook them. He aches all over, from his blistered feet to his sunburnt ears.

Anyone for cheesecake? Leslie says.

Nodding heads, yes please, lovely.

Over cheesecake there is further discussion of jigsaws, and Ella Fitzgerald, the resurgence of vinyl, how Sherry and Leslie have taken up speed-walking, how Sherry has a mobile kitchen called Dolly's, which she owns with a friend who is obsessed with Dolly Parton. Like a burger van? Daniel says. Goodness no, this is a *mobile kitchen*, Daniel, we're known for our quality ingredients, we do gluten-free, vegan, all that malarkey. We used to run a cafe but the rent was so high we took it on the road. You can come out with me one morning, if you like.

Coffee? Leslie says, standing up. But I warn you, Daniel, I make it strong.

Daniel loves how they keep using his name. It makes him feel real, less papery, less sketchy.

Leslie returns with a cafetière, a box of After Eights and a plate of chocolate biscuits shaped like animals. Over his shoulder, he is carrying a pink woolly blanket.

Are you cold, Daniel? he says, putting down the tray. It's just that you look a bit shivery, I think, like maybe you have a virus. He walks around the table, lays the blanket across Daniel's shoulders, followed by his big hands, just for a second or two. There, he says. It's lambswool, from M&S.

And the weight of Leslie's hands on his shoulders.

Daniel will feel it through these clean clothes.

He will feel it through pyjamas.

He will feel it through painter's overalls, a smart suit on his wedding day, the same smart suit on the saddest day.

He will feel it through all the years ahead of him, and all the years behind him as they surface like a dream.

These people are so sweet, so trusting, he thinks. They don't even know me. It makes him want to howl again. He summons every ounce of strength to hold it back, to say thank you that's very kind.

Leslie changes the record, says how about something from the eighties now, for old times' sake?

No thank you, Sherry says.

More Ella then, he says, as though Ella Fitzgerald has nothing to do with old times, as if she's as modern and alive and relevant as ever, which in so many ways she is.

So what happened with this Erica, if you don't mind me asking, Sherry says, tipsy now, less careful.

Erica? Rae says, as if her mother hasn't already told her everything.

My ex, he says, yawning. There's nothing to tell really. We were together and now we're not, end of.

Rae was supposed to be doing yoga with goats tonight, Leslie says, to change the subject, protect the boy.

Really? That sounds great, Daniel says. I love goats. Do they help with yoga?

They're more a fun hindrance than a help. The receptionist at work persuaded me to go. I think I quite like it, Rae says, surprised by her own words.

So *you've* missed yoga, and *you've* had to put away your jigsaw, Daniel says. I'm so sorry.

No, I wanted to come and see you, Rae says. The goats can wait. To be honest, I've often wondered about you and your mum.

Daniel glances at Sherry, just for a second.

I googled her once, Rae says.

Who? Sherry says.

Eve, Rae says.

And there it is, the actual word: *Eve*.

Why? Sherry says. Why would you do that?

And what did you find, Daniel says. The words *compulsive liar*?

Sorry?

That's what she is, I'm afraid. I don't want anything to do with her.

What? Rae says. Why not?

She's not a good person, let's put it that way, Daniel says.

Sherry feels sick, cold, terrified. She wants to grab the pink blanket and run.

Rae's mouth is wide open.

She lied to me, Daniel says. She's been lying for years, keeping secrets. But the truth always comes out, everyone knows that.

'Dream a Little Dream of Me' is playing now.

Leslie sips from a tiny cup of black coffee.

All of them, looking down. As if the boy in the turquoise fleece has placed a hand grenade on the table.

Which he has.

Daniel leans forward, picks up an elephant biscuit half coated in milk chocolate, dips it in his coffee.

It's a funny thing, the whole idea of truth, Leslie says. It's something I think about a lot.

Is it? Sherry says.

A lie doesn't make someone a bad person, Leslie says.

Oh really, Daniel says. Just wait until you hear the lie.

Ella Fitzgerald, glorious and soulful and melancholy and deep, is singing about April in Paris.

The record player sits on a long sideboard, beside a lamp with an abundance of tassels dangling from its shade.

Sometimes, life is all about the tassels.

Sometimes, life is all about hanging threads.

The lamp is now on, giving the room a reddish-brown tint like an old sepia photograph.

The tall candles have been lit.

It's late evening.

There are two men and two women, sitting at a dining table. They have eaten chicken and cheesecake, drunk a lot of wine, dipped animal-shaped biscuits into coffee.

One of the men has a pink woolly blanket draped over his shoulders and his eyes are closed.

Just wait until you hear the lie, this man said, before leaning back in his chair and falling asleep, as if this sentence had taken a toll on him, knocked him out.

Now the people who are not asleep are watching him.

Oh, Rae says. Has he actually dropped off?

He's exhausted, Leslie says.

Probably hasn't had a big meal for a while, Sherry says.

They feel like visitors around a hospital bed, waiting for the patient's eyes to open.

Each of them has a different set of feelings about the patient waking up.

Sherry: Let him sleep all night and all through tomorrow. When the secret comes out I'll deny it. I'll call it fake news. No one knows what's true and what isn't any more. Then, I'll stage a medical emergency.

Leslie: What does the boy need, what can we do?

Rae: Eve's not a bad person, she would never lie. Wake up and explain yourself! And why must Dad keep calling you a boy? You're a fully grown man, responsible for your actions and words, your misunderstandings and messes. The urge to slap you awake is so strong, my hand is tingling.

What did you find when you googled Eve? Sherry says.

She teaches anatomy at the University of Edinburgh, Rae says.

She doesn't, Leslie says.

She does.

Well I never. She must've gone back to school.

Well obviously, Rae says. For a *long* time. Years and years, probably.

She's in Edinburgh, Sherry says to no one.

Why has that made you cry? Rae says.

I don't know, Sherry says. It's just weird isn't it, knowing where she is.

Not really, Rae says.

They sit in silence, looking at the man, the boy, the stranger, their trampish old friend, who has now become what exactly, apart from a shadowy figure stepping across the years, pulling at loose threads.

Rae's foot accidentally on purpose juts out.

The man in the turquoise fleece opens his eyes.

Oh my God, he says. Was I? I mean, did I –

256

It's fine, Leslie says, I do it all the time, sometimes in the middle of a sentence.

You dissociated, Rae says. That's my theory.

Do you think that's what *I* do? Leslie says.

Nah, you're just old, Rae says. Then she turns back to Daniel. You were telling us about your mum, she says. How you thought she'd lied.

I didn't *think* she'd lied. She had.

About what? Rae says.

Daniel is foggy and sore. He shuffles about in his chair, straightens his back, tries to stretch himself fully awake, fully here and now in Abigail Gardens, May 2018, the month that is neither agonising April nor disgusting March nor treacherous fucking February.

It all began in February, he says.

And Leslie leans forward, because he can't remember the last time someone told him a good story.

Which, for the record, Daniel says, was one big shit-show from start to finish. Excuse my language, Leslie.

You're excused, Leslie says. Do remember, I live with the biggest fishwife, so I hear much worse on a daily basis.

Less of the *big,* please, Sherry says, lightened by the phrase Daniel just used, *it all began in February,* which can't be anything to do with her and Eve, who began mid-summer, the moment they met across a garden fence, they always said that was when they began. This is not about me, she thinks. Which quite possibly is a thought she has never had before.

Treacherous February began like any other February, cold and easy.

Daniel turned the page on the kitchen calendar, which was something he always enjoyed doing.

Erica said her usual thing about preferring to use iCal on her phone these days.

And wasn't it just typical that he wasn't even there when it all started to go wrong. He was in their local Tesco Express. Erica had sent him out for gluten-free bread, said she was feeling bloated. And while he was gone, there was a knock at the door.

There was a woman, in her eighties probably, soaked from the rain. Does Daniel Berry live here? she said.

He does, Erica said. He's not here right now, can I help?

May I come in? the woman said, glancing up at the falling rain.

I'm sorry, I don't know who you are, Erica said.

My name is Gail Berry. I'm Daniel's grandmother.

Oh, Erica said. But –

And you are? the woman claiming to be Gail Berry said.

I'm Erica, Daniel's girlfriend. I'm afraid he doesn't have a grandmother, so –

Well what am I, an apparition? the woman claiming to be Gail Berry said.

He doesn't have any family apart from his mother. I'm so sorry, I know it's raining but I can't let a complete stranger in.

The woman claiming to be Gail Berry said this was very rude. His mother's name is Eve, she said. She ran off with Daniel soon after he was born. I wanted to find them but my husband wouldn't let me. And now I'm a widow. A drenched widow. I hired a private detective and have travelled for miles by train and I didn't bring an umbrella. So there we are. May I *please* come in?

Oh God, Erica said.

She made tea, fetched towels, offered Gail Berry a dressing gown while she dried her clothes.

It's fine, Gail said, I'm not a fan of dressing gowns.

Okay, Erica said, wondering if there's any such thing as a person who would call themselves a fan of dressing gowns, and if so, would they wear them all the time, day and night, indoors and outdoors.

I'll just sit by the radiator, Gail said. What's that accent of yours, are you Australian?

That's right, Erica said, as she switched on the heating.

Gail seemed to be chewing this over, the fact of Erica being Australian, and was clearly finding it unpalatable.

Erica texted Daniel: *Where are you? Someone's here for you X*

He texted back: *I'm waiting for a teenager to bring out some gluten-free bread. None on the shop floor. Want anything else? xXx*

Just hurry home, someone is here to see you x

Are you playing a naughty game?! XXXXX

NO.

Who is it?

Bring Maltesers and a lemon cake.

Who is this sweet-toothed person?! Your bread is here, it's bloody expensive, we should make our own really xXx

He won't be long, Erica said.

So was she really your grandmother? Rae says.

She was, Daniel says.

And could you tell, as soon as you saw her?

That's him, Erica said, relieved to hear Daniel's key turning in the door.

Gail Berry, if that was her real identity, had been talking about Jason Donovan for the past ten minutes.

They both stood to greet him.

Gail had wrapped a towel around her head and her little green cardigan was damp around the shoulders. Daniel, she said.

He handed his David Hockney tote bag to Erica. Who's this? he said.

I'm Gail Berry, the stranger said, holding out a tiny hand.

Sorry, who?

I'm your grandmother, dear.

My what?

I'm sorry to just turn up. I probably should have called, but I hate the telephone, it does nothing for me.

Daniel looked at Erica, who was looking at Gail Berry. This was the first time he had ever heard that name.

Do you have any proof of identity? he said.

She rifled through her handbag for her bus pass.

This wasn't really what I meant, he said. It says Gail Berry obviously, but that doesn't mean you're my grandmother.

Blimey, you're a tough nut, she said. Just like your mother.

What would you know about my mum? he said.

Well I did bring her up, she said.

So how old is she now? he said.

Eve will now be fifty-six.

And what year was I born?

Oh that one's easy, it's imprinted on my mind. The year I lost my daughter and grandchild was 1978.

Gail Berry removed the towel from her head with a wild flourish as if the truth was held beneath it. But there was no truth, only white hair, curly and damp.

That gesture, the way she threw the towel on the floor for no good reason apart from a sense of personal drama, a moment of intensity –

Bloody hell, he said. You're my grandmother?

He picked up the towel from the floor and hung it on the back of a chair, because the Berrys may be intense creatures, but they are also very sensible.

They drank tea, ate lemon cake, Gail told them about her husband, Roger, who apparently had a good heart until it failed him during an episode of *Midsomer Murders*, and you mustn't think badly of him, he thought it best if we left things alone, left you and your mother alone. Can you imagine having a child who turns against you from day one, scrappy little thing she was, not quite right. Roger was buried in December on a misty morning, just a small funeral, but that's what you get when it's flu season.

Couldn't you have found us anyway? Daniel said. If it meant that much to you, why didn't you just try?

You don't understand, she said. He wouldn't have liked that at all. And where would I have said I was going?

Gail Berry was frail but loud. Daniel swayed between liking and loathing, believing and disbelieving. Was this how his mum had felt as a child?

Is Eve really a professor? Gail said. I can't imagine that being possible.

She is, Erica said, which startled Gail and Daniel. She had been so quiet until now. Edinburgh, she said. But she's in New York for a year, working on a project.

Erica, Daniel said. He was angry with his mother, but he felt protective too; something about Gail Berry made him want to hide Eve's whereabouts, keep her safe.

What? Erica said.

It's all right, I already know, Gail said. The investigator was good, and so he should've been for that amount of money. But I wasn't quite sure he'd got that bit right.

Which bit? Daniel said.

The part about Eve being a professor. She left school at sixteen, she was never a high-flyer. She was always a bit scratchy, emotionally unstable. We knew she wasn't fit to be a mother. We told her we'd look after you, bring you up as our own, while she got on with her life.

I beg your pardon? Daniel said.

She ran off with you from the hospital, Gail said. Hours after you were born. You never even came home.

No she didn't, Daniel said.

I'm not joking. She said she'd make sure we never found you. It worried us sick, how she'd make ends meet, put a roof over a baby's head. Especially with her being unwell, mentally speaking.

Why didn't you go to the police?

She wasn't a missing person, Daniel. She just cut us off. Got one of her teachers to pass on a message. *Leave me alone*, it said. Broke my heart. Bet she didn't tell you that, did she. She's selective with the truth, my daughter.

Her teacher? Daniel said.

That's right, Feegensomething. She was a rampant feminist.

Erica laughed.

She was in with a dodgy crowd, your mother. She was always running around with an awful girl called Robbie, who dressed as a boy.

I don't like the sound of Gail, Rae says.

Shh, Leslie says.

Daniel could hear his mother's voice: *They're monsters. We're better off without them.*

What's true and what isn't?

All these years we could have known each other, his grandmother said.

There was a clicking, coming from Daniel's throat.

You all right? Erica said.

Daniel blinked hard.

Kitten-boy in a potato sack, pillar to post on a scratchy girl's back.

Why would his mum lie, tell him his grandparents hadn't wanted to know him? It made no sense.

Enough of this, Daniel said. You need to leave, I need to speak to Mum. Can you give me your phone number?

You want me to go? Gail said. I've only just got here. I thought I could stay for a few days. Erica won't mind, will you, dear?

Stay *here*? Daniel said.

Yes.

No, I'm sorry. Can you go? I need you to go.

Daniel, Erica said. She's come all the way from Derby on the train.

To tell me my mum's a mentally unstable liar, he said. I'm sorry, Gail, but getting on a train, turning up unannounced, to say something like that. I think you're the unstable one.

When she had gone, he slammed the front door and stood in the shock of everything she had told him.

What the hell's wrong with you? Erica said. She's an old woman, she's travelled for miles, where's she supposed to go? Jesus, Daniel. Why did you have to be so rude to her?

Erica pushed all the kitchen chairs back under the table. The chairs scraped against the floor, made a sound they had never made before, like furniture in pain, like damage being done.

Out in the garden, Daniel saw a robin hop along the fence and fly away.

In a dining room in East Anglia, Ella Fitzgerald and Louis Armstrong are singing 'A Foggy Day'.

No one is listening.

Because Daniel is telling a story.

And Leslie, Sherry and Rae are wholly tuned in, he has their wholehearted attention.

And he can feel it.

As he speaks, he feels more and more awake.

Good listening will do this to a person.

So there you go, he says when the story is done. The one about a visitor, soaked from the rain.

Eve is in New York? Sherry says.

Which isn't the response he expected. Of all the things he had just said, surely his mum being in America was the least shocking part?

Yes, he says.

But Daniel, Leslie says. All that stuff about your mum being a liar, it simply wasn't true.

It was, he says. It was.

New York

A man's face appears on the screen of a woman's laptop.

This man is the woman's son.

In the place where the laptop sits, it's 3pm.

In the place where the man sits, it's 8pm.

And there is something quite fitting about this woman and this man being in different time zones, about them being oceans apart.

Anger is a rare sight on this man. He is usually mild, either smiling or on the verge of a smile, but not this evening, not this afternoon. He is flushed, fuming, a red-hot version of himself, full of accusations.

She wants to turn down the volume, click the little minus sign, send him floating to the bottom of her screen.

Did you or did you not, he is saying. Run away with me, lie.

She stares at her laptop as if she is watching TV, some horrible show, nothing to do with her. And this sense of distance, is it the shock of his words? Or is it because he is digital, one step removed, thousands of steps removed.

Inside his rant there are two hard facts:

1. Her father has died.

2. Her mother has finally found Daniel, her grown-up son, her baby.

Fact number 1 hits her with unexpected force. And after that, it's impossible to gauge the impact of fact number 2, the thing she always feared and ran from, here right now like a mouse with a giant shadow.

She says nothing, what can she say.

I feel like the rug's been pulled from under my feet, her son shouts.

And she thinks about this, about the idea of security as underfoot tapestry. Who made that rug in the first place, Daniel? Who worked night and day to bring it to life? And also, rugs wear out. They are by their very nature temporary, decorative, warming, soaking up sound. Rugs are not the earth itself. *I feel like the earth's been pulled from under my feet* is what you should have said if you wanted to convey real pain. Or, *what was solid is now liquid, what was fixed is now shifting*.

All the things he doesn't know and can never understand.

She plugs headphones into her computer, puts them on.

Now his presence is smaller. The sound of him no longer fills her apartment.

How could you do this? he is saying. Tell me I wasn't wanted. And did Anna know too? Answer me, Mum. *Say something*.

And now she enters another time zone. What she sees as he speaks from his evening into her afternoon, as he travels through time with only fury for luggage, is a boy in a faded yellow T-shirt. On the front of this T-shirt there is a smiling lion, mane like a cartoon flower all around its head. This boy is adorable. He has the kind of floppy hair that she always wanted to touch; it drove him mad, how she was always ruffling his hair. She would lift his T-shirt and kiss his belly, which also drove him mad, and sometimes made

268

him laugh, depending on his mood. He was beautiful, he was hers.

I fought for you, is all she wants to say.

Instead, she says nothing. And it seems on the surface that nothing is happening, she is so quiet and still, but look:

Her memory is building bridges all over this moment, and she crosses them happily, the here and now always the now and then.

In her own youth, she flew the nest for this boy. Scrappy, hungry, she pulled him close, migrated east.

What you've done is unforgivable, he says to her now. Don't contact me for a while, I need some space. I mean it, okay?

She takes off her headphones, puts her laptop on the coffee table.

She stands up, turns around.

She has her back to him now, she is walking towards the door.

Mum, he says. Where are you going?

Mum?

He is livid.

He crosses his arms and stares at the screen, at the empty space where his mother had been.

Only a sofa now, royal blue.

His mother has left her apartment, is walking to a cafe nearby.

And now there are two faces close together on the screen of her laptop.

– Has she cut you off?

– No, it's still on.

– Where is she? Is she still listening?

– I don't know. Mum, are you there?

– She's a strange one, your mum.

– Erica, shh.

– Just close it down.

– She might come back in a minute.

– I like her sofa, do you? Ours needs replacing.

– There's nothing wrong with our sofa.

– We've had it for five years, Dan.

– It still looks brand new.

– It's sagging a bit.

– No it's not. Jesus, how did we get onto this? I've just had a really upsetting conversation with Mum and now we're arguing about our sofa.

– We're not arguing, Dan, we're having a discussion. Stop being so overdramatic.

A man in a cafe in Greenwich Village is concerned about one of his favourite customers.

You okay, Eve? he says.

Had better days, she says.

Ah, well, I've got something that'll fix that, he says. And he brings her a large slice of lemon meringue pie. Made with love, he says.

She eats it while gazing out of the window, waiting for Niesha.

When Niesha arrives she tells her what happened, how her father is dead and words wouldn't come and Daniel will never forgive her.

Niesha listens with deep concentration, as she always does. She never looks away when there is trouble. Her loose grey T-shirt, her gold chain. Her hands, gentle and strong.

They walk with takeaway coffee by the river, the sky heavy with cloud.

And Eve wonders how much worse she would feel if they weren't together, if Niesha wasn't cooking her dinner tonight, if tomorrow they weren't meeting friends for breakfast, if this kiss right now wasn't simple and fierce.

She hopes Erica takes the edge off Daniel's pain.

She hopes he feels loved.

trippy

Daniel wakes to a bright room, sunshine streaming through a gap in the curtains.

He is in a saggy single bed, once occupied by Rae Marsh.

Aren't these curtains the ones his mother made? Brown with orange flowers, hideous but pleasing. He is sure he can remember her at the sewing machine, talking about orange flowers, talking about curtains for Rae.

Admirable, he thinks. Flowers at a window lasting thirty years, perfectly functional, not replaced merely for the sake of it.

The alarm clock beside his bed says 10:04.

He never sleeps this late, always wakes early.

The house is silent.

He gets out of bed, goes over to the window. He is at the front of the house, looking down at the street below.

How stupid to expect his mother, in her twenties, to be out in her front garden.

Their old bungalow is still standing, and there is a woman in its driveway, washing her car.

He watches her for a while.

Then the soft mumble of voices coming from downstairs.

He sits on the edge of the bed, takes a long deep breath, notices a change in his body. He has grown used to the quick beat of his heart, the tiny shakes in his face and hands, the frantic orchestra of his gut. Anxiety, the unhinged percussionist.

But this morning, for now, he is quiet.

Hello sleepyhead, Leslie says.

Morning, Daniel says. I'm sorry I slept for so long.

Don't be sorry. I'm just about to make coffee, would you like some?

Yes please, Daniel says.

And some toast? Leslie says. Or we have crumpets too. Actually, I quite fancy a crumpet myself.

You make the coffee, I'll do the crumpets, Daniel says.

Then you can help me with my jigsaw, Leslie says. I've set one up already, made a little start. To appease my dear wife, this one's the cover of a Beatles album.

They are halfway through their crumpets when the front door slams shut.

It's Rae. She bursts into the kitchen and drops two tote bags on the table.

Ooh lovely, I'll have a crumpet, she says, emptying her bags: a bunch of roses, a French stick, a pot of olives, some kind of cheese. Can I borrow your car today, Dad? she says, putting flowers in a vase, more crumpets in the toaster.

Why? he says. Where are you going?

I'm taking Daniel to the coast.

And does Daniel *want* to go to the coast? Leslie says. Maybe he's tired of being outside. Maybe he just wants to sit for a while, do a jigsaw.

Well I wasn't suggesting a long walk, Rae says. Just sitting on a blanket in the sun, listening to the waves. It's restorative.

Daniel wants to laugh, he doesn't know why.
Being here is easy and astonishing, uncannily normal.
Trippy.

He watches her collect four large pebbles. She shakes out her blanket, lets it flap in the air between them and drift down onto the sand. Then she places a pebble on each corner.

There, she says.

It's strangely moving, watching her make a place for them to sit, the way she arranges the pebbles so carefully.

She has brought a flask, a picnic, sunscreen, towels, more blankets, a newspaper and books. Even a first aid kit, she says. Because you never know what you're going to step on these days, cut my foot last time I was on a beach, blood everywhere.

Oh dear, he says, sitting down.

Behind them, reeds bend in the wind.

Knees to their chests, they watch the sea.

I haven't been here since you moved away, Rae says.

Really? Daniel says. But we used to come here all the time.

Mum took us to other beaches, but not this one.

Oh, he says. That's a bit odd.

Well, things were different after you left, she says.

She hugs her knees closer, listens to the waves, the seagulls, a laugh, a cough.

I never understood why you went, she says.

Guess that makes two of us, he says. But maybe it's like Gail said, Mum was messed up.

That's not how I remember her at all.

You probably saw a different side of her.

Maybe, Rae says. So what happened after you left? Dad said your mum sold all your things.

Oh, Daniel says. Well, Anna came and took some of it, for safekeeping.

Anna?

Auntie Fig, you remember, she used to come and stay.

Oh yes, Rae says. I'd forgotten about her.

But the rest of it was taken by some kind of house clearance company.

God, that must've been horrible. So where did you go?

Daniel lets sand run through his fingers. He pictures the motels, the bed and breakfasts, all the brown, purple and paisley, a tight perm behind a reception desk offering him a sticky lolly.

We just seemed to travel for ages, he says. It was awful.

Travel? Rae says.

He remembers how he had yelled at his mum: *I'm not going, I won't, I hate you.* But once they were on the road, his anger morphed into a frightening tiredness. She handed him a tin of boiled sweets and they drove for days. He felt like he had been stolen, snatched, kidnapped. He felt cold and damp, as if he had just been out in the rain and couldn't get dry, but there had been no rain. The car was dripping with tension, and all the trees they passed were dripping with tension, and the windows of all the houses were steamed up and dripping with tension.

We lived with another family for a while, he says.

Another family? Rae says, not liking this picture at all. Where? she says.

In Wales, he says, Pembrokeshire. They'd advertised in the local shop. We shared a room.

Who did?

Me and Mum, he says. To be honest, it's a blur. But I remember it flooding every time there was a storm. And there was a massive photo of John Wayne in the lounge.

I can't imagine anything worse than having to share a room with my mum, Rae says.

I don't think it was for too long, he says. We moved around a bit after that. We were in a caravan for about a year, that was quite fun. Mum was working as a cleaner in a holiday park. Eventually, Anna moved down, and we lived with her.

So life got better after that, Rae says.

He pictures himself as a teenage boy, always by the river, never at school.

He pictures himself and his mum playing cards in the evenings; he would make daft jokes, she wouldn't laugh, his need for her was nothing more than graffiti on the wall of her sadness.

Sort of, he says.

Rae is shaking her head.

What? he says.

Do you remember how our mums would drop us off at the library and leave us there by ourselves for a couple of hours? That would never happen nowadays.

I loved it, Daniel says. You were always hunched over old maps, hardly said a thing.

And you were always with Betty, she says.

Oh my God, I'd forgotten all about Betty, he says.

Chief librarian, Rae says. You were her favourite, she always gave you a Milkybar.

What can I say, I'm adorable, he says.

Yeah right, she says.

Did I tell you about the woman I met in the library? he says.

And she expects to hear a story about another ex-girlfriend, someone he met in the fiction aisle. Instead, in this story he is crying, he's sitting on the floor and a woman walks up to him, puts her hand on his shoulder.

That's why I came here, that's why I got on the train, he says. Seems I always meet good people in libraries.

For a while, Rae watches him sleep.

She sips tea from her flask and watches people walk along the beach, creep gingerly into the water, beckon each other in.

He sleeps for at least half an hour, twitching through his dreams. He looks innocent, childlike. She wonders if she also resembles a child when she sleeps, and if anyone has ever noticed.

Daniel's face, already pinkish brown from his days in the sun, is starting to redden. She squeezes sunscreen onto her fingers, rubs it over his cheek in small circles. She expects him to jump, be startled or cross, but he opens his eyes, looks at her, then closes them again.

She pulls one of the blankets from her bag, lays it across his bare arms, which are also turning red.

Then she stands up, undresses down to her swimming costume.

This stretch of sea was the last she swam in. Once Eve was gone, she had no desire to go in.

Now she walks towards the water.

There is no tentative dipping of toes, no cautiously wading in, up to the stomach first.

Rae begins to run.

She is noisy, splashy, here we go, all in.

She goes right under, and the freezing wide-awake shock of it.

When she surfaces, she turns to face the beach.

And there he is, sitting up now, waving.

She waves back.

She has salty hair. She is dripping. Wrapped in a towel, she unpacks a late lunch. Baguette, brie, olives from a tub. Vinegary crisps, Tunnock's Teacakes.

As they eat, they sift through their lives, show each other fragments. The fragments are like pieces of broken pottery, some plain, some patterned, some sharp.

I don't remember us talking much as kids, he says.

We didn't, she says. We were more interested in each other's parents.

True, he says. I loved your parents.

I loved your mum, she says.

They laugh, it's not funny, their laughter is Savlon, bandage, nurse.

It's not only that, Rae says. I don't know how to explain this really, but I sort of loved *my* mum more when yours was around.

She sits and thinks about this. How she has always sensed that there is more to her mother than all her bluster and brassiness, her never fully listening, her perfume and mascara. She misses the mother she only briefly met, longs for her, the woman she glimpsed thirty years ago, the woman who was friends with Eve.

That's really sad, Daniel says.

They stare ahead of them, he is seven and she is nine, just for a moment.

And now he misses his mum.

And he refuses to miss his mum.

Can I tell you something really bad, Rae says.

Does it involve me? he says.

No, it only involves me, and a man I slapped in the face. That's how I got my job at SOM. By slapping an employee, she says.

Well that's different. Must've been an unusual interview.

I'm a pacifist, Daniel. I'm not the kind of person who slaps another person in the face. I'm not like the rest of my family.

Your family aren't violent.

Dad and Pauline, no. But Mum would probably slap someone. Bailey and Carol, they definitely would.

Who are Bailey and Carol?

Oh, she says. I forgot. You never met them did you, the twins. They were born the year you left. To be honest I can't stand them. They're a bit, well, thuggish.

Blimey, Daniel says.

He remembers now, finding out that Sherry was pregnant, yet somehow he never imagined other Marsh children arriving, the landscape of the family changing so dramatically. It was just Leslie and Sherry, Rae and Pauline, in his mind at least.

How old are they? he says.

Twenty-nine, she says, then grimaces. Oh no, they'll be thirty in October, I can't face another party.

Twins, he says. He is stunned, lightheaded. How could he have forgotten?

Yep, sadly there are two of them, she says. But the good news is, they live miles away. Bailey's in Manchester, Carol's in Cardiff. They came for Dad's eightieth last month. Hopefully I won't see them again until Christmas.

You'll probably meet Pauline soon enough, she's nearby and still fairly eccentric, but Bailey and Carol are something else.

In what way? he says.

Okay, I'll give you an example, she says. Last year, on Dad's birthday, Bailey got into a row with one of the guests at the party. He ended up setting fire to the man's coat with a lighter and shoe protector spray.

What?

Needless to say, he ended up in hospital.

The man?

No, Bailey. He's an idiot. I've spent my whole life trying not to be like my family, apart from Dad obviously, and now it turns out I'm just like them.

Because you slapped one person?

That was at a family gathering too, in front of Mum of all people. She looked so proud.

Daniel laughs, can't help it. Shall I tell you something that'll make you feel better, he says.

Please, Rae says.

A few days ago, I twisted a man's arm. I think I might've broken it.

Oh my God, we're disgusting, she says.

I know, he says. We are.

They are chest-deep in dappled sea.
    They are swimming side by side, breaststroke, slow.
    They are floating on their backs, talking, still talking.

and the river
speaks back

Here comes the boy again, marching hot through the fields, he pauses to take off his school jumper and wrap it around his waist, to loosen his tie and unbutton his shirt, then he sets off again through the warm haze until he comes to the river.

He kneels down, dips his hands in the water, the current against his fingers, his fingers against the current. Look at all this sparkle and swim, this boy is the river and the river is him, that's how it feels when he's here, when he looks at the water so constant and clear, all the tough golden pebbles, all the soft leaning reeds, straightforwardly good, it fills him with hope.

He listens very carefully. Can you hear that?

Someone in the distance is playing a trumpet. To Daniel it sounds old-fashioned, like a moment of great importance, a time to stand up straight, something to do with honour and nostalgia, something to do with respect.

All this, from a solitary trumpet.

He instinctively stands, brushes the grass from his knees, looks straight ahead of him.

Now the trumpet is joined by other wild instruments, playing from the forest at the other side of the river.

Music rises, sweeps through the sky.

And he is alive, he can breathe, this boy on the bank, skipping school again, playing truant in the sun with his dear watery friend, his only friend, if you discount Aunt Fig, if you discount the boy who sits with him sometimes at lunch, who he doesn't really like.

He speaks to the river and the river speaks back.

Do you think the music is real, Daniel says.

Of course, the river says.

I mean, do you think everyone hears it when they come here, he says.

Ah, well those are two different questions, the river says. And by the way, happy birthday, Daniel.

How do you know? he says.

Of course I know, the river says. Sixteen eh? You're getting on a bit now. Doing anything nice?

We're going to the cinema.

Who's we?

Me, Mum, Fig.

And how are things with you, Mum, Fig?

Same as ever.

Meaning?

Well it's like I told you. She's always studying isn't she. Mum, that is. Even when we're doing something nice, it feels like we've just had an argument.

In what way? the river says.

Dunno, Daniel says. There's just this atmosphere all the time, or maybe it's just me.

Well it's not going to make things any easier, coming here, the river says.

It is actually, Daniel says, it always does.

But playing truant, the river says. You know the school will call her again.

I don't care, Daniel says.

He opens his rucksack, takes out sandwiches wrapped in foil, a bottle of diluted orange squash.

Me and Fig have started playing badminton at the sports centre, he says.

That's nice, the river says.

It's a bit weird, Daniel says. It's only because Mum's got all her new uni friends.

He unwraps his lunch, and inside the foil, on top of white bread and sandwich spread, there's a small square of paper. He unfolds it. YOU CAN DO THIS, is what the paper says. His mum's handwriting, red biro.

He folds it back up, leans close to the river, lays it gently on the water.

Technically that's littering, the river says.

As his mum's words drift away.

That was sweet of her, the river says. But what does it mean, *you can do this*?

Daniel sighs. It means, *you can get through a whole day at school without leaving*. It basically means, *don't leave the premises*.

So she does care, the river says.

No she doesn't, Daniel says. She just wants me to do what she asks.

And now he is tired. He doesn't want to walk all the way back through the fields to the bus stop, then home to a birthday cake made by Fig, then fake cinema smiles.

He hears the boy's voice, the one from this morning: Why are you such a fucking weirdo, Berry? Look at your twitchy nose, like some dumb rabbit. Come here, rabbit boy.

And maybe this is it, he thinks now. The day when he lowers himself into the river and lets go. He is a good swimmer, but this water is deep and strong, he likes the idea of it wrapping him up.

Truth is, he can't be bothered. That's what stops him every time. Laziness.

He puts on his sloppy jumper. You'll grow into it, his mum said when she bought it.

You off? the river says.

Can't miss the bus, Daniel says.

Well you go careful, and don't you worry about those boys, all right? What goes around comes around, the river says.

I don't know what that means, Daniel says.

You will, the river says. Anyway, I see good things ahead for you.

Really? You can see the future?

I can see everything, the river says. And that's why I'm not worried.

About what? Daniel says.

About you, the river says.

wildly and
infinitely
interesting

Daniel strolls along the beach to the cafe, buys two ice creams, rushes back.

Vanilla with raspberry sauce, he says.

Perfect, Rae says.

She waits for him to sit back down, get comfy, before she asks her next question. There are so many things she wants to know, she's worried there won't be time.

So you were in Wales, she says. How did you end up living in the South West?

I stuck a pin in a map, he says.

You did what? she says.

Me and Mum had a massive row. She wanted me to go to university, I didn't want to. Things just sort of blew up. I told her I was leaving, and I did, he says.

He laughs in a way that isn't laughter at all, only sadness and disbelief, a staccato sigh. He remembers that summer, how his mother had dyed her hair red, how she was heavily into anatomical art, kept bringing home drawings of skin, muscle, bone.

She told me I wouldn't go, he says. She said I was being *silly*.

His memory was close, but it wasn't quite true.

You're throwing toys out of your pram, that's all you're doing, is what Eve Berry had actually said.

And this phrase, this sickening phrase. She knew he hated school, so why did she think he'd want to go to university? He wasn't like her. And her response was to reduce him to a screaming toddler.

Fuck you, he said. I'm leaving.

Eve was close behind as he ran into Anna's study, pulled a map of Great Britain down from the wall, placed it on the floor and stamped his foot on the glass. He turned the frame on its side and shook it, shards of glass came loose and fell, exposing one jagged area of paper. He grabbed a drawing pin from Anna's desk, pushed it into the gap: Somerset.

You're being ridiculous, Eve said. And you've cut your hand, look.

He was surprised to see his own blood. He hadn't felt the cut happen, he was hot and numb, an arrow mid-flight, that was all. He had yet to leave, but his leaving had already begun.

And that was it, Rae says, you just left home?

Pretty much, Daniel says. It wasn't completely random, we'd been arguing for ages.

Why?

Well, she was either studying and never there or bossing me about. You can't be absent *and* expect to tell a person how to live their life.

He tells her how Anna had bought him an old Fiat Panda when he was learning to drive, not knowing it would become his temporary home.

Meaning what, Rae says.

Meaning I slept in it, he says. Until I found a job, could afford to pay rent. I put a little card in a shop window, did some painting and decorating. I got more and more work until I started doing it full-time.

Daniel, that's awful, she says.

No I liked it, he says. It's really satisfying to see a building transformed.

I didn't mean that, she says, it's great that you had your own business. But you've been homeless twice. I'm so sorry, she says.

Let's not go into all that. Let's talk about you, he says.

So last week, when you were sleeping rough, she says, ignoring his attempt at diversion. Your mum didn't know about that.

No, he says.

Do you mind if I ask what happened?

The landlord kicked us out, gave us two months' notice, he says.

You and Erica, she says.

Yeah. Our home is now a holiday cottage. It was the third time that's happened to me, although usually they want to sell. He came round to tell us in person, brought us six bottles of craft beer in a posh wooden caddy.

Soft soap, Rae says. Did you drink it?

Of course, he says. It was good beer. Also, Erica had just dumped me. *On the same day.* I'd have drunk anything to be honest.

He thinks of the robin that was always in their garden, the one that loved it when he pulled out the weeds, turned over the soil, planted something new. It would hop about on the flowerbeds as soon as he was done, searching for worms, assessing his work, and was often still there long after he had gone inside to change and make dinner. Mikey's still busy, Erica would say, as she stood by the kitchen window, washing up. It was irritating, how she always called the robin Mikey, as if this bird was hers to name.

Rae looks deep in thought, she's shaking her head. That Erica knows how to time a punch, she says.

It wasn't like that, Daniel says. She didn't want to live with me again, sign her life away. I guess for her it was an opening. Anyway, it's Mum's fault really.

How is it your mum's fault?

After my so-called grandmother turned up, we argued non-stop. If Mum hadn't lied, none of this would've happened.

Wouldn't it? Rae says. What were you arguing about?

Apparently she'd been unhappy, he says. But she never told me, I had no idea.

He pauses, wonders if somehow he *had* known, if he'd had an inkling.

He loves that word, *inkling*, how it's all about the truth of things, and how it places truth where to him it belongs: below the surface, with all the mysterious undertones, and every now and then we glimpse what lies beneath through a hint, a hunch, an inkling.

He imagines Erica's unhappiness as a tiny figure, standing at the entrance to a festival. It stamps the back of his hand with dark ink. Now you can enter the Festival of Unhappiness whenever you like, it says. Feel free to come and go as you wish.

Yes, he'd had an inkling that something was wrong, of course he had. But isn't there always something wrong? What he means is, isn't it normal to feel that way?

Are you all right? Rae says.

Yeah, he says. Sorry, I was just thinking about Erica. She's the sort of person who's always reaching for something, you know? She's never properly still.

Rae takes a pack of wet wipes from her bag, wipes her fingers. Want one? she says.

Please, he says.

He likes that she carries wet wipes.

Why didn't you sleep on a friend's sofa? she says. Sofa surfing would've been better than sleeping under a tree, surely.

Blimey, what is this? he says, pretending to be bothered by her cross-examination.

Sorry, she says. Tell me to shut up if it's too much.

I hate that phrase, *sofa surfing*, he says. The implication that having nowhere to live is like surfing, is somehow leisurely, is somehow connected to riding a wave.

I take your point, she says.

Also, he says, eating his ice cream, mint chocolate chip. I'm not that good at making an effort with people, if you know what I mean. Don't judge me, I can see you doing it.

I'm not, I'm the last person to judge, Rae says. Do you know how I ended up working for SOM?

You said, you slapped someone.

Yes, but not only that. I helped the company develop, became a bit of an *expert*.

Daniel looks confused.

I was their number-one customer, she says. I was always hiring Strangers.

Oh, he says, surprised.

Don't get me wrong, I do have friends, she says. But I don't seem to have as much enthusiasm for friendship as you're supposed to have.

Enthusiasm, he says, nodding. It's not that easy to come by, is it. I mean, it's no small thing.

I know, she says. To be honest, I have a chronic lack of enthusiasm for most people.

Me too, he says, liking how often she says this, begins

a sentence with *to be honest*. Don't get me wrong, he says, I'll go wild for a good tree, I'm not unemotional.

She smiles. That much I've gathered, she says.

As he dozes again, she wonders how sleepy he is when he has not been sleeping rough. When his life is on track.

Then she wonders what she even means by this. By the idea of a life being on track, like a tram or a train, on schedule, on course.

Preposterous, she thinks.

And yet she knows what derailment feels like.

And it's interesting, sitting here watching the sea beside this sleeping man.

It's wildly and infinitely interesting.

They are lying on their backs, watching the clouds.

Daniel is wearing Leslie's sunglasses, wraparound, they give the sky an amber tint.

They can hear gulls, voices, a ball being thrown and caught, thrown and caught.

What you asked me earlier, he says. About why I didn't stay with friends.

Hmm, Rae says.

Thinking about it now, since you asked. If I'd stayed on a friend's sofa, an *acquaintance's* sofa, it would've been hard to end it, should the thought have crossed my mind.

End it, she says. As in –

Uh huh, he says. As in, the end of me.

So that was your plan? she says.

He expects her to be shocked, appalled, darkened by his darkness.

There was no plan, he says. But maybe it was some-where in the mix.

I see, she says.

Also, he says. It was like my whole body just said no, like I wasn't even thinking, I was somehow shutting down.

He looks up at all the birds, shrieking overhead.

A squabble of seagulls, he says.

Which reminds Rae of Eve. And one memory frees another like a monkey loose from its cage, running through corridors, a bunch of keys in its hairy hand: a pandemonium of memories.

Do you remember when your mum got really drunk that Christmas, and tried to ride one of the flamingos in our front garden? Rae says. We've still got the photo. You were always sitting on those things.

What happened to the flamingos? he says.

They're in the shed. Dad wouldn't let them go. They weigh a ton, you wouldn't believe. Anyway, we digress, she says.

He asks her if it pays well, working for SOM, and she tells him it does. Her boss, Sally Canto, she's good that way.

I haven't made good decisions, he says. About anything really, but especially about money. I should've bought somewhere tiny years ago, before my *great decline*.

She asks about his job, if it's hard to get work as a decorator.

Word of mouth, he says, that's what you need. I've done all right, I think. Thing is, I haven't worked for three months now. Cancelled jobs, pretended I was ill.

Maybe you *were* ill, Rae says. It's not a crime.

Malaise, he says.

That's such a good word, she says. It manages to describe so much with so little effort. Which is fitting really isn't it.

The man is suffering from *acute malaise*, Daniel says in a posh accent.

If you ask me, Rae says, that should be used more often. I see a therapist sometimes, her name's Camille. She refuses to use the word *depression*. She has this bee in her bonnet about the importance of language, says the right words are a kind of release, and sometimes the words need some drama. So if someone feels terrible, like they don't care if they live or die, she would say they had a profound case of melancholia, inconsolable sadness, crippling down-heartedness, a debilitating sense of dread and foreboding.

Interesting, he says.

Daniel can't remember the last time he used this much language in a day. He isn't a great talker. This is one of many things he believes about himself.

And this language today, it feels like air, blowing through his aloneness.

Rae leans forward, runs her finger along the sand, draws a line about an inch thick. The line is wavy and fun. It's not a hard, straight, undeviating sort of line. It's like a sound wave, vibrations in the air. There's a high and a low and another high; a peak, a drop, then up we go again. It's a line full of change, a line full of hope.

She turns around.

How do you draw a line, she says. That's the question isn't it. You nearly drew a hard line, it could have been the end of Daniel Berry. Which means I'm spending the day with a man who almost wasn't. And then what would I have been doing? she says.

Something better, he says.

No, she says, definitely not.

He smiles.

And she watches this particular smile pass across his face.

Like something she wants to keep hold of.

Like something really quite beautiful.

How it changes him, makes him look older and younger at the same time.

Have you ever been through a terrible breakup? he says.

If you mean have I ever had my heart broken, then no, not yet, she says. But there's always time.

Don't even joke, he says. It's no joke I'm telling you.

What's Erica's full name? she says.

Erica Yu, he says.

That's better, she says. I think you should use her full name from now on. Unfamiliarity's good for the brain. Do something different, however small. Rethink her. Shake things up in there.

She knocks on his head, one two three.

You must think I'm such a loser, he says.

Daniel, you need to know who you're talking to here.

And who's that? he says.

You're talking to someone who hired a Stranger to go with them to see Leonard Cohen, she says. That was 2008, and I've been doing it ever since.

Why didn't you go on your own?

I have no idea. It's not like I mind going to things on my own.

I love Leonard Cohen, he says.

Me too, she says. Do you fancy another Tunnock's Teacake?

Go on then.

They take it in turns to go off to the sand dunes. Closer than the public toilets, it's what everyone does.

And the nudists are in the distance, just part of nature, no costume.

Daniel hears Rae's voice in his mind: *do something different, good for the brain.*

So this afternoon, what the hell, he steps deeper into the dunes.

And now he too is starkers, just for a few minutes.

He has always loved all the words for nakedness: in the raw, in the nuddy, in the altogether.

He's as naked as the day he was born, and there's sand beneath his feet, and why today this appreciation of words? They're coming from nowhere, these unlikely words, pushing through his barren mood like a shock of bright flowers on a shingle beach.

Sherry is wearing purple velour. It was an instinctive decision, a reaching into her ottoman, a moment of digging deep.

While her best clothes live inside two wardrobes, her favourite clothes live in the ottoman at the foot of her bed. This box has been upholstered twice over the years, first in maroon velvet, then in deep blue. It contains indecently transparent blouses, patched-up jeans, five Beatles T-shirts, two old hoodies and a purple velour tracksuit that she bought in the eighties.

Sherry is the proud owner of eleven tracksuits. She is a fan of sportswear in general, but mainly sportswear with sequins, spangles, glitter, the outfit that tells the world she is glamorous *and* energetic, oh yes.

So here she is all zipped up in purple velour. And okay, it's a little bit tight. But is this really a bad thing?

She decides it isn't.

Anyway, who cares, she has the house to herself. Well, sort of.

I can't *believe* you still have that tracksuit, Eve says.

They don't make them like they used to, Sherry says.

Leslie has gone to the market, as he always does on a Saturday. He likes to chat to the stallholders, buy fruit and veg, sift through old vinyl. Then he will go to a cafe,

305

the livelier the better, where he will order coffee and a slice of cake, read the paper by himself.

Daniel is at the beach with Rae. Even though he only arrived yesterday, Sherry can feel his absence. No, it's more than that: she can see and hear it. Because he hasn't taken Eve, the woman he brought with him.

Did Leslie see her too, strolling in behind Daniel, or was it just her?

Funny thing: Eve hasn't changed one bit. She is still twenty-six, the age she was when she left. Which is making Sherry feel horribly old.

Now that I'm back, I'm *really* back. I'm all over you, I'm everywhere, Eve says from the contours of Sherry's mind, its rolling hills and ominous skies.

Sherry goes into the kitchen, opens a pack of Wagon Wheels.

She eats one, then another. She is restless, jumpy, tense. One minute you're just living your life, then *this*. A blast from the past. *Prepare yourself for the blast*, no one said. Should've turned the cellar into a panic room, she always thought that was a good idea. And maybe it's going to get worse, she thinks. What does Daniel know, what will he say to Rae? He's like a time bomb, or one of those memory boxes that people bury, what are they called?

Time capsules, Eve says.

Yes, that's it, Sherry says, taking another Wagon Wheel from the pack. He's a time capsule, a box of memories, he's the walking talking past.

Maybe he's also the present and the future, if you let him be what he is, Eve says.

*

306

Sherry doesn't remember leaving the kitchen, yet here she is in the lounge, walking around the sofa then doing it again, mindless circuits, humdrum exercise.

She thinks about visiting Bailey or Carol for a few days, getting away. Now there's a good idea. But what if something happens while she's gone?

She picks up her town crier's bell, rings it hard. The bell sounds louder than usual and not loud enough.

You've still got it, the bell I bought you from that car boot sale, Eve says. Do you still have the Russian dolls too? I don't see them anywhere.

Now Sherry is in her bedroom. She opens a drawer, reaches to the very back of it.

Oh charming, Eve says. You could at least've kept them on your windowsill.

Sherry tries a second drawer, then a third.

Here we are, she says, relieved and disappointed to discover the past in her knicker drawer. I knew I hadn't thrown you away, she says, holding a matryoshka doll.

She pulls it open, lifts out another, keeps going until there are seven dolls lined up on the windowsill.

She thinks about parallel lives, and choices, how each doll is a version of the same doll.

Now she is on the floor, her hand reaching under the chest of drawers. Ah, there it is, the envelope attached to the bottom with masking tape, the one she rereads every year, then seals back in place with fresh tape.

Oh, Eve says. I'd forgotten about that. I hate to think what I wrote, I was in such a state. Bit risky wasn't it, the way I stuck it to the painting. I don't think it was deliberate, I didn't really know what I was doing.

Sherry opens the door to Rae's old room, sees Daniel's

rucksack in the corner, the clothes he borrowed from Leslie neatly folded on a chair.

May as well give him these clothes, she thinks. And the ones he's wearing today. And what's that over there on the bedside table, beside Rae's old alarm clock? That wasn't here before.

It's a tiny sheep.

Sherry picks it up, turns it upside down, there are no markings underneath.

What does Daniel know? she says. Does he know about *us*?

Of course not, Eve says. I always said you could trust me, didn't I?

But can I, Sherry says. All this stuff about your mother turning up at Daniel's door. She said you were unwell, that you ran away. That isn't what you told me – you said *they* were unwell. Now I don't know what to think. You ran away from here, didn't you? You went so quickly. It was terrible, for all of us. You didn't have to go.

I never said they were unwell, Eve says. I said they were *cruel*.

Sherry sits on the bed. If you hadn't gone, she says. Daniel could've been happy. *We* could've been happy. You should've stayed.

And the feeling in her stomach, it's always the same when she sees Eve's handwriting.

Too many Wagon Wheels, that's all, she says.

You're emotionally stunted, Eve says.

That's not very nice, Sherry says.

My dearest Sherry,
    Please accept this painting as a goodbye from me and Daniel. I can't bear to let it go with everything

*else. I don't know if you'll want to keep it, I doubt it
somehow. I saw some graffiti on a wall once, it was
around the time we first got together. It said: We were
real, we were amazing, please don't say it isn't true.
I wonder now if that was some kind of omen from a
broken-hearted soul to a foolish soul (me), a soul who
was about to give herself more truly than she knew
possible to the most beautiful woman (you). I couldn't
believe my luck, it felt like a once-in-a-lifetime thing –
you grab this, Eve Berry, you take it now or you may
never have the chance again to experience something
so perfect. And so I said yes. And all the mornings,
afternoons, in bed with you. That day in the forest,
do you remember? All those matinees at the cinema,
I could never concentrate on the film, I was just waiting
for you to give me a sign, to say now, let's go, come on,
off to the women's toilets, always the same cubicle, ours.
And that night we went camping by ourselves, just us –
I can still hear the rain on the roof of our tent, I can
still hear everything you said. We were, weren't we?
Real and amazing. But the way you've been lately,
I feel like I imagined it. Having to let you go is one
thing, but thinking that you're fine, untouched, not upset
at all, is a hurt I have no words for. And I know this is
your way, it's something I love about you, how breezy
and unfazed and aloof you can be. But bloody hell. The
thought of you having another child together, sharing all
that, getting on with your lives as if we never happened.
Maybe this will sound terrible, but if I knew you'd miss
me, think of me, desperately wish things could've been
different, that you'd never met him, that when you first
said hello over the garden fence, you had been free.
I don't know how I could've let this happen. Generally*

speaking, I'm a sensible person. What a cliché I am, the other woman, hands full of outlandish expectations. You started this, darling. And I don't regret a day of it. And that doesn't mean I'm not sorry, that I don't feel guilty. Leslie is one of the most precious people I've ever met. But I wanted you so much, I still do. It's bigger than me. All I can do is say what I feel. I love you, Sherry. I'll miss you terribly. I wish you all every happiness, and somehow I do mean it, I realise now how many different things we can feel at once. Please tell Rae I'm so sorry I had to go – will you try and think of a good reason? I'm really going to miss her.

With all my love, always,
Eve
xxxxx

Totally naked? Rae says.

Yep, Daniel says. Only for a few minutes.

Her eyes are half closed in a hard stare. She is messing about, pretending to study him, calling him weird without having to say it.

And he likes it.

Her face is kind, full of fun, he thinks. And it's a good look on her, the whole silly and studious thing. He can imagine enjoying it, Rae Marsh making fun of him on a regular basis. The warmth of her jokes, their gentleness.

I did it to surprise my brain, he says, sitting on the blanket beside her. Do something different, that's what you said, wasn't it.

It was, she says, but that wasn't quite what I had in mind. Interesting start though.

I thought so, he says.

They watch the sea, silvering now, its bluish green fading as the clouds blow in. It's turning cold. People are packing up for the day, putting on jumpers and hoodies. After the past week of humid days it's easy to forget that it's only May, still spring, the season of fleeting heat, of never knowing what to wear.

It's a bit chilly, Daniel says, reaching into a bag for Leslie's sweatshirt. He puts it on, it's so thick and soft. He lifts his arm to his nose, breathes it in. How does a person make laundry feel and smell like this? Like sandalwood and honey. Like everything is in order, taken care of.

You all right? Rae says, wondering what he's doing as he gazes at her father's sweatshirt, sniffs its sleeve.

I am, he says. I love the feeling of putting on warm clothes when I've been outside all day.

That always feels best at the beach, she says.

True, he says. Simple pleasures, he says.

She asks him to pass her a jumper and some socks.

Now they are cosy, all wrapped up.

They are windswept, clear.

I'm hungry, she says. Fancy some fish and chips? My treat.

The pub is called the Handy Sailor.

I've heard of places called the Jolly Sailor, Daniel says, but never Handy.

Rae tells him it's named after Rebecca Wilson, who built sheds and was always out sailing. Her granddaughter, Louise, owns this pub.

I'd love to build a shed, he says. I mean, a really good shed, from scratch.

Me too, Rae says. I'd happily live in a shed. A really good shed, obviously, with windows, water, electricity.

A proper wooden house, he says. A cabin in a forest.

Exactly, she says. Well maybe not *in* the forest, but at the edge of the forest.

Hmm, he says, picturing this place, what it might look like and feel like.

They are sitting at a table in the corner, talking about freedom and nature and belonging, without mentioning any of these things.

312

Rae is drinking ginger beer, Daniel a pint of ale.

The pub is dark, it smells of wood and vinegar and school dinners.

Their food arrives. Fish and chips for Rae, pie and chips for Daniel.

That pie is enormous, Rae says.

Nah, he says. It's just a regular-sized pie.

No, it's enormous. You should probably give me at least a quarter.

Ah, I see, he says.

You can have some of my fish, she says.

As they eat, they're visited by a hopeful hound, a grey whippet called Frida who lives here with Louise, according to the woman drinking bourbon at the next table.

Named after Frida Kahlo, this woman says.

She's lovely, Daniel says. Just look at those sad eyes.

I don't think she looks sad, Rae says. Just soulful.

Only you know the answer, don't you, Frida, he says, stroking the dog's head, bending close. Are you sad, soulful or both?

Frida lies down, settles by Daniel's feet, as if his voice, or maybe his question, has won her over.

He is touched by this, it makes him feel something he hasn't felt in a long time.

Wanted, chosen, peaceful.

Something along these lines.

The kind of lines you might draw with a soft pencil, as you let your hand move freely across a sheet of paper.

Daniel can't remember feeling this relaxed. His senses seem heightened. He is aware of everything at once, this chair beneath him, Frida's chin now resting on his foot, all the voices and music, the smell of food and drink, this sweatshirt, the air around them.

313

The more he becomes aware of, the calmer he feels.

Do you mind if I ask about your mum? Rae says.

If you like, he says.

It's just that you never told us what she said.

About what?

About your grandmother turning up. All that stuff you said about your mum having lied.

She didn't say a word, Daniel says, sipping his pint. I asked her outright, said did they want to meet me or not? She literally didn't speak, it was really shocking. She didn't contradict any of it. She was right in front of me, onscreen that is, on FaceTime, saying nothing. So there you go. What kind of mother tells her child he's unwanted when he isn't?

I'm sorry, Rae says. To be honest, I can't even imagine.

Which is true. She is trying and failing to imagine. It's impossible to believe any of this.

Because Eve Berry belongs to her too.

In the way rock stars belong to their fans.

In the way superheroes belong to children.

In the way a town misses a library, a park, a pear tree.

In the way a daughter misses her mother.

And what strikes her now is how passive she has been. Who lets people go without putting up a fight?

Not any old people, Rae. People who evoke immense enthusiasm.

Yes, people like that, she thinks.

What an idiot, what a waste, what a journey she could have taken. Years ago, a train to Edinburgh. She had known where Eve worked for a long time.

Briefly, she is pure regret. Then, she is pure excitement.

She dips a chip in ketchup, watches the man in front of her, who is talking to Frida now, saying hello sweet girl, aren't you lucky not to be a human being.

But it's only something to say, he doesn't mean it, not really.

In this moment, he quite likes being human.

New York

Is it wrong to be feeling what she is feeling right now?

This is the question in the chair beside her as she sits in the New York Public Library, supposedly working.

This question is twitchy, horribly physical. It keeps nudging Eve with its elbow, brushing up against her, rubbing the dirty soles of its sneakers over the top of her shoes.

Because she is having a good day, and here is the rub: yesterday's conversation was something she had spent four decades running away from, running with the weight of a boy in her arms. And it's an odd sensation, when something you have dreaded finally happens. And now her son is distraught, and she should feel guilty, but she feels something else instead.

I feel sort of, well, *free*, she said to Niesha in bed this morning. That sounds awful, I know.

And this afternoon she looks up at the ceiling of the library, all the painted clouds and chandeliers, and the beauty of this reading room, this city, this year; all these days they have spent away from home.

She takes off her reading glasses, tries not to cry.

Outside, she drinks coffee at a table in Bryant Park. She checks the time on her phone; Niesha won't be here for an hour. She scrolls through her list of contacts, her Favourites:

Niesha, Daniel, Anna, Robbie; Niesha's brother and parents; her friends Elena, Nigel, Maggie; then Franklin, Peter and their daughter, Alison.

She always feels lucky when she looks at this list.

She presses the little photo of Anna, waits for her to answer. In this photo, Anna is about to blow out candles and make a wish. She is in one of her favourite places, a tiny French bistro that's always busy, always noisy and dark. Daniel has emerged from the kitchen with a brightly lit cake, and everyone in the bistro is singing.

Hello you, Anna says now.

Hi, Eve says. I just wanted to hear your voice.

Everything all right? Anna says.

Sort of, Eve says.

Hold on, Anna says, just give me two ticks.

Eve waits. She can hear Anna speaking to Percy, her German shepherd: In you come, that's a good boy.

Okay, Anna says now, as she settles into her chair by the window. What's going on?

Eve tells her about Gail Berry, turning up at Daniel's door.

No, Anna says. I don't believe it.

I know, Eve says. She hired a private detective apparently, how weird is that.

But why now, after all this time?

My dad died.

Oh, Anna says, I'm sorry.

Are you? Eve says.

It can't be an easy thing to hear, Anna says.

They let me down, they were bad parents, that's what she told him.

She said that? Well I never. She's obviously changed.

Ah, wait for it, Eve says. They let me down because I

320

needed *treatment*. Mentally unstable. They held on to that one. Told him they had wanted to raise him themselves.

Oh for God's sake, Anna says. Well Daniel won't believe that, she was just pissing into the wind.

He did, actually.

Of course he didn't.

He did. And now he wants some *space*.

Space?

Yes, that's what he said.

I'll ring him, Anna says. I'll talk to him, explain.

No, Eve says. Thank you, but no.

That woman, honestly, Anna says. You'd think she might have gained just a little wisdom by now.

It's so strange, Eve says. I feel really shocked by all this, shaken up. But at the same time, I also feel completely fine. I don't know how to explain it. It's like, this news has *tried* to push me over, and I feel bruised by that, but somehow I'm steadier on my feet than before. Maybe I feel relieved, I don't know.

In Wales, Anna is smiling.

In New York, Eve can hear it.

What are the waves doing today? she says.

Oh, they're fairly subdued. But honestly, I still can't stop watching them. Every morning, I can't wait to see what they're doing. It's like being in love, Anna says.

Eve laughs. If my mother could hear us now, she says, she'd definitely say we were crazy. You're in love with the sea and I'm in denial.

I don't think you're in denial at all, Anna says. Do you want to talk again later?

I'll be all right, Eve says.

I know, Anna says.

*

In Bryant Park, Eve listens to a group of young people at the next table, discussing their writing. They sound earnest, optimistic.

She drinks the last of her cold coffee while thinking of Anna, probably out walking on the beach now with Percy.

She pictures Daniel on his sofa with Erica, trashing his mother.

Then her own so-called mother, alone somewhere, trashing her daughter.

Eve's life, her decisions, rubbished.

Then she remembers that expression, *one man's trash is another man's treasure*, and it makes her feel better.

She watches two men playing chess.

It starts to rain, the softest drizzle from a bright sky.

And here comes Niesha, walking through the rain, wearing her sunglasses, her hands deep in her pockets.

And it happens again, this thing that keeps happening since they came to New York. The sight of Niesha, just walking towards her, can make her lose all sense of where she is. For a moment she is adrift, impossibly light. And she loves these moments. It's as if something has been let loose from their beginning, from their early days, and is swimming through the years with all its muscle and fire, and every now and then, it's here.

What are you grinning at? Niesha says.

Nothing, Eve says.

my beautiful boy

The love she felt. For a bump, for a kick in the night, for the soft beginnings of a person suspended in fluid, held in place by her skeletal frame, a skeleton in service of new budding bone, *I love his bones, I am his bones,* Eve said to a friend from school.

He grew for eight months, three weeks and a day.

Her hand so often on the belly of his forming.

Her quiet voice singing him a song.

Good morning watery boy, is how she would open each day.

The tenderness of a sixteen-year-old girl, keeping herself calm and steady and his, inside a house creaking with tension.

Is it time? Eve whispers to the pain, whispers to her readying son. Are you ready, is this it?

She is in agony.

She goes downstairs to call for an ambulance.

What are you doing? her mother says.

Mrs Gail Berry. Always waiting and watching. Bag packed, car full of petrol, such a doting mother.

Eve hadn't heard her, thought she was out. She is wearing her pain, it's impossible to hide. She is sweating, bending, *go away, get lost.*

325

Don't talk to me like that, her mother says. What's happening, is this it?

Eve says nothing, refuses, won't. She wants to handle this herself, has been insisting for months. *I don't want you there when he's born, it's my body, my choice.*

Now her waters break. Her secret is properly out.

It's happening.

He is coming.

Ford Cortina, back seat, she watches a cardboard tree dangle from the rear-view mirror.

What the fuck is that smell? she says.

Don't swear, her father says. *What* smell?

It smells like a forest in here, but not in a good way, she says. And don't tell me not to swear, you can't control what I say.

Foul humans in the front seats. Her father's sports bag beside her in the back, the one he takes to squash. Why couldn't she have brought her *own* bag? Instead of the one that usually holds his sweaty towels, the odour of competition, his pathetic need to prove himself.

I'm not sure this is the best route, her mother is saying now.

Of course it is, her father says, because he knows best, always has, this is the order of things.

Shit, I forgot the rabbit, Eve says. Why did you have to rush me?

I don't think the baby will care about a toy rabbit, her mother says.

That's not the point, I wanted it with him from the start, Eve says.

She had bought the little rabbit from Woolworths, named it Kevin.

326

Mistake number one, she thinks, picturing Kevin alone on her bed.

She tries not to look at her father's puffy hands on the steering wheel, the sight fills her with rage, the fact of him controlling the journey as her son shifts bravely inside her, reaches for the world.

There's a strange noise coming from the passenger seat; incongruous, ill-fitting. It's Eve's mother, opening a bag of sweets. She holds it in front of her husband, their fingers dip in and out. They crunch their way through the start of their daughter's labour as if they are watching a film.

Holy fuck, Eve shouts over a contraction.

Don't *swear*, her father says.

Her schoolfriend Robbie is waiting outside the hospital. Eve phoned her before they left, said hey there are you ready, can you come?

Don't be so ridiculous, her mother said. You can't have another girl in the delivery room, especially not *that* girl. I won't allow it.

It's nothing to do with you, Eve said.

So here is Robbie, whose actual name is Roberta, which is a name she really hates. She called herself Rob for a while, then Robert, and during an experimental phase she opted for Robot. Now she is Robbie, standing outside the hospital in her older brother's jacket, his big brown boots. She has put a vast amount of wax in her short hair, made it stand to attention. Robbie means business.

Eve tumbles out of the car, staggers over to her friend.

Their embrace makes Gail Berry stiffen from head to toe.

You're not to leave my side, Eve says. Not once, all right? Even if they try and make you go. Even if it gets really gory or I shit the bed.

Got it, Robbie says. And you *will* shit the bed. I got a book from the library, I'm prepared for all eventualities.

That makes one of us, Eve says.

Roger Berry waits on a hard chair that's too small for his body.

He waits for a boy to come into the world.

He reads the *Daily Mail*, eats a Mars bar.

Now he stands up, steps forward.

He greets a man and a woman, who join him on the hard chairs.

How long? Mrs Jenkins says.

Can never tell, Roger says.

Robbie wonders if her fingers have just broken. Tears stream from her eyes. This is the job, she tells herself, as her friend's screams engulf her like a terrible nightmare. She stands firm, imagines herself as a guard or a soldier, imagines she is in the army, a whole new world depends on her.

She looks at Eve's mother, standing at the other side of the bed, arms tightly crossed, hanky in hand. Every now and then she lifts the hanky, dabs her eyes and nose. There is a word, sewn across the corner of this hanky. The word is GAIL. Robbie wonders if Mrs Berry sewed it on herself or if a special kind of shop does it for you. Either way it's weird. And why is her handbag still over her shoulder, why hasn't she put it down?

One more push, come on, Eve, you're doing so well, you can do this, Robbie says.

The following scream is gargantuan. This is how Robbie will describe it later. *I swear it was the size of a country*, is what she will write in a letter to Eve Berry, c/o

Miss Anna Feigenbaum. *I miss you, dear friend, will you please let me know where you are?*

It's the most unbearable thing, seeing her friend in pain like this. Because Eve is supremely lovable. She's just one of those people who is clever and kind and inventive.

It's a boy, the nurse says.

I know, Eve says, red and drenched and exhausted, impossibly bright-eyed, laughing at the idea that she wouldn't know her baby was a boy.

Here he is, the nurse says.

As skin meets skin. His upon hers for the first time.

Well done girl, Robbie says.

Couldn't have done it without you, Eve says.

Look at his tiny fingers. Just look at him, Robbie says.

My beautiful boy, Eve says.

It's too soon, Gail says. Why don't you come back in the morning – go home, get some sleep?

We'll wait, Mrs Jenkins says. We'd rather not leave.

I can sleep anywhere, I'm like a bat, Mr Jenkins says, shuffling about on the plastic chair.

Bats sleep upside down, Gail says. Her tone is sharp, new, confusing.

Is he all right, is he healthy? Mrs Jenkins says.

He's perfect, Gail says.

And Mrs Jenkins begins to pray. Thank you, dear lord, she says.

That night, Eve dreams of galloping horses.

Their muscle, motion and grace.

Robbie sleeps in the chair beside Eve.

This is highly irregular, the nurse says.

Please? Eve says. She's our bodyguard.

And why do *you* need a bodyguard? the nurse says.

Maybe everyone does, Eve says.

By morning, the Jenkinses are ravenous, impatient.

We've just had a second breakfast, Mrs Jenkins says, reappearing in the waiting room.

There's no such thing as a second breakfast, Gail says. You've just had *more* breakfast.

Gail, Roger says. You're overtired. Go and get some coffee.

Robbie, Eve says. Will you do me a favour?

Name it, Robbie says.

Will you go and make sure they're not here.

Project Motherfucker? Robbie says.

Yes, Eve says.

And so Robbie checks the area for any sign of motherfuckers.

Her task is too easy to fulfil.

There's a huddle of sticky grey faces. A plot of nylon. A heist waiting to happen.

Project Motherfucker goes like this:

The moment I go into labour I'll call you. Tell your parents, tell them to expect it – the message has to reach you. Next, you must call Miss Feigenbaum. If she doesn't answer, leave a message. Tell her I'm in labour. Tell her you'll be with me and if anything goes wrong you'll phone her again. Next, get to the hospital. Maybe your brother could drive you. Don't rely on buses, you know what they're like. Most important thing: do not leave my side whatever you do. Well, unless you need the toilet. Second

330

most important thing: if you see a man and a woman speaking to my parents who are not in medical uniforms, run to a phone and call Miss Feigenbaum again. Tell her the Jenkinses are here, that's all you need to say. Make sure you have some change for the phone. Have you got all that? Eve said.

Got it, Robbie said.

The thing is, Gail says, at 3am. The thing *is*.

What, her husband says.

She has woken him up, dragged him outside to the car park, pulled him into the thick of night, all for this:

I've changed my mind, she says.

What about, he says.

Eve, the baby, everything, she says.

He sighs, and she recoils. His constant mothball mouth.

Jesus, Roger, she says. Your breath's getting worse, you need to see a doctor.

We're not changing our minds, he says.

Why not?

Because she's just a kid. But not only that, she's irresponsible, she can't be trusted.

Is she? Or is she just a teenager.

What?

You must've felt something when you saw them together. She looks like a mother, doesn't she?

Any woman would look like a mother with a newborn sleeping on her chest.

Would they? Gail says.

He sighs again. Airborne attack. We can't afford a baby, he says.

But how much do we even know about the Jenkinses? she says.

We know plenty, he says. They're good solid people.

She tells him that's been said about a lot of people who went on to do terrible things.

He tells her she is tired and emotional. If we bring it home, you'll live to regret it. I'm standing firm for both of us, he says. You'll thank me, I know you will. When things settle. When Eve's back at school.

Robbie's face is an emergency. I'm sorry, Eve, she says.

Oh my God, Eve says.

They're in the waiting room. The nurse says they've been there all night. I've called Miss Feigenbaum, she answered, she's on her way, Robbie says.

I don't believe it. They said it was over, they'd got rid of them.

Lying bastards, Robbie says, gathering Eve's things, stuffing them into a bag.

How could they? Eve says. They promised me I could keep him. They promised me.

When Eve was eight months pregnant, Anna Feigenbaum began her preparations. She cleaned her car inside and out, then did it again every few days, making sure the Mini was fit for a brand new life. This physical activity was a way to channel her anxiety, burn it off. Hopefully she wouldn't be needed. Hopefully Eve would go home with her baby, drama sidestepped, no intervention required.

But if not, she would be there. Eve was a girl, a young woman, who was capable of doing something important, Anna just sensed it. And so knowing her was a kind of waiting, and that too felt important, lent a hopeful charge to the air.

*

There is a hot kerfuffle of voices:

GAIL: Miss Feigenbaum? Why are you here?

ANNA: What you're doing, Mrs Berry, what you're *trying* to do –

GAIL: Roger, get in here now. Quickly.

ROGER: What the hell's she doing here?

ANNA: I'm here for Eve. It's *her* baby.

ROGER: She's not keeping it, it's not happening. This is nothing to do with you, it's family business.

ROBBIE: He's not an *it,* he's a baby. She's going to call him Daniel.

GAIL: It's not up to her.

ROGER: Give him to me, Eve.

EVE: No.

ROGER: You're just a child.

EVE: He's *mine*.

ROGER: Oh come on. You're not fit to be a mother, everyone knows you're crazy.

EVE: I'm not crazy, what do you mean?

ROGER: We could have you locked up. You're a liability, you are. You're a danger to yourself, let alone that kid.

EVE: Excuse me?

GAIL: Roger, stop –

ANNA: No one'll believe that, Eve. Don't listen.

ROGER: You reckon? They don't let stupid teenagers look after babies.

EVE: We're leaving. I'm going with Anna. Robbie, bring my bag.

GAIL: You're being overdramatic. It's the hormones, that's all. You'll thank us for doing this in a few weeks.

EVE: Anna, can you take Daniel? It hurts, it hurts to –

ANNA: Of course, it's all right. Lean on Robbie, I've got him, here we are, *here we are little one*.

GAIL: Just stop this, sweetheart. Listen to your father. Where do you think you're going to go?

EVE: Don't you *sweetheart* me. You're evil. Both of you are evil.

ANNA: I'm sorry, but this is despicable. You can't force her to do this. Please get out of the way.

ROGER: Don't you talk to my wife like that. We'll report you to the school.

ANNA: And I'll report you to social services.

ROGER: You interfering bloody –

ANNA: Mr Berry, step away from me.

GAIL: He's not yours to take.

EVE: He *is* mine. If you touch my son, if you *ever* come near him.

GAIL: You don't know what you're doing.

EVE: How could you do this to me? How could you? You said I could keep him, you promised. But they're outside aren't they. You're fucking liars.

ROGER: We're fixing *your* mess, that's all.

GAIL: Roger, do something. Roger –

ANNA: Take your hands off me right now, Mr Berry.

ROBBIE: Come on, just lean on me, that's it, take it slow.

GAIL: You're not leaving.

EVE: I never want to see either of you again.

GAIL: Don't be ridiculous. We'll find you, you can't do this on your own.

EVE: I'll never forgive you for this, Mum.

Turner

Hey Dad, Rae says, poking her head into the lounge.

Hello love, he says, getting up from his armchair in slow motion. Did you have a good day?

We did, she says.

And Daniel, is he all right?

Better for some sea air, Daniel says, appearing in the doorway.

Marvellous, Leslie says.

You weren't waiting up, were you, Dad?

Oh no. Just nodded off in front of the news, as usual, Leslie says.

There are footsteps on the stairs. They turn to see Sherry in a Beatles nightie and long cardigan, no make-up.

Rae is shocked. She has never seen her mother like this, purely herself, no paint, no great cover-up. This is a woman who wears heavy make-up in the day and light make-up at night. She is rarely without it.

Wow, Rae says. You look lovely.

Don't take the piss, darling, Sherry says.

I wasn't.

How was the beach?

Really good, Daniel says.

We swam, slept, went to the pub for tea, Rae says. This guy can *talk*.

Only because you ask so many questions, he says.

Daniel had a little go at nudism, didn't you, Rae says.

Sherry is wide-eyed. Is their houseguest a raging natur-ist? What have they let themselves in for?

Are you a raging naturist? she says.

I'm not sure I know what that is, he says.

And where were you while this was going on? Leslie says to Rae.

I was reading, she says, trying not to laugh.

She and Daniel look at each other. Both of them, in this moment, feel like teenagers.

Well, I'd better let you all get to bed, she says. She turns to Daniel, tells him she'll call him.

I don't have a phone, remember, he says.

Oh, I forgot. I'll call you here then, she says.

And then there are three.

Leslie and Sherry feel like much younger parents to a boy who isn't their son, who has just been on a date with a girl who is their daughter, when there has been no date at all.

It's confusing, standing here in this hallway. The con-fusion is light-hearted and heavy-hearted; it's easy and fun and poignant and sad. Daniel, with his week-old sunburn. Sherry, without her make-up. Leslie, in his baggy pyjamas.

She didn't even ask if she could go home in my car, he says.

Since when is it your car? Sherry says. Isn't it *our* car?

You know what I mean, he says.

And it's over. The confusion, its loveliness, its strange stab of pain, slipping away.

Fancy going for a little run with me in the morning, Daniel? Leslie says. And by run, I mean a brisk walk, obviously.

I thought I should probably leave in the morning, Daniel says. I don't want to outstay my welcome.

Don't be silly. We've only just got you back, haven't we, Sherry?

Absolutely, she says. Anyway, I have to practically force him to do anything. Then you turn up and he wants to go *running*.

She shakes her head, and winks, pretends to be cross and isn't.

Her mischievous expression, still the same after all this time, makes Daniel ache.

All the years they could have been making mischief.

All the things his mother had taken without asking.

Rae drives home with the windows down.

In her flat, she feels out of sorts. As in, discombobulated. As in, ruffled.

She fetches her laptop from the lounge, takes it to bed.

She types four words into Google: *Eve* and *Berry* and *New* and *York*.

What comes up is Edinburgh University, the page she has seen before, with Eve's photo, research interests and publications. Her email address.

Dear Eve,

I don't know if you'll remember me. My name is Rae Marsh, I used to know you when I was a girl, when you lived next door to us for a while. My parents are Sherry and Leslie Marsh.

I'm sorry to email out of the blue like this, at your work address, and after such a long time. I'm writing because of your son, Daniel. He turned up yesterday at my parents' house – they still live at 4 Abigail Gardens. We haven't seen Daniel since you left, it was quite a surprise.

He came here looking for something, I think. For help of some sort. He's not in a good way, Eve. He's staying with Mum and Dad for a while, so if you'd like to be in touch you can contact him there. I've listed their phone number and email address at the bottom of this message.

I hope you don't think I'm meddling or interfering. I am, of course. But Daniel is off-grid, his girlfriend left him, he had to move out of his house, I think it's been too much. He ended up sleeping rough. He got rid of his phone, says he even closed his Gmail account. I keep imagining you trying to find him, and not being able to, and how awful that would feel.

He says that you and your wife are in New York for a year, so I don't know if this email address still works. No one knows I'm sending this, so if you choose not to respond, it's okay. I won't be telling Daniel – I don't want to put either of you under pressure.

I hope you're well, Eve, and that life has been good to you over the years. I missed you so much after you moved away! We were all very sad.

With love,
Rae Marsh

Daniel is watching a flower, a yellow rose.

This rose is flamboyant and peaceful. It's vigorous, bold, unworried.

And what if this is it? Daniel thinks. The exact moment of this rose reaching full bloom, holding its head high, becoming everything a rose can be before it starts to fade.

If so, what a thing to witness.

And here is Leslie, stepping into the front garden with two mugs of tea. One mug says ALL YOU NEED IS LOVE. The other has a cartoon sloth hanging from a tree, and says THE SLOTH IS MY SPIRIT ANIMAL. It's not difficult to guess which belongs to Sherry and which she bought for her husband.

Not looking so bad out here is it, Leslie says.

It looks great, Daniel says.

They sit in silence, drinking tea, contemplating the garden.

Funny how things go, Leslie says after a while. Then he closes his eyes, as if the sun is too bright or he's taking a nap.

Daniel watches him, and while he is watching he thinks about the books he used to read as a boy, the ones where you choose your own ending.

If you would like Daniel and Leslie to travel back in time and make a different choice, turn to page –

If you would like Eve to travel back in time and make a different choice, turn to page –

Now his mind is full of Cher, singing that song, 'If I Could Turn Back Time'.

He remembers how he used to picture his mum as the captain of a ship, able to turn their boat around. But she never did. She was focused, determined, they sailed onwards. Once she had made her choice, that was it.

And for a moment, he admires her for this.

And for a moment, he hates her for this.

But here comes another mother, marching along, waving, *woohoo!* She is back from work, her hair is a mess, she looks tired and wired and pleased to see them.

Oh my God, she says, people were *really* hungry this morning.

She takes a seat on the bench, squeezes into the gap between her husband and Daniel, tells them to budge up.

It was crazy, she says. The queue went on for miles.

Miles, dear? Leslie says.

Maybe not *miles*, she says, pulling off her shoes. But right down the street, honestly. By half nine we'd completely sold out of facon butties.

What's facon when it's at home? Leslie says.

For goodness' sake. How many times do I have to tell you what facon is. It's *fake bacon*, isn't it. Memory like a sieve, you have.

Well maybe if you fed *me* facon I'd be able to remember what it is.

Fed you? You're not a pet or a farm animal.

My ex, Erica Yu, she used to eat a lot of facon, Daniel says.

342

Figures, Sherry says.

Fake it till you make it, Leslie says.

I tried that, Daniel says. Didn't work for me.

What are you two going on about?

It's a self-help slogan, Leslie says. You're supposed to pretend you feel capable as a way of becoming capable. Something like that.

I never know how you know the things you know, Sherry says.

I'm a man of mystery, Leslie says.

That, my love, is an understatement, she says.

Daniel could listen to this all day, their sparring with soft gloves.

Anyway, what have you two been up to? Sherry says.

I've been making marmalade, using the frozen oranges, Leslie says. Thick cut, with whisky.

I've been gardening. Just a bit of weeding, I hope you don't mind, Daniel says.

Well that's all very impressive, she says. I could get used to this.

To what? Leslie says.

To you not being slumped over a jigsaw, she says.

He tuts. You're obsessed with my jigsaws, he says.

You're obsessed with your jigsaws, she says.

Daniel glances at Sherry's pink T-shirt, the word *Dolly's* printed across it. She has ordered him a black one, says it might do him good to join her sometime, be out in the world, meet different people.

Rae has offered him work as a Stranger at SOM. She thinks it would be good for his brain, his malaise, his hurt and his wallet. No pressure if you don't want to, she said.

But far more inviting than either of these things is the task offered to him by Leslie. I don't suppose you'd help me decorate a couple of rooms? he said. The lounge and hallway are the main issues. But no worries if you're too exhausted. And I'm talking about paid work, obviously. I know you're a professional.

I'd love to do that, Daniel said.

Really? Well that's wonderful.

On one condition.

What.

I do the work, you give the orders and make tea, and you don't pay me a penny.

Hmm, Leslie said. I don't know about that.

Daniel shrugged. Oh well.

Leslie smiled, which made him look sleepy, Daniel thought. He has the sleepiest smile, this man.

Thing is, Leslie said. I'd really *enjoy* stripping that wallpaper. So if I make the tea and don't pay you a penny, can I be your ineffectual assistant?

All right, Daniel said.

But we won't start for at least a couple of weeks, Leslie said.

Why not?

You need some space, a proper rest. I'll put the date on the kitchen calendar. Good to have a plan I always think.

I don't know where I'll be in a couple of weeks, Daniel said.

Leslie looked confused.

You've been so kind to let me stay, but I don't want to take advantage. I need to sort out what I'm going to do next.

What's the rush? Leslie said. Why don't you just take some time before you make any decisions? We're happy to have you here. Anyway, you'd be doing me a favour.

*

It was a curious and unusual feeling, having three people, individually generating ideas about what was good for him, without being asked.

Human generators.

All that energy, going into him.

Their attempts to revive him, give him a place in the world.

How could anyone not be touched by this.

Seriously, you want to turn the house upside down? Sherry had said when her husband revealed his plan.

Only the lounge and hallway. I thought you'd like the idea.

I do, but it's going to make such a mess. I don't know if I'm in the mood for it.

But mess is good, isn't it? Don't you think we need some messing up?

Do you? she said.

Yes, Leslie said, his voice louder now, defiant.

Defiance isn't something Sherry associates with her husband. He's a follower, an audience, generally compliant. He isn't what you'd call a disrupter.

Maybe we need disrupting, he said.

Meaning what? she said.

Nothing drastic, he said. Just a change, that's all.

Oh, she said.

Anyway, it's good to alter your environment. That wallpaper's been with us since the eighties, God only knows how many bugs are living inside it.

Sherry grimaced. Bugs in wallpaper? she said.

Probably, he said. I think it'll be helpful for Daniel, give him something physical to do. It might make him feel more

345

positive, keep him busy, give him a fresh start. That's what he needs, I think.

You've obviously given this a lot of thought, Sherry said, wondering who the fresh start was really for.

It's now been a week since Leslie scribbled his plan on the calendar. In that time, Daniel's hosts have treated him like a convalescing patient. They have made him fresh bread, soup, hearty meals; insisted on long walks, naps in the afternoon.

But one of their biggest gifts is what they haven't done: asked him about the future or the past.

Just take one day at a time, Leslie said.

I'll try, Daniel said.

What *is* a staycation? Sherry says.

It's a vacation, but at home, Rae says.

Like being off sick, Sherry says.

Well no, because I'm not ill, am I? I've booked next week off work, as holiday.

Can you do that without any notice? You've only just started that job.

Sally was fine with it, she knows I haven't had a break this year. She thinks it's important to nurture your well-being, let your brain recharge. Anyway, I thought I'd do some fun things with Daniel before he starts painting the house. He's basically eaten and slept since he got here, he needs to get out and about. I've made a list of places to go and things to do that might help him.

Him? Sherry says.

Yes, Rae says.

They are in row G of the cinema at two in the afternoon.

A small bottle of wine, a bucket of popcorn.

This feels really decadent, Daniel says.

I know, Rae says. Last time I was here I hired a Stranger to come with me. He didn't enjoy my choice of film.

Were you lonely? he says. Is that why you hired someone?

She doesn't know how to answer his question, to explain why she hired a Stranger to go with her to the cinema, the arboretum, the theatre, the concert in the park. It wasn't about loneliness. It seemed to make sense at the time, that's all. It met a need, made it easier to do these things, visit these places. She had craved company, but of a highly specific kind. The kind with no past or future. The kind with no expectations.

Well I suppose it's a bit like alcohol, she says. Some things feel better with a drink.

The trailers are so bad it makes them laugh.

Think we'll give that one a miss, Rae whispers.

And the way she says this, as if they are two people who often go to the cinema, who share an ongoing pattern, simple as that.

He is a boy in water being thrown a rope.

Afterwards, they step outside into sunlight.

Well, how would you describe that film? Daniel says.

I would call it a noir murder mystery about the nature of existence, she says.

Whatever it was, I bloody loved it, he says.

Really? she says.

It was dreamy, ambiguous, the music was stunning. I could watch it again to be honest, he says.

Rae is delighted, but tries not to show it. She loves films like the one they've just seen, so hazy and enigmatic, gripping but also drifty, intense and meandering, like getting lost while knowing where you are. The Stranger had called the last one *painfully incoherent, two hours we'll never get back*.

Shall we stretch our legs, take a walk? she says.

Sounds good to me, he says.

The following day they are surrounded by outdoor plants.

It's really good of you to help me with this, Rae says. I've been meaning to do my bit, keep the garden looking nice, but you know how it is.

No problem, Daniel says, I love a trip to a garden centre. I used to have a great garden.

You will again, she says. But for now, you can make your mark on mine. I'm crap at gardening. I wish I wasn't, but I am.

Okay, he says, rolling up his sleeves.

An hour later, Leslie's car is full of compost, bursting with foliage.

Better hoover this old thing before I take it back, Rae says, glancing at the soil all over the floor.

There's also a tin bath, behind them on the back seat. A spontaneous purchase, made by a woman who never makes spontaneous purchases. Daniel had egged her on, said she couldn't go home without it.

I can't believe I paid that much for an old bath, she says.

It's so much more than an old bath, he says. It's a piece of history. And if you ever get bored of your bathroom, you can soak under the stars.

Yeah right, she says. While seriously contemplating this idea.

They bought succulents too, for indoors.

My God this is *spectacular*, Daniel said, as they entered the greenhouse full of nothing but succulents.

Side by side they looked down at all the tiny plants.

Goodness, Rae said, to their natural brilliance and artistry.

They were the most intricate things she had ever seen. They were rubbery, tactile, ornate. They were purple, jade, olive, violet and the softest of blues. They were pink-tipped, orange-tipped, their unfolding geometric shapes so perfect she could cry.

They're quite nice, aren't they, she said.

Certainly are, he said. How many would you like?

Let's go for ten. We can have five each, she said.

I have nowhere to put them, he said.

Of course you do, she said.

Now they carry all the plants into Rae's garden.

Next, the old tin bath.

Here's good, she says, when they reach the patio.

Their backs ache.

Daniel climbs into the bath, sits down.

I like it in here, he says, pulling his knees to his chest, making room for another body.

Rae squeezes in too, and they face each other.

Daniel closes his eyes, Rae copies him.

She opens hers again, just for a second, to see if his are still closed, which they are.

Sitting out here in the garden, it's one of those times when Rae would normally drift away to her island. She would take the slow boat from here to Petula, from real to unreal.

But as she sits here now, listening to birdsong and breeze, she feels connected not only to the man she is sharing a waterless bath with, but to all the other people who once sat in this bath, who used it to get clean, back in the days before plumbing and instant hot water. She pictures once-a-week bath times in front of the fire, water heated in pots and carried through, everyone taking their turn. One day, way ahead in the future, she says to these people, this bath will be bought from a place that sells old things for a lot of money, objects that have seen and known far more than those who buy them, and a man and a woman will place it in a garden and sit in it for a while, and that woman will be me.

When she opens her eyes, Daniel's are already open.

She wonders how long he has been watching her.

Next on her list is the art gallery.

Daniel has been looking forward to this one.

He is wearing new jeans and a new jumper, new to him at least, pre-loved, bought last week from the charity shop. Leslie had gone with him, bought two records, a blazer and a pair of yellow candlesticks for Sherry.

Rae arrives at ten, drives him to a cafe on a farm, a converted barn full of fairy lights.

On every table there is a teapot full of flowers.

He eats bacon, poached eggs, roasted tomatoes and mushrooms, fried potatoes.

Rae eats an omelette with asparagus, spinach and parmesan.

They drink coffee and plan their day.

You still up for the gallery? she says.

Definitely, he says.

If this is all a bit much, me dragging you around every day, I really am happy to drop you back at Mum and Dad's, she says.

It is, it's overwhelming, he says. In fact I'm miserable.

Oh really, she says.

Totally, he says, finishing his coffee, glancing up at all the tiny lights. Look, they do a supper club, he says, squinting at a poster. Big Indian feast next week. Do your mum and dad like Indian food?

Of course.

Well maybe we could all come, my treat, as a thank you.

You don't need to do that.

It's okay, I can afford it, he says. And I love Indian food.

Or, she says. We could make an Indian feast at mine and invite them over. Are you a good cook?

He thinks about how to answer this. *Is* he a good cook? He used to enjoy cooking, before he met Erica Yu. Which seems a strange thought to have, doesn't make sense, not yet.

Possibly, he says.

As they stroll through the gallery, Daniel feels tearful, he doesn't know why.

He stops to look at a photograph of a boy, or maybe the boy has stopped to look at him. This boy is wearing shorts and a white shirt, he's standing alone in front of red-brick terraced houses, his chest raised, elbows bent, fists on his hips. He's a superhero in a school uniform, acting proud and strong, he doesn't seem to have noticed that it's beginning to snow, or maybe he just doesn't care. The snow is coming down fast, any minute now it will cover the pavements and rooftops, and everyone in this city will look out of their windows, look up at the skies; everyone in this city will talk about snow.

Rae is tugging at the sleeve of Daniel's jumper. Come this way, she says, there's something I want to show you.

He follows her into another room, then another.

She is still pulling his sleeve, dragging him like he's a boy, or maybe like she is a girl.

Look, she says when they get there, when they stop.

In front of the ocean at its wildest.

In front of a steamboat in a storm, caught inside a swirling vortex.

The boat is barely visible, almost lost to the storm.

It's terrifying and beautiful.

I love this so much, she says. It's Turner, she says.

Daniel is speechless.

She slips her arm through his and they stand in front of the ocean, the boat, the storm, for a long time.

This gallery and all its weather.

It's awesome, Rae eventually says.

She looks proud of herself for bringing him here, and he notices what this pride does, how it makes her seem more dishevelled than before, sort of happy and crumpled, as if she has just woken from a good sleep.

Or maybe Turner is doing this. Who knows, who can tell.

Making her look like she used to when she was young.
Making him feel like he used to when he was young.

Rae walks into her parents' house, calls hello, waits for an answer.

Anyone in? she says.

Nothing.

Then she hears laughter coming from upstairs.

Dad? she says, up on the landing now.

Hello love, he says, stepping out of his bedroom. Didn't know you were coming round again.

You all right? she says. You look a bit rosy.

Daniel appears behind him, also red-faced.

We were just moving the wardrobe, Leslie says.

Why?

I've been wanting to do it for years. I hate where it is. I asked Bailey to help me when he was last here, but he said his back was too bad.

Why do you both have wet hair?

We've just got back from the pool, Daniel says.

You've been swimming? Rae says to her father.

We have, Leslie says.

I thought you didn't like it, said it gave you ear infections.

That's your mother, not me, he says.

Well don't overdo it, she says. You should pace yourself, have a cup of tea when you get home, instead of immediately moving a wardrobe. There's no rush is there.

Isn't there? he says.

That evening, Rae makes Daniel a risotto.

As they eat at the little table in her kitchen, she decides to tell him about Petula.

Well, it's not really a decision. More an impulse, an accident.

So there's this place, she says.

Go on, he says.

And he listens to her description of a remote place.

If I don't go there for a while, she says, I get twitchy. What a freak, eh?

I don't understand, he says.

She looks down at her plate.

What I mean, he says, is I don't understand why that makes you a freak.

Oh, she says.

Firstly, he says. When you've been to Petula once, why wouldn't you go again? Seems perfectly natural to me.

But isn't it a childish thing? she says.

No, he says. It sounds a bit like meditation, or those visualisations people do to relax. People pay a fortune to feel calm, you get it for free.

I suppose, she says.

You're only saying it's childish because you first thought of it as a child, he says. But you also first wore shoes as a child. So are your shoes just childish things? Is a bed a childish thing? Is a house, a home?

Yes but it's not *real*, is it. Shoes and beds and homes are real.

It's a dream, he says, a vision. If you were a painter or a writer you'd call it a beginning. You'd take it seriously, base an entire piece of work on trying to depict it as truthfully as possible.

Rae is nodding, trying to comprehend his curious sentences. His words are like sculptures, something to walk around, view from many angles, surprisingly tactile.

I get what you're saying, she says.

It's a bit like that song, he says. 'The Whole of the Moon'.

The Waterboys? she says. I love that song.

Some people have to travel miles to see beautiful islands, to find really peaceful places, he says. All you have to do is close your eyes. It's the sort of thing people write songs about.

Elbows on the table, chin on her hands, she watches him.

And also, he says. I used to talk to the river. I'd skip school, go down to the river and tell it everything. And sometimes I'd hear music, coming from the forest. And also.

Hmm.

When I spoke to the river, it always spoke back.

What did it sound like? she says. What kind of voice?

He thinks about this. Its voice was deep, he says. It was deep, honest, cheeky.

Cheeky?

Yeah. It would say whatever it wanted, it didn't hold back, but it had a sense of humour.

Interesting, she says.

And by the way, he says. Your eyes are quite rivery.

She laughs out loud, and he blushes.

Rivery? she says. I've never heard that one before.

I just mean, he says, they're pale green, and they really remind me of the river.

Are they deep, honest, cheeky? she says.

Maybe they are, he says.

He leans back in the chair, into the cushioning fact of how she isn't tricky or sharp. Things seems to shift and move as they talk, this is the only way he can describe it. The sand shifts beneath them but he doesn't lose his footing. Yes, that's it. Spending time with Rae Marsh is sandy and serious and like playing a really fun game.

If he were to tell her this she would laugh.

Because she has never thought of herself as a *fun person*.

Now they are on the sofa in her lounge.

She is proud of this sofa. It's new, courtesy of SOM and Sally Canto.

I know it's stupid at my age, she says, but this is the first sofa I've ever bought. I always wanted one like this, a gold velvet settee. Try it, go on.

He sits down, places his hands flat on each cushion to his left and to his right.

Oh this is *nice*, he says.

Isn't it, she says. Shall I put on some music?

If you like, he says.

There's a song, she says, her voice trailing off as she searches Spotify on her phone. It's a song I keep thinking of from when we were kids.

Now she hits Play, and music comes from a little speaker in the corner of the room.

It's impressively loud for a small speaker, he thinks, as he tries to name the song. Oh he knows this, come on, what is it?

She is smiling, embarrassed, waiting for the song to burst into life.

Which it will, any second now.

It's the one from *Flashdance*, he says when it does.

Irene Cara, she says. 'What a Feeling'. I used to love this song when I was little. I was obsessed with it.

She jumps to her feet, she is wriggling her shoulders, holding out her hands.

Shall we? she says.

Dance? he says. God no, he says.

Why not?

I don't dance.

Okay, she says.

She sits down again, feels silly, rejected.

But not only that, he says. It has really bad connotations for me. So I just can't do it, I'm sorry.

It's fine, she says.

Now I feel like an idiot, he says.

If it helps, she says, I can't sing. I might be able to, if I actually tried, but I can't and won't. As you say, *bad connotations*. It's a long story, there's a very good reason, I just –

Shh, he says, the smallest hint of a smile returning to his face. You know what you said at the beach, about doing something different.

Hmm, she says.

Well, how about you sing, and I'll dance, and we'll do it really badly right here at the exact same time, he says.

What? No, she says.

Why not? he says.

She buys time with a long sigh.

The time she buys isn't hers to keep, but it is.

Only if we close our eyes, she says.

Deal, he says.

And she sets Irene Cara playing again from the start.

And in her living room they do it.

He's a stilted wooden dance, she's an out-of-tune song.

He's a creaky puppet, she's a creaky voice.

He dances like a boy in drama class, a flower blowing in the wind.

He dances like it's 1967, hippy and trippy, the Summer of Love.

Rae's singing was quiet at first, barely audible, but now she's ramping it up.

Which is putting it mildly.

If there is a ramp here in this room, then Rae has just taken a running jump and leapt right off it.

Blimey, she's really going for it.

What a shock, what a voice, what a heart full of song.

Daniel wants to open his eyes, but doesn't.

Because he promised, remember.

How has she lived without making this sound when this sound has lived inside her?

He wants to laugh, because it's just so bloody good, but laughing would be catastrophic.

Her singing makes his dancing even bendier.

Yes, that's pretty much it: he's a bendy kind of dancer, anything goes.

I bend this way and that way I am only the weather.

When the song ends and the room falls silent, they stand still and open their eyes.

Again? he says, out of breath.

She laughs. She is red from the neck up. Different song, she says, fiddling with her phone again, looking for one of her playlists.

Oh, he says, as a new song begins.

'Landslide', Fleetwood Mac.

That's quite a change, he says. How do I dance to this?

Don't think, she says.

She steps towards him, puts her arms around his waist, her head against his shoulder.

And slowly they sway from side to side, in a living room in East Anglia, in the middle of spring.

When the song ends, another automatically begins.

'Just Like Heaven', The Cure.

They go wild, obviously, who wouldn't?

Eyes open now, they are a brilliant mess.

Rae's hair, flying in all directions.

Daniel, dancing like a tree growing in time-lapse.

He is a thousand moments over forty years.

He is the bending of time, time as living thing, his body only a free-flowing river.

He is a flourish, a kick, a whirl.

A dancing ampersand.

&

You are bloody ridiculous, he says when the dancing is done.

Why am I? she says.

Because you can actually sing, you idiot, he says.

The next day, dancing is all Daniel sees.

Butterflies ballet dancing in mid-air. Leaves pirouetting from branch to ground. An old man at the bus stop, shifting position to ease his aches, doing a little jig. Cat on a rooftop, dogs in a chase, children in fluorescent vests swarming into a park – did you ever see so much dancing? The quick-stepping commuters, the enraged tango of couples, pretty much everyone dancing around the truth. But small talk between the lonely is the sweetest dance of all, quick and shy, let me spin you around in good morning, how are you, nice to see you, cheerio bye-bye.

For a moment, Daniel's life feels silly, cinematic.

Well, this is something to write home about, he finds himself thinking.

But where would he send his letter?

Daniel lies in bed and listens to the rain.

It's 2am, he can't sleep, his shock is here again in the dark, luminous, fizzing.

Perfectly understandable, he says to himself.

He is repeating something Rae said, when he told her this kept happening in the middle of the night, even after good days, relaxing days. I fall asleep just fine, he said, but then I wake up a few hours later in some weird state of emergency.

It's okay, it makes sense. It's perfectly understandable, you've been through a lot, she said.

He felt relieved to be in the company of a person who was so straightforward. This was something he had felt a lot over the past week, and every time it made him think. These waves of relief, like moments of being able to breathe. But since when *hadn't* he been able to breathe? Why hadn't he noticed his breathing was tight, shallow? He looked up *straightforward* in the dictionary, was interested only in its antonym: *difficult, complicated, evasive,* these were some of the words listed to describe the opposite of straightforward, to describe the company he had been keeping for years.

Here, borrow this, Rae said. It's about a woman called Catherine Sullivan, she travels to an island off the coast of

Finland. You can read it in the night, I think you might like it. It's called *Undone*.

Daniel reaches for the bedside lamp. He opens the curtains, opens the window, gets back into bed.

Now the rain is loud in this room, and he picks up Rae's book, which he has almost finished, only two chapters to go.

Catherine Sullivan is eighty-four years old, or she was when she wrote *Undone*, when she sat pencil in hand, trying to capture and release her life. Catherine had always been a troubled soul – dark moods, anxiety. In bed each night, Daniel has read all the chapters about her troubles, enjoying the hints about what happens when she reaches the island, dotted over the pages like pebbles on a winding path. And what happens to Catherine is this: she has the strangest sense that she is coming undone. And it isn't at all unpleasant. After years of struggling with her past, attempting to overcome it, she no longer needs to try. As her days slowly pass by foot, bicycle and kayak, by sea, rock, forest and meadow, all the events that had shaped her seem to loosen. She likens her past to a trawl net, in which she had been caught, this net now floating beside her.

She writes:

I am in awe, I suppose. There is no better way of putting it. And I had forgotten what awe does to the body, the mind. I had forgotten uncomplicated love. But to be in awe requires openness. And the surprise of this place! I have never seen so many different shades of blue and green and yellow.

Look at me, a beginner in old age, barefoot, excited.

I had no idea that I needed to come undone. And maybe we are all undone by different places, people, influences. As I sit here now I can smell a thousand trees, and I am green as moss.

That was quick, Rae will say when Daniel returns this book. What did you think, did you enjoy it?

And he will shake his head ever so slightly. He will sigh, in a sad and happy way, in a super impressed way.

I've never experienced such stillness while reading a book, he'll say.

I did a few little sketches, tried to draw the stillness of the island in miniature, is something else he'll say.

And a shyness will pass across him, a fleeting cloud.

Later, when Rae opens the book and finds his sketches tucked inside, she will fold one into her purse in the slot for a photo of a loved one, or a driving licence maybe, who knows what all the pockets are for.

and the river
speaks back

Ha, the river says. Well isn't this a turn-up for the books.

I love that phrase, Daniel says. Did you know it originally comes from gambling? Well, that's what my aunt once said. When an unlikely horse won a race, and many bets were lost, it delighted the bookie and his or her book. The book in this case being the log of bets placed.

I like that, the river says. The idea of a book being delighted by an unexpected event, the event in this case being a windfall. And also, isn't *that* a good word, while we're on the subject of words we love. Windfall, Daniel: fruit brought down by the wind.

Anyway, Daniel says. We digress.

But do we? the river says. Do we digress, or do we in fact land on the very topic we should be discussing?

Which is what? Daniel says.

The fact that you're here, sitting beside a river, not the river you used to speak to, but what does it matter? A river is a river is a river, the river says.

Meaning? Daniel says.

Meaning, the river says, I think there's something you need to do. Give it to me, Daniel, go on.

Daniel reaches into his coat pocket, and there it is, the small ceramic sheep.

He places it on the grass, right beside the river.

Symbolic sheep, the river says.

Symbolic of what? Daniel says.

Well, the wise old river says. You bought this sheep with Erica, didn't you? Then you gave it away, then you bought it all over again. So it's a symbol of holding on to your life with Erica Yu, and I'm afraid it has to go.

Excuse me, the little sheep says. I'm just here you know, I can hear you.

Well I never, the river says. I like you very much, Daniel Berry. I like how you give everything a voice.

I haven't given it a voice, exactly, Daniel says.

I beg to differ, the sheep says, and I still don't see why I should be sacrificed.

Ha, sacrificial lamb, the river says.

But why should I? the sheep says. Do I symbolise his life with Erica Yu, his *time* with Erica Yu, or do I symbolise his capacity to salvage something good? Personally, in my humble opinion, I think I symbolise the fact that he isn't dead, if I symbolise anything at all, which I probably don't. A sheep is a sheep is a sheep.

You're a very dramatic ornament, the river says.

How dare you, the sheep says. I'm not an *ornament*, I'm a miniature depiction of one of the finest woolly mammals.

Whatever, the river says. Have you noticed that he's been making sheep's eyes at Rae Marsh?

I certainly have not, Daniel says. I'm a broken man, just look at me, tell me what you see.

What do *you* see? the river says, for it knows that this is the most important question.

Turner, Daniel says.

Turner? the sheep says.

I see a painting by Turner, a boat in a storm, and the boat is me, Daniel says.

370

Nah, the sheep says.

Nah, the river says.

What do you mean, *nah*? Daniel says.

You're a wounded man, full of love, the sheep says.

The thing is, the river says. If he's going to get better, if he's going to start healing, *you* have to go.

Maybe it's for the best, Daniel says.

And he picks up the sheep.

No no no! the sheep says from the middle of a man's palm.

Throw him in! Throw him in! the river says.

And then there is a noise, it's unexpected.

Saved by the bell, the river says.

Hello? Daniel says.

Hello son, Leslie says. Just checking it's working.

All good, Daniel says. It took me by surprise, I forgot I had it.

He is referring to Sherry's old phone, flip-top, bright red, with a new pay-as-you-go SIM.

Thanks again, Daniel says.

Well, Leslie says. It's given me peace of mind, knowing you have a phone. I thought I'd make a pie for tea, mushroom and ale, what do you think?

That sounds great, thanks so much, Daniel says. I'll do the washing up.

After the call, the river and the sheep stare at Daniel.

Well isn't that a windfall, the river says.

I love mushroom and ale pie, the sheep says.

Daniel pats his stomach. I'm eating a lot of pie right now, he says.

So I see, the river says.

I have a proposal, the sheep says. How about, instead of selling me down the river, instead of labelling me as a symbol of emotional breakdown, you consider me a lucky charm? Turns the whole thing on its head, doesn't it, if you see me differently.

You sound like Rae, Daniel says.

I was thinking, the sheep says, that we could go to that vinyl shop in town, we could see what records they have that Leslie might like.

And instead of *talking* to me in future, the river says, why don't you actually jump in, have a swim? My future is long and deep, it might do you good to swim in me.

Oh my God, *look*, Daniel says.

What? the river and the sheep say at exactly the same time.

Just look at that, Daniel says. I haven't seen one for years, have you? It's so beautiful, almost unreal. It's magical, he says.

I see them a lot, obviously, the river says. Did you know that the collective noun for a group of kingfishers is a realm?

Makes sense, Daniel says. Because looking at this one now, it's like being lifted into a bright new realm.

Isn't this a lovely day, the sheep says.

Oh I love that song, the river says.

What song is that? Daniel says.

'Isn't This a Lovely Day?', the river says. It's from the film *Top Hat*. Fred Astaire sings it to Ginger Rogers, tries to get her to dance with him, even though the weather is terrible.

I like the Ella Fitzgerald and Louis Armstrong version, the sheep says.

Oh yes, the river says. You *have* to go to the record shop and look for that song. You have to. Go now, go on.

Shall we? the sheep says. We could buy a little something for everyone while we're out – Leslie, Sherry, Rae – and maybe even stop for a quick beer on the walk back, what do you think?

Go on then, Daniel says.

It's a good thing he's so suggestible, the sheep says to the river as Daniel gets up.

It's one of his strong points, the river says to the sheep. I do like a person who's easily swayed, it makes life so much more romantic.

They are playing the Pretenders in the record shop, 'Don't Get Me Wrong'.

Daniel and the sheep are soaked from a heavy shower that came from nowhere.

Invigorating, the sheep called it.

Daniel sifts through old vinyl, listens to the song.

And here she comes again, the woman from the library, wandering through his mind.

He often wonders where she is, what she's doing.

Sometimes he imagines her as a farmer, tending to lost and arid land.

Or a gardener who bends to save what's almost dead.

Or a dancer, following the beat of bad weather.

flamingo

Now is the time, the time is now, Leslie says.

Really? Sherry says.

That's what she said, those exact words.

But what did she mean?

She just wants to do it now, I suppose.

Our Rae, she says. Well I never. I didn't know she had it in her.

Didn't you? Leslie says.

He has started doing this lately, answering everything she says with a question. Really? he will say. Are you sure? Is that true? Questions to that effect.

It's his way of telling her that something has changed, and this change has made things look different, *truly* different, and now he is wondering what else is other than it seems, or could be. It's doing funny things to his eyes, whatever this change is. It's altering how he sees. Even his cataracts feel less annoying.

Sherry is finding this behaviour irritating. He's like a teenager who has just discovered philosophy, who keeps musing and wondering, dismantling and disrupting, no stone unturned, and what is a stone anyway? But also – go on, admit it, Sherry – as well as being infuriating, she is finding it a tiny bit attractive. Her husband has found his mojo, got into the groove, this is what she thinks.

377

I can't believe it, she says. She's never sung a word in her entire life. She's been like a mouse.

Has she? he says. I'm not sure you've chosen the right animal there.

It's just so sudden, I don't understand it, she says.

Don't you? he says.

No, I really don't. And what *sort* of choir?

It's one of those community things, where it doesn't really matter if you can sing or not.

Oh that's good, that's very good, she says. But why aren't I invited? I'm the singer of the family, aren't I.

Look, don't be upset, it's something she wants to do with Daniel, that's all. Some sort of dare, apparently.

A dare?

I think so.

For God's sake, it feels like you're all regressing. It's chaos.

Leslie laughs at how a dynamic can shift, one you never really noticed, it was simply the way things are, your invisible reality.

His whirlwind wife, downgraded to a breeze.

The winds are changing, he thinks. And it's *fun*.

She knew we'd want to go too, he says. But we can't, we're banned.

He is rolling out one of his well-worn tricks, using the word *we* where *you* would be more accurate.

Banned? she says. That's outrageous.

As I say, she anticipated this. But we're not invited. She doesn't want to be overshadowed.

Is that what she said?

Something like that. You may not realise, but you have quite a vocal presence. Very powerful, he says.

Oh thank you, darling, she says.

She'd be intimidated if you were there, he says.

Sherry is nodding, looking sympathetic. I get it, she says, I do. It's like me being unable to sing in front of Cher. I'd be frozen, I know I would.

Cher? he says.

Uh huh, she says. I'd just love to be there, that's all. To see Rae open her mouth and sing. The amount of times I've tried to get her to sing with me.

Hmm, Leslie says, fighting the urge to say the word *overbearing*.

He closes his mouth, traps the truth.

She leans forward, kisses him hard, takes him by surprise.

Today is one of life's surprising days. It's in the air, like pollen on the wind.

On the kitchen table there's an orange polenta cake, sitting pretty on a stand. The stand itself is new to this house but not to the world. Leslie bought it yesterday from the charity shop, his new favourite pastime, buying pre-owned objects for next to nothing, objects with history.

We're not to touch this until three o'clock, he says to his wife, as he drapes a Beatles tea towel over the cake stand.

Why not? she says. And that looks odd with the tea towel over it, like you're about to do a magic trick.

Maybe I am, he says.

Last week, while they were stripping the old lilac wallpaper from the hallway, Daniel mentioned the flamingos.

Leslie lit up. They're still here, he said. Come with me.

And there they were, poised in the dark of the garden shed, three lonely figures from the past.

Hello there, Daniel said to them.

They look a bit sad, Leslie said. I feel guilty now, for keeping them locked in here.

Don't worry, they're not real, Daniel said.

But they were and they both knew it.

Not real flamingos, but real emblems, real gateways to a time when life was impossibly good.

They were mascots, symbols of hope.

Something for a boy to confide in.

They spoke of then and now, time being quick and slow.

They spoke of love, welcome, sadness and waste.

But mainly of *urgency*.

These flamingos need to go back on the front lawn, Leslie said.

I completely agree, Daniel said.

So what's happening at three o'clock? Sherry says.

We're eating this cake with Rae and Daniel, Leslie says. On the front lawn.

Okay, she says.

And, he says. We'll have three other guests.

Really? Who?

Guess, he says.

Well give me a clue, she says.

They're very pretty, he says.

What? Who is?

The guests, he says.

Three women? she says.

No, he says.

Three pretty men? she says.

No, he says. Try again.

I will not try again, just tell me who's coming, I haven't got all day.

The flamingos, he says.

Her face changes. Excuse me? she says.

The pink flamingos, he says.

I know what colour they are, Leslie. What do you mean?

Isn't it obvious? he says. We thought we'd release them from the shed.

We?

Me and Daniel.

You can release them from the shed and take them *straight to the tip,* she says. They're tacky as hell.

No they're not.

Yes they are, Sherry says, it's a ridiculous idea.

Well they're coming out. I want them in the front garden again. They're good company, those flamingos.

Is that why you're wearing that old suit? she says.

Thought I'd make an effort, dress for the occasion. I'm the perfect colour, am I not, he says, brushing a crumb off the lapel of his crumpled linen suit, faded pink.

She sniffs. Are you wearing my perfume? she says.

Might be, he says. I don't have any aftershave, do I.

Sometimes you are very weird, she says.

Sometimes *you're* very weird, he says.

Well we're perfect for each other then aren't we, she shouts.

Yes we are, he says.

They have always sparred, bickered, dipped in and out of a running joke about what he is like and what she is like, while playing by the number-one rule: Sherry always emerges as the winner, gets her own way, or believes she does.

But the power is shifting.

And how does this woman feel when she is no longer always the winner?

She *loves* it.

And they are free.

A flamboyance of flamingos, released from captivity after almost three decades.

Oh well, at least we've got more storage space now, Sherry says, as she watches Daniel, Leslie and Rae do all the heavy lifting.

It takes a long time to position all three in their proper places on the front lawn.

No, not there, to the left, no too far, bit more to the right again, that's it, now a bit closer to the house, Sherry says.

She is doing it on purpose, doesn't really care where the awful things go, is enjoying the orchestration.

Oh good word, she says to herself. He may have won this time, but I am still the conductor.

Power, such a confusing force, flowing this way and that way then back again, never in anyone's possession for long.

She stands with her hands on her hips. Good job, she says. Time for some cake?

They drink tea and eat cake on the grass, with all the bills and feathers, the long winding necks, legs like stilts.

Did you know that flamingos are monogamous? Daniel says.

I did not, Rae says. Did *you* know that flamingos aren't really pink? It's the pigment in what they eat, it colours ~~th~~eir feathers, all the algae and shrimp and whatnot. So in they get fed a special diet to keep them pink.

Well, Sherry says, I read that they apply make-up to themselves, to attract a mate.

Make-up? Leslie says.

Natural oils from their bodies, she says. They dab it about to enhance their plumage.

Trust you to know that, he says.

Oh, I meant to tell you, Daniel says. I met one of your neighbours earlier, I think his name was Rod.

That'll be Rod Stewart, Rae says.

His name's Rodney Stewart Green, Sherry says. He calls himself Rod Stewart for a bit of fun.

Oh, Daniel says. Well he was very nice, he asked if I'd paint his front door and his windows, maybe even the kitchen.

Did he? That's great. Make sure you charge a good rate, he's minted, Leslie says. He owns Cleaning Rod, you've probably seen their vans around. His cleaners wear Rod Stewart T-shirts.

No job too small, no stain too big, Sherry says.

Dad, this cake, Rae says. It's amazing.

Why thank you, he says.

And he is about to describe it in detail, the making of this cake, when he hears footsteps, a passing neighbour probably, he turns his head to see.

There is a woman, walking down the street, coming towards them.

She stops right at the edge of the garden, as if there's an invisible barrier, a sign saying keep off the grass.

But there is no barrier, no sign.

He turns himself around to look at her properly.

She lets her rucksack drop to the floor and stands perfectly still.

Must be admiring the flamingos, is what Leslie first thinks.

Which she is, and isn't.

This woman he knows, and doesn't.

Daniel stops eating, puts down his plate and stands up.

Mum? he says.

Daniel, Eve says.

ACKNOWLEDGEMENTS

Love & thanks & deepest gratitude:

Gaia Banks (agent & guiding light) and all at Sheil Land Associates

Imogen Taylor (editor & visionary), Amy Perkins and the team at Tinder Press

Siân & Nick (boundless generosity)

Nigel (mischievous compassion)

Rosalind (inspirational maverick)

Henry (hungry muse, background music of soft snores)

Dad (builder of boats in the sand, will miss you always)

Jacquie (kindness, silliness, bright flowers on a shingle beach)

You are invited to join us behind the scenes at Tinder Press

TINDER
PRESS

To meet our authors, browse our books
and discover exclusive content on our
blog visit us at

www.tinderpress.co.uk

For the latest news and views from the team
Follow us on Twitter

 @TinderPress